NEW PENGUIN SHAKESPEARE
GENERAL EDITOR: T. J. B. SPENCER
ASSOCIATE EDITOR: STANLEY WELLS

DISCARD

WILLIAM SHAKESPEARE

*

ANTONY AND CLEOPATRA

EDITED BY
EMRYS JONES

PENGUIN BOOKS

PENGUIN BOOKS

Published by the Penguin Group
Penguin Books Ltd, 27 Wrights Lane, London W8 5TZ, England
Penguin Books USA Inc., 375 Hudson Street, New York, New York 10014, USA
Penguin Books Australia Ltd, Ringwood, Victoria, Australia
Penguin Books Canada Ltd, 10 Alcorn Avenue, Toronto, Ontario, Canada M4V 3B2
Penguin Books (NZ) Ltd, 182–190 Wairau Road, Auckland 10, New Zealand

Penguin Books Ltd, Registered Offices: Harmondsworth, Middlesex, England

This edition first published in Penguin Books 1977
19 20 18

This edition copyright © Penguin Books, 1977
Introduction and notes copyright © Emrys Jones, 1977
All rights reserved

Printed in England by Clays Ltd, St Ives plc
Set in Monotype Ehrhardt

CONTENTS

INTRODUCTION

NOTHING is known of the early performances of *Antony and Cleopatra*, though there is a strong likelihood that it was duly performed – with a boy as Cleopatra – at the Globe and Blackfriars playhouses. But whatever success it may have had on the stage was probably confined to the Jacobean era. In 1677 Dryden wrote a free adaptation of it, *All for Love*, which was so much more to the taste of the time – for instance, its female roles were written for actresses – that it ousted Shakespeare's play from the stage for the best part of two hundred years. In the Romantic period the best-known critical tribute paid to the play was Coleridge's praise of its style: '*Feliciter audax* . . . happy valiancy . . .'. It was, significantly, a reader's tribute. For throughout the nineteenth century *Antony and Cleopatra* remained, as it still does, far more of a reader's play than a play for audiences. Few actresses have made their name as Cleopatra (Mrs Siddons refrained on moral grounds from trying); still fewer actors are remembered as Antony. Even today, stage productions, though less rare than they once were, are not common. Of all Shakespeare's major tragedies, it remains the least performed.

Antony and Cleopatra might have more success on our stages if it were seen as essentially a small-theatre work. Shakespeare himself may have conceived it as primarily a Blackfriars play – as written for an indoor theatre, with a fairly small, intimately placed audience. It is not a play with a wide popular appeal, and certainly should never be thought of in terms of cinematic or operatic spectacle.

7

INTRODUCTION

Although it abounds in imagery of cosmic vastness, it
works through short scenes and small groups of characters
and through verbal effects of often minute delicacy. Unlike
Shakespeare's other Roman plays, it has no crowd scenes:
it is in many ways a quiet play, conversational rather than
declamatory. In all this it might be thought readily acceptable to modern taste; and so it is. Nevertheless the play
undoubtedly presents difficulties – not only to the theatre
producer but to the reader intent on imagining a performance. For to Coleridge's praise of its style must be added
the strictures of many other critics on its apparent formlessness, what A. C. Bradley called its 'defective construction'. This is perhaps the biggest problem presented by
Antony and Cleopatra. How does one grasp a work so
extensive, so various, and so fluid?

Its opening scene gives a foretaste of its dramatic
procedure. Two Roman soldiers appear, in the middle of
an argument. Demetrius, it seems, has arrived in Egypt
from Rome. He has apparently just spoken, for Philo is
answering him and trying to convince him of something:

> *Nay, but this dotage of our general's*
> *O'erflows the measure....*

The argument is about Antony, and perhaps the first thing
to notice is the simple fact that Antony provokes argument.
Not even his own soldiers can agree about him: 'Nay,
but ...'. And Philo's words seem curiously at odds with
themselves. 'Dotage' is a plain term of disapproval and
scorn, but 'O'erflows the measure' is more doubtful. It
might suggest not so much a vicious excess as an abundant
overflow. Already one is uncertain whether there may not
be something similarly ambiguous about Antony's so-
called 'dotage'.

Of course no theatre audience could pause to examine

words in this way. But at a performance, using our eyes
as well as ears, we would pick up a good deal of information in a moment. Before any words had been spoken we
would see that an argument is already in process, and by
the end of Philo's speech we would have the essentials of
the entire situation. Antony, the great soldier, is now no
more than

> *the bellows and the fan*
> *To cool a gypsy's lust.*
>
> I.1.9–10

At once Antony and Cleopatra approach. 'Look where
they come', bids Philo. 'Take but good note. . . . Behold
and see.' And, taking the hint, we judge for ourselves. The
lovers too are in the middle of an argument, not a quarrel
but a love-debate, in which Cleopatra – significantly
speaking first – is setting the pace:

CLEOPATRA
   If it be love indeed, tell me how much.
ANTONY
   There's beggary in the love that can be reckoned.

> I.1.14–15

Then, with the abrupt appearance of a messenger, Cleopatra changes style. She now presses the claims of Rome:
the messengers are waiting, their business is urgent, why
doesn't Antony get on with it?

> *You must not stay here longer. Your dismission*
> *Is come from Caesar. Therefore hear it, Antony.*
> *Where's Fulvia's process? Caesar's I would say! Both!*
> *Call in the messengers.*   I.1.26–9

Of course this is the last thing she really wants, and the
more she needles Antony, the less inclined he feels to get

down to his Roman responsibilities or go back to his scolding wife. He does exactly what Cleopatra wants. He rejects them all:

> *Let Rome in Tiber melt, and the wide arch*
> *Of the ranged empire fall! . . .*   I.1.33–4

His speech, the centre-piece of the scene, superbly asserts his sense of love's value. But at once it is challenged by Cleopatra: 'Excellent falsehood!' She doesn't believe a word of it, or so she says. He must have loved Fulvia once if he married her. Is she herself no more than another Fulvia? Will he leave her too one day? More protestations from Antony follow, while he and his 'wrangling queen' move on, leaving the stage once more to the two watching soldiers. Demetrius admits regretfully that Antony 'approves the common liar' – another phrase with an oddly equivocal effect. Still, Antony may change: 'I will hope | Of better deeds tomorrow.'

For all its brevity, the scene has conveyed a wealth of information, but has done so in such a way that it leaves us not only informed but perplexed. To begin with, it has established a sceptical viewpoint which hints that no one's words are completely trustworthy. Philo is not wholly aware of what his metaphors mean; he is not saying quite what he intends. Antony's magnificent hyperboles may be undercut by anyone who refuses the invitation implied by such rhetoric, while Cleopatra's own words show her a virtuoso of deception: here, as elsewhere throughout the play, her words float and shimmer in a haze of tonal ambiguity. She even pretends – or seems to – that she herself is at the mercy of words, artfully simulating a slip of the tongue so as to make her point: 'Where's Fulvia's process? Caesar's I would say! Both!' We are left finally with the paradox that what Antony does proves what the liars say true, as if the true and the false may somehow, or sometimes, coincide.

The scene leaves us without any clear directives as to what to think. Prompted by Philo, we view the lovers with a kind of spectatorial detachment, something which Cleopatra's artificiality does nothing to diminish. In any case she and Antony are before us for so short a time that little rapport is possible. Yet Antony's love-assertion can hardly be dismissed as the 'dotage' of a 'strumpet's fool' – it speaks with too imperious an authority; it commands respect. And in doing so, it divides us, so that we too are enlisted among those who argue about Antony.

Finally the scene prepares for the special dramatic rhythm of *Antony and Cleopatra*, its teasingly discontinuous movement – at its most obvious in its predilection for short scenes. Part of its teasing effect comes from its failure to initiate a plot. What Antony does is negative: he refuses to see the messengers; and when he leaves he gives no indication that he might change his mind: 'Speak not to us.' It is unusual for an opening scene not to lay down clear pointers as to how the plot is going to develop. In that sense we can say that, by the end of the scene, we have got nowhere. Though not without movement it is in a way static; it lacks 'action'.

This opening scene, then, prepares perfectly for the scenes that follow. If, like this one, they offer little obvious action, they supply instead a rich flow of talk, well discriminated and subtly suggestive of personal nuance. Those who do the talking are the top people in the world. They appear only briefly, then disappear while others take their place, and all the time they talk about each other. The talk is endlessly opinionative. Everyone judges everyone else, and is himself judged. And from the ceaseless clash of views, the descriptions and counter-descriptions,

the conflicting analyses, we learn that this is a world awash
with the tide of merely human opinion. 'This common
body', says Caesar, referring to the common people, whom
we never see,

> *Like to a vagabond flag upon the stream,*
> *Goes to and back, lackeying the varying tide,*
> *To rot itself with motion.*   I.4.45–7

In this world there are no absolutes, no ultimate court of
appeal, nor any point of rest to which we can turn for
stable reassurance. (The action of *Antony and Cleopatra*
takes place in the pre-Christian era, while Shakespeare
wrote for a society that was overwhelmingly Christian.)
People are on their own, pushing their opposing interests
and expounding their rival codes of value. The world they
live in is spatially vast: Antony leaves Egypt for Rome at
the end of Act I, scene 3; during the next three scenes he
is still making the journey; only in Act II, scene 2, do we
see him in Rome. The scenic sequence itself helps to
convey a sense of the distance covered. Later, in Act III,
scene 7, Antony finds it almost incredible that Caesar with
his full army could cross the Adriatic in so short a time.
On this occasion, the speed in traversing space expresses
Caesar's astonishing efficiency. This vast world is also
profoundly diverse; it lacks discernible unity. Alexandria
is a long way from Rome – and not only in terms of
distance. But just as the world extends and changes
through space, so also does it move through time. Human
beings – the play shows – are creatures of internal mood
and impulse, changing from moment to moment; they
also suffer the external vicissitudes of fortune. Both within
and without, they inhabit a medium in perpetual movement. Moreover, since the world and the people within it
are caught in a process of ceaseless change, those who set

up as commentators are liable to be out of date or in some way inaccurate whatever they say. This holds good throughout *Antony and Cleopatra*. So Pompey, reflecting on Antony in Act II, scene 1, thinks him still in Egypt, still the 'amorous surfeiter', when Antony is in fact almost in Rome. The immediate irony is at Pompey's expense. But Antony is not going to stay in Rome for long: he will soon be back with 'Egypt's widow' – so to that extent Pompey's diagnosis is not so foolish. Human nature is predictable but constantly surprising, apparently knowable yet finally baffling. Antony once may have loved Fulvia: is Cleopatra just another of his women? Cleopatra herself – as Charmian reminds her – once loved Julius Caesar and Gnaeus Pompey: is Antony merely her latest conquest, and possibly not the last? Like the sea, whose presence is much felt in the play, reality is 'varying' – always the same but different, always different but the same, a process of creation in which new and old are endlessly intermingled.

Such are a few of the features of the world created by Shakespeare in *Antony and Cleopatra*. The purpose behind these features (and others like them) can perhaps be summed up in the idea of a certain kind of historical realism. They remind us what life was 'really' like for the persons concerned, who cannot share our knowledge of the historical outcome. This is one of the functions of the Soothsayer who appears at the beginning of the second scene. His mysteriously charged utterances remind us what is finally to be the fate of Cleopatra and her maids, but at the same time make us realize their utter ignorance of the future. For them, as for the other characters of the play (with the exception, at certain moments, of Caesar), life is a matter of infinite potentiality: the future is open and unsettled, unknown because not yet in existence.

Similarly, their knowledge of each other is necessarily imperfect, since everyone, being alive, is still in a process of becoming. They are not yet characters in history, complete, unchangeable, dead; they are still breathing, making themselves up from moment to moment:

> I saw her once
> Hop forty paces through the public street;
> And, having lost her breath, she spoke, and panted,
> That she did make defect perfection,
> And, breathless, power breathe forth.   II.2.233–7

At such a moment Cleopatra is very far indeed from being an august personage from the pages of classical history: she is caught, unprepared, in the glance of a bystander. It is a moment of becoming – which also 'becomes' her. But it is of course her endless capacity for becoming, her livingness, that most delights Antony, as we have already been told in the opening scene:

> Fie, wrangling queen!
> Whom everything becomes – to chide, to laugh,
> To weep. . . .   I.1.48–50

And it is this quality, in history, that *Antony and Cleopatra* most strives to capture.

*

The idea of writing a peculiarly fluid and intimate history play may have been Shakespeare's own; but he would certainly have found such qualities in the famous Greek biographer who supplied him with his main source. A glance at Plutarch can take us a little further towards seeing why the play is written in the way it is.

When, in 1606 or 1607, Shakespeare turned to the subject of Antony and Cleopatra, it had already attracted a number of dramatists. It was a stock theme, like Dido and Aeneas, and before 1600 had been dramatized in Italy and France as well as in England. The Countess of Pembroke's *Antonius*, a translation of Robert Garnier's *Marc Antoine*, appeared in 1592; Samuel Daniel's *Cleopatra* in 1594. These earlier plays were all neo-classical in conception. They obeyed the three unities (time, place, and action), and used a version of the classical chorus. Off-stage events were narrated by messengers, while everything that had happened before the opening of the play was gone over in detail in retro-spective monologues. Since the unity of time had to be observed, the hero and heroine were shown only on their last day alive – and the effect is usually one of stifling and arbitrary constriction. Some of these plays are less dull than others, but they are all dull to some degree. None of them gives the slightest preparation for what Shake-speare was to do in his Antony and Cleopatra play, for no one before Shakespeare had made any serious attempt to transfer to the stage the narrative movement of Plutarch's *Life of Marcus Antonius*. To be fair, only Shakespeare, after nearly twenty years of writing for the stage and acting on it, had a dramatic technique resource-ful enough for this very difficult task. Certainly only he conveys any sense of the Plutarchan narrative, with its long time-perspectives, its altogether lifelike waveringly inconsistent characters, and its crowded anecdotal feeling for reality.

Plutarch's *Parallel Lives of the Greeks and Romans* were written in Greek about A.D. 100. (Shakespeare used the English translation of 1579 by Sir Thomas North, which in turn was based on Jacques Amyot's French version of 1559.) A typical Plutarchan biography inevitably tells a story, but is not organized primarily with a view to

narrative effect. Its main purpose is ethical. By studying
in detail the life of an illustrious, or notorious, man, we
are invited to increase the store of our moral understanding: we may become wiser men ourselves. And so the
various anecdotes which make up a large part of a Plutarch
Life have an ethical force: they persuade us to admire or
deplore the deeds of the hero. As D. A. Russell remarks,
'the question which is being answered all along is the
rather unsophisticated "What sort of man was he?"' . . .
The facts are therefore presented not so much for their
intrinsic interest as in evidence to support a general
judgment' (*Plutarch* (1973), pages 102–3). Throughout
such a *Life* we are not just reading an interesting story;
we are assessing a moral case-history, awarding praise and
blame according to the way the hero meets the various
crises of his career. But there is also another consideration
to be borne in mind. Plutarch had a special interest in the
private moments of the famous personages who were his
subjects. In his *Life of Alexander* he says that his readers
should remember that

> *my intent is not to write histories, but only lives. For
> the noblest deeds do not always show men's virtues and
> vices; but oftentimes a light occasion, a word, or some
> sport, makes men's natural dispositions and manners
> appear more plain than the famous battles won wherein are
> slain ten thousand men, or the great armies, or cities won
> by siege or assault.*
>
> Shakespeare's Plutarch, pages 7–8

Plutarch had an eye for the informally revealing anecdote,
the intimate detail. Here is a characteristic passage from
his *Life of Antony*:

> *Furthermore, things that seem intolerable in other men, as
> to boast commonly, to jest with one or other, to drink like*

a good fellow with everybody, to sit with the soldiers when they dine, and to eat and drink with them soldierlike – it is incredible what wonderful love it won him amongst them. And furthermore, being given to love, that made him the more desired; and by that means he brought many to love him. For he would further every man's love, and also would not be angry that men should merrily tell him of those he loved.

pages 177–8

Plutarch is as much interested in behaviour, a man's habits and way of living, as in the great events of his life; and this again affects his biographical procedure. It comes out in an abundance of descriptive detail, much of which is difficult to reduce to the simple moral judgements with which every so often he punctuates his narrative. Some of this detail shows a curiosity about human behaviour for its own sake, while sometimes he conveys a strong sense of its perplexing paradoxicality: in the passage just quoted, for example, he makes us feel that things which would be 'intolerable' in other men were not only acceptable in Antony but even had a kind of glory in them. Confronted by such splendidly generous folly, moral judgement seems for a moment disarmed and confused.

These characteristics of Plutarchan biography are more fully reflected in *Antony and Cleopatra* than in any other of Shakespeare's Plutarchan plays, and help to explain some at least of its many puzzling features. Plutarch's ethical concerns – his interest in answering the question 'What sort of man was he?' – left their mark on the play in a way quite central to its structure and meaning. In the first half-dozen scenes, for example, Antony is either at the centre of the stage when he is on it, or the subject of talk when he is not. In the opening lines of the play, as we have seen, he is described by Philo before speaking for himself when he appears with Cleopatra. He is next seen in private with the Messenger and even in a rare moment of self-communing. In the next scene, in a more public vein, he negotiates the difficult feat of taking leave of Cleopatra. These scenes are followed by three in which he is off stage. But while he journeys to Rome, three separate groups of characters – Caesar and Lepidus, Cleopatra and her servants, Pompey and his followers – talk about little else but Antony. The long scene of the triumvirs in Rome (II.2) again centres on Antony, on his past misdemeanours and his present 'greatness'; but as soon as he leaves to see his new bride Octavia, he becomes again the off-stage subject of conversation, as Enobarbus describes the woman who has bewitched him. And so it goes on until his death at the end of the fourth act. He is the observed of all observers in a way that not even Hamlet is, for not even Hamlet is the theme for so much direct commentary elsewhere. All through the long-drawn-out agony of his dissolution after Actium, Antony is observed in close-up by Cleopatra, Enobarbus, and his other followers. Indeed Caesar's words to Thidias –

> *Observe how Antony becomes his flaw,*
> *And what thou think'st his very action speaks*
> *In every power that moves –*   III.12.34–6

serve as an implied injunction to the audience to scan Antony's every movement, every facial expression, gesture, posture. (Thidias himself is not given much chance to 'observe' Antony; only the audience can fully benefit from Caesar's words.) We must look closely to see how Antony takes it, what this 'noble ruin' (III.10.18) makes of each rending crisis when it comes, and, on quieter occasions, with what mood he registers the passing minute. In focusing attention on Antony in this way from a variety of viewpoints, Shakespeare can be seen as responding to a Plutarchan emphasis. We entertain a complex image of Antony, or perhaps a series of different, complementary images of him, in a way that we scarcely do of Hamlet, Othello, Lear, or Macbeth. In this respect the play has much more in common with the two other Plutarchan tragedies of this period, *Coriolanus* and *Timon of Athens*. In those plays, as in this, the hero is subjected to a prolonged ethical scrutiny, in which praise and blame are mixed; in them, too, there is a good deal of personal commentary on the hero, and again the function of the flow of talk is not only to supply information about him but to encourage us to think questioningly about 'what sort of man he is'.

Far more than *Coriolanus* or *Timon*, however, *Antony and Cleopatra* finds a dramatic equivalent for Plutarch's small-scale anecdotal progression. The play, like the *Life*, is rich in anecdote, reminiscence and allusion; we breathe an air laden with trivial social exchange, gossip, competing oral traditions. Charmian reminds Cleopatra

> *'Twas merry when*
> *You wagered on your angling; when your diver*
> *Did hang a salt fish on his hook, which he*
> *With fervency drew up.*

II.5.15–18

And Cleopatra at once rises to Charmian's bait: 'That time – O times! ...' Or Pompey touches incautiously on a delicate topic:

POMPEY
... And I have heard Apollodorus carried –
ENOBARBUS
No more of that: he did so.

19

POMPEY   *What, I pray you?*
ENOBARBUS
    A certain queen to Caesar in a mattress.   II.6.68–70

At such moments the play seems to presuppose an audience especially quick to take a point, perhaps one already well-informed on the private history of Rome.

Another sign of Plutarch's influence, perhaps, is the peculiar drifting movement of Shakespeare's play. For a Renaissance tragedy, it comes remarkably close to doing without a plot. In its first half particularly, as we have seen, there is much talk but little decisive action. Antony breaks away from Cleopatra, but by the end of the first half has returned to her again. There have been minor episodes, like the disposal of Pompey, but everything else seems a matter of aimless movement, activity rather than action. The concern is more with ethics, even manners, than with the growth of passion. Significantly, many passages border on the comic: an audience will be frequently roused to laughter, not only by Enobarbus's satirical hits but by Cleopatra's self-indulgent airs. The inclusion of this kind of material in a tragedy perhaps also reflects Shakespeare's reading of Plutarch. The kind of biography written by Plutarch is associated, as D. A. Russell remarks, 'with the realism of comedy rather than with the grand topics of epic or, for that matter, history. ... One might almost say that biography stood to history as the comedy of manners stood to tragedy' (page 102). This is exactly the effect of at least a few passages in the first half of the play; Cleopatra's scene with her servants (I.5) and her two scenes with the Messenger (II.5, III.3) contribute nothing essential to the action but brilliantly put on show her ethical character. Elsewhere in this first half, our attention is persistently directed to the tangle of good and bad, honourable and dishonourable, in the conduct of the characters – not only of the chief antagonists Antony and Caesar but of subordinate figures like Sextus Pompey, the man who feels he deserves worldly success but is not of the stuff of which winners in this world are made. Antony's shabby behaviour over the affair of the elder Pompey's house and Pompey's hurt reproachfulness form one of several minor strands delicately and allusively woven into the play's fabric. All the time the dramatist is conveying exact ethical information about his characters of a kind which would allow us to make a judgement on them were it not that the play's movement encourages judgement to be indefinitely suspended. It is perhaps not judgement but a sympathetic, even tolerant, though open-eyed, comprehension that is the final goal of the play's audience.

Shakespeare had used a similar method in his earlier Plutarchan play *Julius Caesar*, where sharply distinguished characters were placed in a series of juxtapositions inviting comparison and appraisal. (Plutarch's entire plan in the *Parallel Lives* was of course based on such comparisons.) But the special structure of *Antony and Cleopatra* allows far more speed and economy. An example is the splendid galley scene (II.7), which needs performance for its full quality to be brought out. Six speakers – Antony, Lepidus, Pompey, Menas, Caesar, Enobarbus – interact in a series of brief exchanges which call out the idiosyncrasies of each. As the feast mounts to its climax, attention is held by the helpless Lepidus; as it sinks to its close, Caesar emerges into his usual position of controlled power. And in each phase Antony forms the focal point of contrast, in the first with the weak Lepidus, in the second with the strong Caesar. Set over against the conviviality of the occasion is Menas's offer to his master of 'the whole world'. It is a moment when, it seems, the entire course of world history might have been changed. But it passes off with scarcely a vibration, and the surrounding good humour is undisturbed. Lepidus, 'the third part of the world', is carried drunk to bed, and the rest join hands for a ring dance. The entire scene – world-sharers in a drunken party, floating on the sea – creates a wonderfully suggestive image of the paradoxes of political power. It arouses sharply contradictory feelings, and yet the prevailing one is a sense of Olympian geniality. More than any other scene, it encapsulates the vision of the play.

*

Plutarch's *Life of Antony* is one of the most absorbing of all his *Lives* and is especially brilliant in its descriptive detail. Yet there is little in it that suggests dramatic form. Apart from the deaths of Antony and Cleopatra, the events narrated by Plutarch might indeed have struck a prospective dramatist as suffering from two disabilities. They were either too big to be put on the stage – like the sea-battle of Actium. Or they were possibly too small – like the practical jokes played on each other by the lovers or the various incidents involving Antony's followers and allies in the wars. For one of the impressions likely to be carried away from Plutarch's *Life* is of a multiplicity of small incidents. The life of Antony as told here does not present itself as a clearly visualizable shape: apart from his first riverside meeting with Cleopatra, his flight at Actium, and his death, there were few notable events around which a drama might be organized. (And of the three events just mentioned, Shakespeare could stage only the last: the other two were of their very nature off-stage affairs.) Far from attempting to disguise this paucity of big event, however, Shakespeare seems to have decided to accept it and even exploit it – partly in the interests of a certain kind of historical realism which, as we have seen, may have been derived from Plutarch. The result is a play which seems often determined to flout the expectations of an audience. Harley Granville-Barker defended the great number of short scenes in the play by appealing to the conditions of the Elizabethan stage, with its special opportunities for easy continuity between scenes. But despite the force of his argument, many would still agree with A. C. Bradley's charge that, of all Shakespeare's tragedies, *Antony and Cleopatra* is 'the most faultily constructed'. The question arises why the mature Shakespeare should have designed a play which, on the face of it, looks so like a regression to the primitive shambling structures of his Elizabethan predecessors. He could easily have reduced the number of scenes if he had wished, so as to achieve a design more conventionally concentrated. If he did not, the likelihood is that he had other aims in view.

The five-act division which modern texts of *Antony and Cleopatra* inherit from the early eighteenth-century editors is no help in grasping the play's design; if anything, it is a hindrance. In the first Folio, our only authoritative text, the play has no act division whatever. We must look for the natural divisions, the breaks which would have been observed in the theatre by Shakespeare's own acting company. They are the only divisions that matter.

Like most of Shakespeare's other histories and tragedies, *Antony and Cleopatra* seems to fall into two major movements. Other less important divisions may also be discerned, but the play as a whole seems to have one major break. The point at which this break comes – or so it could be argued – is at the end of Act III, scene 6. This is the scene where Caesar in Rome describes the imperial ceremonies of Antony and Cleopatra in Alexandria, and is then surprised by the unexpected arrival of Octavia. Shakespeare is usually careful to arrange close narrative links between scenes so as to maintain continuity, but the chain set going at the beginning of the play comes to a stop here, as if a break in the play's performance were envisaged at this point. The new sequence, begun in the next scene (III.7), continues to the end of the play.

In the first movement, Antony leaves Cleopatra for Rome, marries Octavia, but then abandons her for Cleopatra. This prompts the war between Antony and Caesar, which, together with its aftermath in the deaths of the lovers, occupies the second movement. Both movements open with Antony and Cleopatra together, and both of them end with Caesar. He has the last word in both sequences – an arrangement which can be interpreted as having an expressive value. It is a way of dramatizing the actual historical outcome – for since Caesar survived Antony and Cleopatra, he can be said historically to have had the last word. At the end of Act III, scene 6, he speaks as if he had foreknowledge of what is to happen:

> let determined things to destiny
> Hold unbewailed their way.

He is the heir of Aeneas, the man chosen to fulfil Rome's destiny. And on this elevated, decisive note, the first movement ends. The second movement ends with his final summing-up, in which, once again transcending his merely historical role, he speaks with a more than personal voice:

> their story is
> No less in pity than his glory which
> Brought them to be lamented.   V.2.359–61

In dividing his material in this way, Shakespeare was in fact being faithful to what he took from Plutarch. His first and second movements correspond to two massive blocks of Plutarch's *Life*, where they are separated by the long account of Antony's Parthian campaign for which Shakespeare had no use.

A glance at Plutarch may explain a few things about the play's design, but the final shaping is Shakespeare's own. The question is whether enough shaping was done. Dr Johnson put the structural objection long ago in his editorial note on *Antony and Cleopatra*: 'The events, of which the principal are described according to history, are produced without any art of connexion or care of disposition.' Johnson was wrong to deny artistry to the play's plotting, but right in suggesting that it looks as if it does without the usual forms of dramatic organization. The play seems to insist that it is not art but life – life at least in certain of its aspects: untidiness, haphazardness, wastefulness, inconclusiveness. In what is perhaps the earliest critical essay on the play, Hazlitt saw this quality very clearly. Shakespeare, he said,

> *brings living men and women on the scene, who speak and act from real feelings, according to the ebbs and flows of passion, without the least tincture of pedantry of logic or rhetoric. Nothing is made out by inference and analogy, by climax and antithesis, but every thing takes place just as it would have done in reality, according to the occasion.*
> *Characters of Shakespear's Plays* (1817)

In other words, the play establishes a level of realism according to which most other plays of its time would have been found somewhat stagey, their colloquies and confrontations and big climaxes arranged with an implausible neatness and regularity. If *Julius Caesar*, for example, proceeds through a series of massive waves (its big scenes), *Antony and Cleopatra* heaves ripplingly like the sea in a quiet mood. Most of its scenes are short and circumscribed; they have no room for the grander movements of feeling, such as occur in most of the other great tragedies (like the forum scene in *Julius Caesar* or the temptation scene in *Othello*). With one possible exception, the last scene of all, there is nothing like this in *Antony and Cleopatra*. It makes its effects in quite a different way.

Shakespeare's technique of short scenes lends itself to a number of expressive purposes. In the first place, the practice of clearing the stage every hundred lines or so forbids – in the first movement of the play, at least – any very deep emotional engagement on the part of the audience. The constant changes of location (Egypt, Rome, Misenum, Syria, Athens), the contrasting evaluations of Antony's behaviour, as well as the fluctuating play of mood within the individual personality, all work to encourage an ironical comparative response, not quite detachment (because the play kindles a keen interest), but not a profound attachment of feeling either. The setting of the play is the entire world – the Roman empire and its Levantine neighbours, which *is* the world as its inhabitants see it. The dramatist may show us, in one scene, what is going on in that part of the world, but we can be sure that elsewhere, in many other places, many other things are also going on. From its opening scene the play establishes the simple fact that there are as many viewpoints as there are human beings. This is one of the points made by the scene, hardly necessary to the plot, in which Antony's lieutenant Ventidius is shown in Syria (III.1). We have scarcely met him before, and never see him again, but for a few moments we see Antony and Caesar through his eyes – and from this angle they look

different. Public actions will always be interpreted in
different ways, since every human being brings his own
experience to what he sees, and what he sees may not be
instantly intelligible to him. Indeed in this world, for all
the crystalline clarity of the play's poetic vision, human
beings are intelligible neither to each other nor to themselves. Everyone moves in a mist of passion, driven by
obscure pressures which may erupt in action seemingly
involuntary. In the first scene Antony rejects the messengers, declaring himself wholly for Cleopatra and love. In
the second, his mood has changed: he is all for breaking
away and returning to Rome. When he takes leave of
Cleopatra in the following scene he protests his fidelity,
and in Act I, scene 5, we hear that he is still doing so
through messengers. As soon as he arrives in Rome, however, he enters into a new understanding with Caesar and
promptly agrees to marry his sister. We next see him
assuring Octavia that he is a reformed man: 'that to
come | Shall all be done by th'rule.' But a few moments
later he has accepted his Egyptian destiny: 'I'th'East my
pleasure lies' (II.3.6–7 and 41). Throughout the first half
of the play the technique of short scenes is essential for
putting across this view of human activity, with its stress
on discontinuity and multiplicity, volatility and impul-
siveness.

One effect of this technique, then, is to induce a
moderately critical and ironical frame of mind: we keep
on making comparisons. But there are other effects too.
The short scenes are often atomistically constructed: they
are often made up of even shorter discrete parts. In Act
IV, scene 4, for example, Antony is shown going out to
battle. The scene, though very short (under forty lines),
contains several distinct units of action: Antony, in high
spirits, is helped into his armour by Cleopatra; he is then

27

greeted, first by a single soldier, and then by a number of *'Captains and soldiers'*; he takes a soldier's leave of Cleopatra and leads away his men; finally, alone with Charmian, Cleopatra muses on Antony's chances and shows that her real mood is one of low-spirited, clear-eyed detachment: 'Then Antony – but now. Well, on.' Such a technique makes possible a kind of quick close-up view of the speakers like the abruptly discontinuous shots of a news-reel. An illusion of intimacy is created, although we seldom if ever penetrate beneath the surface or overhear a speaker's unspoken thoughts. At the same time the illusion of life in free spontaneous motion is very powerful: the action becomes a succession of moments with a dream-like vividness. This is what life seems like, preserved in memory – brilliant snapshots surrounded by darkness.

By committing himself to a life of sensations rather than thoughts, Antony is choosing to live his life precisely as a succession of moments:

> *Let's not confound the time with conference harsh.*
> *There's not a minute of our lives should stretch*
> *Without some pleasure now.*   I.1.45–7

Life on such terms is a matter of intense experience, immediate excitement, 'pleasure now'. The value of Shakespeare's short-scene technique becomes particularly clear in the play's second movement, the scenes beginning with Act III, scene 7, the first of the war scenes, and ending with Antony's death in Act IV, scene 15. This long sequence, which includes a number of very short battle scenes, has often been uncomprehendingly maligned. It should rather be recognized as a great imaginative achievement, made possible only by a formidable technical resourcefulness. Now that attention is focused unwaveringly on Antony's decline, the short scenes are used with a far greater effect of continuity. We now have a vague impression of unity of place: Actium, Alexandria, and the monument are all sufficiently ill-defined to be acceptable as different spots in more or less the same region, an effect quite different from the use of place in the first half, where Alexandria, Rome, Syria, and the rest were clearly denoted as widely scattered points in a vastly spacious world. Time is also used with a new urgency in the second movement. It no longer seems to stand still, as if people were under no pressure: time is now running out and passes, or seems to pass, with greater and greater rapidity. In keeping with the stress on continuity, this second sequence engages the emotions far more intensely. If the first was often critical in temper, at times sardonic, at others even comic, the second is tragic throughout. Our cue is given us by Enobarbus. In the first movement he maintained a certain detachment; in the second, he can no longer keep up his commentator's role but is compelled to become himself a participant in the tragedy. We too are now drawn into the action and live through with Antony the extreme vicissitudes of his fall.

Antony has surrendered to passion, to a life dominated by will and impulse. He is consequently at the mercy of fortune. When he insists on fighting the crucial battle on sea instead of 'standing on the earth | And fighting foot to foot' (III.7.65–6), he is making yet another symbolic choice. He is throwing away his 'absolute soldiership' (III.7.42) and committing himself to the unstable element. In the scenes that follow he struggles for life in a formless watery void, engulfed by a growing sense of unreality. Life has become a succession of phantasmagoric moments in which mere phenomenal experience is all he has. The series of brief scenes in the fourth act (IV.1 to IV.10) evokes with great economy and power the racing passage of time, as day gives way to night, night to day and day to night again, and as we swing to and fro between one camp and the other. Antony is at his most moody and change-able, at one moment almost embarrassingly pathetic with his servants, at another romantically valiant as he goes out to battle on a fresh early morning, at another sadly but superbly magnanimous as he sends Enobarbus's treasure after him, and at yet another radiantly heroic from his last taste of victory. But each mood is held only for a moment. We catch glimpses of the experience as it was, but no more. When finally he approaches the moment of his last defeat, he has collapsed into a bundle of incompatible impulses, wholly at odds with himself:

> *Antony*
> *Is valiant, and dejected, and by starts*
> *His fretted fortunes give him hope and fear*
> *Of what he has and has not.*　　　　　IV.12.6–9

Suddenly everything is over. His army surrenders to Caesar, and Antony is left alone, raging at Cleopatra. Nothing is left – not even his rage can last. In an ex-hausted calm, he acknowledges his own dissolution: 'Sometime we see a cloud that's dragonish . . . .' He is no more than insubstantial vapour, unable to hold 'this visible shape' (IV.14.2 and 14), decomposing into that sea of matter out of which all life comes – and which in the play is imaged in the formless but fecund mud of the Nile.

At this point we can return to the larger question of the form of *Antony and Cleopatra*. It will be seen that its form is one that asks to be considered as a special case. Superficially, the play looks an undisciplined and shapeless work, desultory and episodic in its first half, and there-after succumbing at length to disjointed battle routines.

Yet one of Shakespeare's purposes seems to have been precisely to imitate disorder and formlessness as they manifest themselves in life. For example, an unusual feature of the play is that its hero dies in the fourth act (or what editors call the fourth act). The play goes on without him, transferring attention to Cleopatra. (This feature has no doubt weighed against the play in the theatre: the role of Antony requires a heroic actor, who must consent to being finally 'upstaged' by his female co-star.) But the untidy-looking arrangement serves to bring out the untidiness of life. The ragged sequence of events was supplied by history and Plutarch, and Shakespeare accepted it, deliberately spacing out the deaths of his two main characters. He also wished to imitate the immense capaciousness of the world, its endlessly receding vastness. The play shows us that reality – all that is – may contain meanings, systems of belief, codes of value, but is itself mysteriously vaster than any of them. As the Soothsayer knows, 'Nature's book of secrecy' is 'infinite' (I.2.10). In a comparable way, the play contains the tragedy of Antony, but is itself more than his tragedy. And so it includes material – like the scene of Ventidius in Syria – which seems at first irrelevant to the main business. But again, the lack of relevance, the digressiveness, is the point – but a point made with unlifelike, wholly artistic, economy and rhythm.

A consideration of the play's form will inevitably end in paradox. The play is in fact much interested in paradoxical formulations, many of which cluster around Cleopatra. She is a 'Royal wench', she makes 'defect perfection' (II.2.231 and 236). The ultimate paradox perhaps is the play itself. It goes out of its way to break the rules of dramatic writing. But its 'primitive' appearance is assumed for a purpose. Though it runs the risk of looking structurally incompetent, it is in fact a marvel of formed dramatic writing. Like Cleopatra, we may say, it too makes 'defect perfection'.

∗

In most traditional accounts, Antony was stigmatized as a great man ruined by sexual passion. This is clearly what Plutarch thought:

> *Antonius being thus inclined, the last and extremest mischief of all other (to wit, the love of Cleopatra) lighted on him, who did waken and stir up many vices yet hidden in him, and were never seen to any; and, if any spark of goodness or hope of rising were left him, Cleopatra quenched it straight and made it worse than before.*

Plutarch sees nothing but dissipation in Antony's first long stay with Cleopatra, and later refers to ' "the horse of the mind", as Plato termeth it, that is so hard of rein (I mean the unreined lust of concupiscence)' (page 222), which destroyed Antony's character. From a prudential point of view, Antony's was plainly not a success story, and a moralist could hardly have come to any other than an adverse verdict. The question for readers of *Antony and Cleopatra* is whether the play as a whole endorses this traditional view – the view of Plutarch – or whether a more complex assessment of the famous love affair is required.

Many modern readers hold that Shakespeare's play departs from the moralistic tradition in that, so it is argued, Antony's love for Cleopatra is justified by its transcendence, whereas the values of the World, embraced by Caesar and his success-pursuing followers, are shown to be mean and hollow. This argument about the value and status of the love relationship has by now long divided readers, and will surely continue to do so. For it is important to see that, in some respects, the play is ambiguous or open on this question, so that differences of response are only to be expected. In Shakespeare's day the depravity of Antony and Cleopatra was probably something to be taken for granted. Cultural pressures in favour of a hostile moralistic position may have led Shakespeare to assume this view in his audience – which he himself may also have shared up to a point. But since he was writing a tragedy, he deliberately and perhaps instinctively went on to modify this view, to show to what extent sympathy and even admiration could be aroused for the doomed pair. The play starts, accordingly, from the assumption that Antony's passion for Cleopatra was a ruinous infatuation, and then proceeds at once to complicate the account by making us see more in it.

The love relationship is presented as both a destructive and a creative force. Its destructive side is obvious enough. No soldier in antiquity behaved more ignominiously than Antony at Actium. By fleeing in Cleopatra's wake in full view of his assembled army, he achieved a never-to-be-forgotten low point in dishonourable conduct: 'Many plainly saw Antonius fly,' says Plutarch (page 261), 'and yet could very hardly believe it, that he . . . would so have forsaken them, and have fled so cowardly'. Or as Scarus puts it:

> I never saw an action of such shame.
> Experience, manhood, honour, ne'er before
> Did violate so itself.   III.10.21-3

For a man like Antony, who staked so much on what others thought of him – his fame, in the present and in the future – this loss of face can hardly be over-estimated.

Throughout the first four acts, the play finds room for a
great deal of adverse, often contemptuous, commentary.
Most of it comes early, where it is counterpointed against
the lovers' own assertions of supremacy: from the Roman
pair whose disapproval frames the opening scene, and
from Caesar and Pompey on their first appearances. And
these Roman accusers receive some support from Antony's
own misgivings in Act I, scene 2, and his admissions of
former misconduct in Act II, scene 2. In the Actium
scenes and after, Antony's stupendous folly is sufficiently
brought out by the chorus of his own soldierly followers,
men who feel a devotion to him personally but can see
where his blindness is taking them. This is made particularly clear in Act III, scene 7, the first of the war scenes.
Antony is astonished by Caesar's speed in transporting his
army from Italy to only a few miles from Antony's camp.
He turns to Cleopatra: 'You have heard on't, sweet?'

CLEOPATRA
 Celerity is never more admired
 Than by the negligent.
ANTONY   *A good rebuke,*
Which might have well becomed the best of men
To taunt at slackness. Canidius, we
Will fight with him by sea.
CLEOPATRA   *By sea; what else?* III.7.24–8

In Plutarch, Cleopatra responds to the news of Caesar's
approach with a flippantly punning joke. Shakespeare
gives her a curiously sententious remark, whose pat
wisdom is unexceptionable. Her purpose in delivering
this out-of-character moral rebuke is clear: she wants him
to do, not the wise thing, but the thing she wants. It
instantly has the desired effect (just as her needling remark
in the opening scene with the messengers also had the

desired effect). He at once announces the fatal plan of
fighting by sea.

The massive weight of this criticism of Antony is
perfectly apparent in the play; no one can miss it. And yet
many readers write it off as being merely the 'Roman'
point of view, something to be balanced dispassionately
against the 'Egyptian' point of view, in favour of which,
they conclude, the play finally settles. It should at least
be a matter for agreement that no one speaks up for their
love except the lovers themselves. It is never spoken of
with approval by anyone else, and it would seem that,
while the play allows its readers to give it their blessing,
it does not by any means require them to do so.

But the love relationship cannot be reduced to Plutarch's
'unreined lust of concupiscence'; even in Plutarch's own
account it is more than that. The sense of spiritual en-
largement experienced by the lovers, at least by Antony,
is established at the very beginning of the play. With only
the briefest of introductions, Shakespeare works up to the
claim made by Antony on behalf of their alternative
realm, the spacious empire of love:

CLEOPATRA
   I'll set a bourn how far to be beloved.
ANTONY
   Then must thou needs find out new heaven, new earth.
I.1.16–17

Antony's phrase echoes a famous New Testament text:
'And I saw a new heaven, and a new earth' (Revelation
21.1). Cleopatra, as we have seen, mischievously urges
him to hear the news from Rome and so provokes his
definitive reply. It takes the form of a proclamation made
to the world, and is Shakespeare's version of a notable
sentence in Plutarch (page 204): 'For they made an order

between them which they called *Amimetobion* (as much to say, "no life comparable and matchable with it") . . . .'

> *Let Rome in Tiber melt, and the wide arch*
> *Of the ranged empire fall! Here is my space.*
> *Kingdoms are clay. Our dungy earth alike*
> *Feeds beast as man. The nobleness of life*
> *Is to do thus – when such a mutual pair*
> *And such a twain can do't, in which I bind,*
> *On pain of punishment, the world to weet*
> *We stand up peerless.*   I.1.33–40

The claims of the actual empire of Rome are dismissed in favour of their own empire: 'Here is my space.' The earth is in any case nothing but dung; its concerns are base. 'The nobleness of life' is to live as they do. But only for *them*, Antony goes on, is it right to live 'thus': it might not be right for everyone, or even for anyone else, but only for 'such a mutual pair | And such a twain'. And they will not admit the relevance of the moral judgements of others: they 'stand up peerless' – their life is an 'Amimetobios'.

The way of life, or 'order', which Antony here proclaims resembles that of a religious sect: it stands against the values of the world, in favour of its own values, which are erotic, personal, and private. Its contempt for the world has points of contact with the *contemptus mundi* of various religious systems, including Christianity. This otherworldly note makes an important contribution to the play, particularly in Cleopatra's speeches after Antony's death. Seen from this point of view, the entire world is no more than a dunghill, a 'sty', a 'shore' (a sewer), a 'little O'. For a moment, therefore, Antony strikes a particularly vibrant chord, to which any traditionally religious member of Shakespeare's audience might be expected to respond. (In his *Apology for Poetry*, for example, Sidney refers to 'Alexander and Darius, when they strave who should be cock of this world's dunghill': the remark has a peculiar relevance to the political concerns of *Antony and Cleopatra*.) Similarly, when, just before their deaths, both Antony and Cleopatra look forward expectantly to an after-life, we are surely invited to respond sympathetically. To a Christian audience, these pre-Christian lovers might seem deluded, but the desire for, and confident belief in, reunion after death cannot be dismissed as contemptible but is part of their final nobility and magnanimity. We admire and even, in a way, approve.

But Antony is not simply and solely a lover. Indeed throughout the middle acts of the play our sense of his personal greatness arises hardly at all from his lover's role. It comes rather from a generosity, a largeness of spirit, that express themselves in quite different spheres. Antony has a great capacity for *giving*. He is never more sympathetic than when providing for his ruined followers after Actium or when, told of Enobarbus's desertion, he at once sends his treasure after him with not a word of reproach, only deep regret that his own fortunes have 'Corrupted honest men' (IV.5.17). Plutarch had opened his *Life* with a description of Antony's father, a man 'very liberal in giving'. It struck the right note for a consideration of his even more liberal son. The same note is struck by Seneca, who, along with Plutarch, was a favourite classical moralist in the Renaissance. In one of his essays he refers to Antony as he was at the point of death, and quotes a line attributed to him by a poet of the time: 'Whatever I have given, that I still possess!' (*On Benefits*, VI.3) – he has been rich in the power of giving, and is now left with nothing but what he has given away. This is the Antony of Shakespeare's conception – Enobarbus's 'mine of bounty' (IV.6.32) – as it is finally of Cleopatra's 'dream':

> For his bounty,
> There was no winter in't. . . .
>
> realms and islands were
> As plates dropped from his pocket. V.2.86–7 and 91–2

Shakespeare succeeds in establishing Antony not only as a powerful man of affairs and a skilled soldier but also as a great human being whose largeness of nature instantly wins him respect, loyalty, and love. He is more than once called 'courteous' (a word taken over from North, who several times applies it to Antony). The word has various connotations: in some places it means he is courtly, particularly with women: 'Our courteous Antony, | Whom ne'er the word of "No" woman heard speak . . .'. But more often it implies consideration for others, being gentle, generous, noble – the qualities expected of a great nobleman. Courtesy in this sense is a quality diffused over the entire play: it shows in the good manners of many of the conversational exchanges and, among the Romans at least, in their civil and decorous dealings with each other. Of course Antony can lapse into behaviour the reverse of courteous, as when he orders Thidias to be whipped. But when he is more like himself, he is feelingly aware of what is properly due to others.

Antony is shown on a number of occasions exchanging words with his soldiers and attendants, with whom – as in Plutarch – he is on easy terms. It is not the least moving part of Antony's fall that innumerable others suffer too, some of whom we catch sight of – in a way made possible by the play's fluidly mobile scenic technique. So, in one scene just before Actium, his soldiers plead with him not to commit their fates to a sea-battle. In another, he asks his servants to serve him at supper, possibly for the last time. In another, after his unexpected victory, he lavishes praise on Scarus, one of his doughty soldiers, and presents him to Cleopatra. She catches something of Antony's own spirit and gives the soldier 'An armour all of gold' (IV.8.27). It is like Antony that he should want all his soldiers around him at the ensuing banquet:

> Had our great palace the capacity
> To camp this host, we all would sup together. . . .
>
> IV.8.32–3

The thought is one of gigantic and yet intimate conviviality. He had said something like it earlier to his household servants:

> I wish I could be made so many men,
> And all of you clapped up together in
> An Antony, that I might do you service
> So good as you have done.   IV.2.16–19

We are never allowed to forget these innumerable others – 'A moiety of the world', as Caesar calls them (V.1.19) – who helped to make up the political force known to history as 'Antony'. It is no part of Shakespeare's conception to insulate his hero's fall from the fates of his nameless dependants. Servants, soldiers, messengers, are part of the ambience in which he lives – and in which he dies. His freed slave Eros, by an act of loyal disobedience, kills himself rather than kill his master, and even while Antony lies dying Decretas is taking his sword to Caesar in the hope of being admitted to his service. Antony's personal tragedy is set within the tragedy of many others. Life is going on all round the central pair, and will continue to do so when they are dead; as always, the play refuses to identify reality with any one viewpoint.

Shakespeare's Antony is a great man certainly ruined by his sexual passion as well as – possibly – exalted by it. However, against the view that he is finally exalted by love must be set the play's insistence on his humiliation, dejection, and appalling sense of personal deliquescence. Nor is he granted a clean and dignified exit from life. Shakespeare follows Plutarch closely in dragging out the process in a wholly believable and lifelike way. Unlike his servant Eros, Antony fumbles in the act of taking his own life and, fully conscious but physically helpless, lies stretched out, a spectacle to his pitying servants. He must be carried to the monument, there to be hauled up by Cleopatra and her women. The full wretchedness of his end is made unmistakably clear in the visually eloquent terms of the stage business. Antony's courtesy and – in the midst of indignity – dignified resolution persist to the end. But there is no hint of transcendence in his last moments. His mind is set on the things of this world – on dying like a Roman, nobly, not basely, and on thoughts of Cleopatra's safety. (But it turns out that the man he recommends her to trust, Proculeius, is eager to capture her for his master Caesar – yet another intrusion of the merely contingent.)

*

With Cleopatra's end, it is quite otherwise. Antony's death was a matter of anti-climax and mess and sharply-focused humiliation. Cleopatra's death goes entirely according to plan, like a magnificently co-ordinated ritual, beautiful and moving, leaving behind it a sense of satisfaction and completeness.

In this last phase of the play, Cleopatra moves into a new role. During the battle scenes she was firmly subordinate to Antony; with his death, she emerges for the first time as the initiating protagonist, something she has never been before. Her new role, which lasts till the end, is defined by the new situation in which she finds herself: with Antony dead, she becomes Caesar's sole antagonist. His object is to secure her for his triumph; hers to find a way out satisfactory to herself – her new Antony-less self. In this contest of wits she, the defeated, the prisoner, must seem to win; her conqueror, fortunate Caesar, must accept defeat. What she wins is a splendid death; what he wins is the Empire. Or, to put it slightly differently, what they both win is their allotted place in history and in fame – something the play has all along assumed. Octavius Caesar becomes Augustus, while Cleopatra with Antony passes into legend:

> *No grave upon the earth shall clip in it*
> *A pair so famous.*   V.2.357–8

The lovers and their memory are treated with the courtesy characteristic of the play. From the viewpoint adopted by Caesar in his concluding speech, there are no losers; everyone wins.

The final scene, by far the longest in the play, is entirely Cleopatra's. Its remarkable power – it is one of the most thrilling scenes in the whole of Shakespeare – comes, in part, from its length and from its final position in this particular play. Cleopatra's words at the beginning give the clue:

> *it is great*
> *To do that thing that ends all other deeds. . . .*
>   V.2.4–5

For the scene is, in the first place, simply an ending. The death of which she speaks will put an end not only to 'all other deeds' but also to the play itself. As we have seen,

Antony and Cleopatra, a work of considerable length, has kept up an endlessly varied, inconclusive, repetitive, wavelike movement. By means of its exceptional number of short scenes, its constantly switching points of view, and the eddying fortunes of its volatile characters, it will have made its audience especially sensitive to the mere fact of change. It has presented life in its perpetual mobility, its seemingly inexhaustible power to prolong itself. It has, in short, so conditioned us that it is inevitably with feelings of relief and pleasure that we now approach what we have all along been denied, a point of absolute rest:

> that thing that ends all other deeds,
> Which shackles accidents and bolts up change. . . .

The scene needs its exceptional length for this effect to be realized: so that, when at last it comes, we can feel to the full the contrast between movement and stillness, Cleopatra alive and Cleopatra dead. This is why the scene's destination is announced in its opening lines; we must be clear as to what we are approaching, so that the series of interviews which fill the middle part of the scene can be contemplated for what they really are: Cleopatra's last transactions with the world.

But the scene also communicates a powerful sense of the marvellous. In it a metamorphosis takes place. Cleopatra changes before our eyes from a breathing human being into an inanimate work of art, something to be gazed at – as Caesar and his men do in fact gaze at her at the end of the scene.

> Now from head to foot
> I am marble-constant. . . .   V.2.239-40

It is perhaps this aesthetic dimension, this transformation of Cleopatra and her story into a 'wonderful piece of work' (I.2.154–5), that explains the absence here of any sense of pain or distress. In her 'dream' – Shakespeare's own addition to the Plutarchan material of this last scene – Antony was already celebrated as a triumph of the truthful imagination:

> t'imagine
> An Antony were nature's piece 'gainst fancy,
> Condemning shadows quite.   V.2.98–100

And imagining an Antony – which means in practice an Antony *and* a Cleopatra – is exactly what the play has all along been compelling us to do.

*

The final impression made by *Antony and Cleopatra* is one of beauty as well as truthfulness. The immediate source for this impression is its style, which has often aroused appreciation for its own sake. It has an economy and an exceptional elegance in the choice of words that give continuous pleasure; it seems in some way incandescent, as if it radiated light. Of course, like any play of Shakespeare's, *Antony and Cleopatra* has a wide range of verbal effects, and in speaking of its 'style' one is selecting some of those which seem dominant and allowing for the presence of others. Even so, one can say of the play as a whole that it has a peculiarly shining surface – what critics later in the seventeenth century would have called 'lustre'. It suggests that the author has been at particular pains to produce an effect of sustained literary finish.

In the course of the play the style becomes almost a presence in its own right, as if we were hearing the voice of the poet himself telling the story (as he does in the Choruses of *Henry V*) – which is one reason why *Antony and Cleopatra* has become so pre-eminently a reader's play.

Moreover all the speakers share in the general eloquence, the lucid, concise, finely restrained utterance – and not only the chief characters but the often unnamed messengers, attendants, and soldiers who surround them. To demonstrate these qualities fully would mean quoting much of the play, but examples would include, among others, the speeches of the Soothsayer and the schoolmaster, Cleopatra's dialogue with Thidias in Act III, scene 13, and most of the final speeches of Cleopatra and her women. In Act IV, scene 5, to take another example, a soldier tells Antony of Enobarbus's desertion:

ANTONY   *Who's gone this morning?*
SOLDIER   *Who?*
  One ever near thee; call for Enobarbus,
  He shall not hear thee, or from Caesar's camp
  Say 'I am none of thine.'   IV.5.6–9

The exchange sounds spontaneous enough, yet a certain collocation of words and sounds gives it an oddly elusive formality, traceable in part to the repeated 'Who', to the internal rhyme, and to the arrangement of the five-syllable phrases in a way suggestive of stanzaic form:

> *One ever near thee*
> *He shall not hear thee*
> *I am none of thine*

At such moments we seem to be reminded that this is not after all 'life' but part of a work of art; the words have an echoing sonority unintended by the speakers. At other times, particularly in the more tragic second movement, Shakespeare often contrives vocalic patterns (for example, 'now the fleeting moon | No planet is of mine', V.2.240–41) to a degree quite unusual for him. Again the effect is to remind us that, despite the play's psychological and

44

structural realism, the actual words that comprise the experience have been chosen by a poet, and that everything we see in the course of the play has been shaped by the poetic imagination. The formal beauty of the lines in which Charmian takes leave of the dead Cleopatra cannot be explained simply in terms of the dramatic situation, powerful and moving though that is:

> *Downy windows, close ;*
> *And golden Phoebus never be beheld*
> *Of eyes again so royal!*   V.2.315–17

Such poetic beauty seems rather the very medium for the play's Apollonian vision, which, while it sees everything as it is in a bright clear light, also transforms it into gold.

Such a style, with its firmly moulded phrasing, its small-scale figurative effects, and its sustained musicality, has many of the qualities of lyrical poetry. The question arises why Shakespeare should have used a lyrical style for a tragedy about Antony and Cleopatra. It might be put in Renaissance terms by asking whom he was imitating. The lyrical style of *Romeo and Juliet*, for example, is sometimes clearly modelled on Petrarch. The style of *Antony and Cleopatra*, on the other hand, in keeping with its Roman subject, points to a Roman model. And the likeliest candidate is Rome's greatest lyric poet, Horace.

The stylistic qualities of *Antony and Cleopatra*, as they have just been described, are very much those of Horace's *Odes* – or those qualities of Horace that could be freely imitated in a modern uninflected language. Neither *Julius Caesar* nor *Coriolanus*, though they often imitate Latin phrasing, could be called Horatian in this sense. But once Horace is entertained as a possible model, the style of *Antony and Cleopatra* seems to be brought into focus. And it is not only a matter of strictly verbal style: some of the themes of the play – empire, love, and wine – were already Horatian themes. Horace was of course a contemporary of Antony's, and – more relevantly – wrote a famous ode on the defeat and death of Cleopatra.

We can hardly know for certain whether Shakespeare was thinking of Horace when he wrote the play. Coleridge, however, said of *Antony and Cleopatra* that '*Feliciter audax* is the motto for its style comparatively with his [Shakespeare's] other works'. By an odd coincidence, if it is one, the source of his Latin phrase is a comment on Horace's *Odes* by the rhetorician Quintilian: '... *verbis felicissime audax*' ('... his boldness in the choice of words is only equalled by his felicity', X.1.96). Indeed Quintilian's phrase not only comments on Horace but itself adapts one of his phrases: '*feliciter audet*' (*Epistles*, II.1.166). The Sentry's words after Enobarbus's death are, like many others, Horatian in just this sense:

> *Hark! The drums*
> *Demurely wake the sleepers.* IV.9.29–30

'Demurely' has just the surprising rightness – Coleridge's 'happy valiancy' – that has always been singled out for praise in the *Odes*.

G. Wilson Knight used the phrase 'imperial magnificence' to describe *Antony and Cleopatra*. It brings to mind not only the splendour of its phrasing and imagery, but its concern with Empire, the lordship of the world. It is perhaps the idea of Empire that might explain Shakespeare's choice of a style reminiscent of the Augustan poet Horace. For the play is an imperial work in a special sense: it was written by the leading dramatist of the King's Men, whose patron was James I, the 'Emperor' of Great Britain. Although no records survive of the early performances of *Antony and Cleopatra*, it is hard to resist the notion that this most courtly of Shakespeare's tragedies must have been performed at James's court. James was England's, or rather 'Britain's', own modern Augustus, for whom Caesar's lines in the play –

> *The time of universal peace is near.*
> *Prove this a prosperous day, the three-nooked world*
> *Shall bear the olive freely –*   IV.6.5–7

would have had a special significance: James was himself an imperial, quasi-Augustan, peacemaker. So the British Augustus may have watched this Augustan tragedy. (He would also, one supposes, have relished the allusions to his predecessor Elizabeth in Cleopatra's scenes with the Messenger – for Elizabeth had questioned her ambassador about Mary Stuart in a remarkably similar way.) Fortunately for us, however, the play transcends the circumstances of its composition. Antony and Cleopatra are still what Shakespeare called them, a famous pair, and not the least factor in the perpetuation of their names is Shakespeare's play.

FURTHER READING

Editions and Editorial Problems

THE most recent scholarly editions of *Antony and Cleopatra* are those by J. Dover Wilson in the New Cambridge Shakespeare (1950) and by M. R. Ridley in the new Arden Shakespeare (1954), which was based on the old Arden edition (1906; 1930) by R. H. Case. Further contributions are made in the Signet edition (1964) by Barbara Everett. To all these, especially the first-named, this edition is much indebted. There are useful and stimulating discussions of particular textual problems by C. J. Sisson in *New Readings in Shakespeare*, Volume 2 (Cambridge, 1956) and by Hilda M. Hulme in *Explorations in Shakespeare's Language* (1962). The Folio text of the play can be studied in *The Norton Facsimile: The First Folio of Shakespeare*, prepared by Charlton Hinman (New York, 1968).

Sources

The fullest collection of sources and analogues is in *Narrative and Dramatic Sources of Shakespeare*, Volume V (1964), edited by Geoffrey Bullough, who also writes a full Introduction. This volume includes not only Plutarch's *Life of Marcus Antonius* but extracts from Lucan, Appian, and others and full texts of the two earlier Antony and Cleopatra plays: the Countess of Pembroke's translation of Robert Garnier's *Marc Antoine*, and Samuel Daniel's *Cleopatra*. For Shakespeare's use of Plutarch, the most useful reprint, with relevant quotations from Shakespeare at the foot of the page, is T. J. B. Spencer's *Shakespeare's Plutarch* (Penguin Books, 1964). M. W. Mac-Callum's detailed study in *Shakespeare's Roman Plays* (1910; reprinted with an introduction by T. J. B. Spencer, 1967) can still be read with profit. For Plutarch himself, D. A. Russell's

Plutarch (1973) may be recommended; it contains a chapter 'From Plutarch to Shakespeare'.

Criticism

Substantial criticism of the play begins with the Romantics, although Dryden could be said to have commented on it by implication in *All for Love* (1678), his very free refurbishing of Shakespeare's play. F. R. Leavis has compared the two plays by examining what Dryden made of the description of Cleopatra on the Cydnus (*Scrutiny* 5, 1936–7). Dr Johnson's brief remarks on *Antony and Cleopatra* occur in his edition of Shakespeare (1765); a selection from the notes is included in *Dr Johnson on Shakespeare*, edited by W. K. Wimsatt (Penguin Books, 1969).

Coleridge has some suggestive remarks on the play (*Lectures on Dramatic Literature*, 1808–19; see *Coleridge on Shakespeare*, edited by Terence Hawkes (Penguin Books, 1969), page 269); his phrases on its style ('*Feliciter audax* ... happy valiancy') have often been used to initiate discussion. Hazlitt's chapter in *Characters of Shakespear's Plays* (1817) has a few fresh observations.

The first major essay on the play is A. C. Bradley's in *Oxford Lectures on Poetry* (1909), where he takes up Coleridge's feelings of doubt – which he meant as the highest form of praise – as to whether *Antony and Cleopatra* was 'a formidable rival' of the four great tragedies. Bradley is firm in stating that it is not their equal, though 'wonderful' in its own right. His essay, one of his best, is an excellent example of his critical procedure, combining judiciousness with strong powers of attention. Bradley took it for granted that the play was 'the most faultily constructed' of Shakespeare's tragedies – an opinion he had already expressed in *Shakespearean Tragedy* (1904). In his *Prefaces to Shakespeare*, Second Series (1930), Harley Granville-Barker met the charge of defective construction by appealing to Elizabethan stage conditions. He is excellent on the battle scenes and especially good at evoking the flow of the play in performance.

In the 1930s *Antony and Cleopatra*, along with the rest of

Shakespeare, became the object of a new kind of intensive study. G. Wilson Knight devoted to it two long essays in *The Imperial Theme* (1931 etc.) which throw a brilliant light on many aspects of it. Even if their general quasi-religious interpretation may be questioned, they are full of new insights into the play's imaginative qualities, its peculiar 'vision', and its poetic style. Above all they insist on the transcendental nature of the love-experience of Antony and Cleopatra, as also did, in a related way, J. Middleton Murry in his *Shakespeare* (1936), who found in the play's final stress on 'royalty' a high spiritual power. As opposed to the enthusiastic self-surrender to the play recorded by these writers, one might range the more sceptical questioning moral note sounded by three critics all associated with the Cambridge journal *Scrutiny*. D. A. Traversi's views were presented first in *An Approach to Shakespeare* (1938; 1968–9) and then, more fully, in *Shakespeare : The Roman Plays* (1963). L. C. Knights's comparably sober, reserved reading appeared in *Some Shakespearian Themes* (1959). In *Shakespeare's Tragedies of Love* (1970), H. A. Mason subjects the play to a sharply-focused examination and refuses to be dazzled by it: he suggests that *Antony and Cleopatra* has more 'organic weakness' than the 'angelic strength' praised by Coleridge. Some of Mason's points are answered by D. J. Enright in the course of a sensible and humane brief commentary in *Shakespeare and the Students* (1970).

Wilson Knight's 'transcendental' interpretation has provoked different kinds of counter-statement, not only from down-to-earth moralists but from historically-minded scholars. Franklin M. Dickey, in *Not Wisely But Too Well* (San Marino, California, 1957), urged the Renaissance's cool attitude to passionate love, and insisted that Shakespeare's play is best understood when traditional appraisals of Antony and Cleopatra, largely unfavourable, are taken into account. Other scholars have made useful comparisons and connexions which have helped to establish a larger cultural context for the play – as did Willard Farnham in *Shakespeare's Tragic Frontier* (Berkeley, California, 1950) and Ernest Schanzer in *The Problem*

Plays of Shakespeare (1963). T. J. B. Spencer's 'Shakespeare and the Elizabethan Romans', in *Shakespeare Survey 10* (Cambridge, 1957), is a brilliant essay on Elizabethan responses to Roman history.

Another group of historical studies centres on the idea of the Heroic and on Shakespeare's conception of his hero. In *The Herculean Hero in Marlowe, Chapman, Shakespeare and Dryden* (New York, 1962), Eugene M. Waith related Antony to the transcendent and morally ambiguous figure of Hercules as it was seen in the Renaissance, while other aspects of the Heroic are treated in Matthew N. Proser's *The Heroic Image in Five Shakespearean Tragedies* (Princeton, N.J., 1965) and in Reuben Brower's *Hero and Saint: Shakespeare and the Graeco-Roman Heroic Tradition* (1971). An original approach to the interpretation of Antony's character is made in Howard Erskine-Hill's 'Antony and Octavius: The Theme of Temperance in Shakespeare's *Antony and Cleopatra'* (*Renaissance and Modern Studies*, edited by J. T. Boulton and R. S. Smith, Nottingham, 1970), which carefully defines Antony's blend of intemperance and magnificence.

Three very different but well considered accounts of the play can be recommended. John F. Danby's essay in *Poets on Fortune's Hill* (1952; reprinted as *Elizabethan and Jacobean Poets*, 1964) interprets the play in terms of its 'peculiarly Shakespearian dialectic' and sees it finally as 'Shakespeare's study of Mars and Venus'. John Holloway's chapter in *The Story of the Night* (1961), in keeping with the thesis of the rest of the book, tries to elucidate a basic tragic pattern involving the progressive isolation of the leading figures. His essay is closely argued, and illuminates a number of other related topics, such as the lovers' concern with their honour and reputation. S. L. Goldberg's '*Antony and Cleopatra*: The Tragedy of the Imagination' (*Melbourne Critical Review*, 1961) focuses suggestively on the play's final phase and, in particular, on Cleopatra's 'dream' of Antony.

A few other studies may be mentioned which treat special topics or particular aspects. In a lecture on *Antony and Cleo-*

patra, reprinted in *Poets and Storytellers* (1949), Lord David Cecil emphasizes its political concerns, and concludes that its main theme is 'success'. In *Character and Motive in Shakespeare* (1949), J. I. M. Stewart defends the characterization of Cleopatra against the charge of fundamental inconsistency. The play's imagery is examined in Maurice Charney's *Shakespeare's Roman Plays: The Function of Imagery in the Drama* (Cambridge, Mass., 1961), and its extended use of paradox in Benjamin T. Spencer's '*Antony and Cleopatra* and the Paradoxical Metaphor' (*Shakespeare Quarterly*, Vol. 9, 1958). Robert Hapgood has some sensitive comments on the style in 'Hearing Shakespeare: Sound and Meaning in *Antony and Cleopatra*' (*Shakespeare Survey 24*, Cambridge, 1971). In *Scenic Form in Shakespeare* (1971) the present editor explores the structure and dramaturgy of the play and its individual scenes. A. P. Riemer's *A Reading of Shakespeare's 'Antony and Cleopatra'* (Sydney, 1968) and Janet Adelman's *The Common Liar: An Essay on 'Antony and Cleopatra'* (New Haven, Connecticut, 1973) are book-length studies; the second is particularly acute on the play's concern with uncertainty of judgement and unreliability of report.

In *Shakespeare Survey 10* (Cambridge, 1957), J. C. Maxwell gives a discriminating account of criticism of the Roman plays. T. J. B. Spencer has a chapter on *Julius Caesar* and *Antony and Cleopatra* in *Shakespeare: Select Bibliographical Guides*, edited by Stanley Wells (1973). The volume on *Antony and Cleopatra* in Macmillan's *Casebook* series, edited by John Russell Brown (1968), reprints some of the best essays on it, including those already mentioned by Bradley, Murry, Holloway, and Dickey, and extracts from those by Granville-Barker and Mason.

ANTONY AND CLEOPATRA

THE CHARACTERS IN THE PLAY

Mark ANTONY
Octavius CAESAR ⎬ triumvirs
LEPIDUS

DEMETRIUS
PHILO
Domitius ENOBARBUS
VENTIDIUS
SILIUS ⎬ Antony's friends and followers
EROS
CANIDIUS
SCARUS
DECRETAS

MAECENAS
AGRIPPA
TAURUS
DOLABELLA ⎬ Caesar's friends and followers
THIDIAS
GALLUS
PROCULEIUS

Sextus POMPEY
MENECRATES
MENAS ⎬ Pompey's friends
VARRIUS

THE CHARACTERS IN THE PLAY

CLEOPATRA, Queen of Egypt
CHARMIAN
IRAS
ALEXAS
MARDIAN } Cleopatra's attendants
DIOMEDES
SELEUCUS

OCTAVIA, Caesar's sister

MESSENGERS
A SOOTHSAYER
ATTENDANTS
SERVANTS
SOLDIERS
A BOY
A schoolmaster, Antony's AMBASSADOR
A SENTRY and WATCH
GUARDS
An EGYPTIAN
A CLOWN

Cleopatra's ladies, eunuchs, servants, soldiers, captains, officers

PHILO

Nay, but this dotage of our general's
O'erflows the measure. Those his goodly eyes,
That o'er the files and musters of the war
Have glowed like plated Mars, now bend, now turn
The office and devotion of their view
Upon a tawny front. His captain's heart,
Which in the scuffles of great fights hath burst
The buckles on his breast, reneges all temper,
And is become the bellows and the fan
To cool a gypsy's lust.

> *Flourish. Enter Antony, Cleopatra, her ladies
> Charmian and Iras, the train, with eunuchs fanning
> her*

       Look where they come.   10
Take but good note, and you shall see in him
The triple pillar of the world transformed
Into a strumpet's fool. Behold and see.

CLEOPATRA

If it be love indeed, tell me how much.

ANTONY

There's beggary in the love that can be reckoned.

CLEOPATRA

I'll set a bourn how far to be beloved.

ANTONY

Then must thou needs find out new heaven, new earth.

> *Enter a Messenger*

MESSENGER

News, my good lord, from Rome.

ANTONY   Grates me! The sum.

CLEOPATRA

Nay, hear them, Antony.
20 Fulvia perchance is angry; or who knows
    If the scarce-bearded Caesar have not sent
    His powerful mandate to you: 'Do this, or this;
    Take in that kingdom, and enfranchise that.
    Perform't, or else we damn thee.'

ANTONY   How, my love?

CLEOPATRA

Perchance? Nay, and most like.
You must not stay here longer. Your dismission
Is come from Caesar. Therefore hear it, Antony.
Where's Fulvia's process? Caesar's I would say! Both!
Call in the messengers. As I am Egypt's Queen,
30 Thou blushest, Antony, and that blood of thine
    Is Caesar's homager; else so thy cheek pays shame
    When shrill-tongued Fulvia scolds. The messengers!

ANTONY

Let Rome in Tiber melt, and the wide arch
Of the ranged empire fall! Here is my space.
Kingdoms are clay. Our dungy earth alike
Feeds beast as man. The nobleness of life
Is to do thus – when such a mutual pair
And such a twain can do't, in which I bind,
On pain of punishment, the world to weet
40 We stand up peerless.

CLEOPATRA   Excellent falsehood!
Why did he marry Fulvia, and not love her?
I'll seem the fool I am not. Antony
Will be himself.

ANTONY   But stirred by Cleopatra.
Now for the love of Love and her soft hours,
Let's not confound the time with conference harsh.
There's not a minute of our lives should stretch
Without some pleasure now. What sport tonight?

CLEOPATRA
Hear the ambassadors.

ANTONY   Fie, wrangling queen!
Whom everything becomes – to chide, to laugh,
To weep; whose every passion fully strives   50
To make itself, in thee, fair and admired.
No messenger but thine; and all alone
Tonight we'll wander through the streets and note
The qualities of people. Come, my queen;
Last night you did desire it. (*To the Messenger*) Speak
        not to us.
                Exeunt Antony and Cleopatra with the train

DEMETRIUS
Is Caesar with Antonius prized so slight?

PHILO
Sir, sometimes, when he is not Antony,
He comes too short of that great property
Which still should go with Antony.

DEMETRIUS   I am full sorry
That he approves the common liar, who   60
Thus speaks of him at Rome; but I will hope
Of better deeds tomorrow. Rest you happy!   *Exeunt*

        Enter Charmian, Iras, and Alexas   I.2
CHARMIAN Lord Alexas, sweet Alexas, most anything
    Alexas, almost most absolute Alexas, where's the sooth-
    sayer that you praised so to th'Queen? O that I knew

this husband, which you say must charge his horns with garlands!

ALEXAS Soothsayer!

Enter a Soothsayer

SOOTHSAYER Your will?

CHARMIAN Is this the man? Is't you, sir, that know things?

SOOTHSAYER

10 In Nature's infinite book of secrecy
A little I can read.

ALEXAS   Show him your hand.

Enter Enobarbus

ENOBARBUS

Bring in the banquet quickly; wine enough
Cleopatra's health to drink.

CHARMIAN (*to Soothsayer*) Good sir, give me good fortune.

SOOTHSAYER I make not, but foresee.

CHARMIAN Pray then, foresee me one.

SOOTHSAYER

You shall be yet far fairer than you are.

CHARMIAN He means in flesh.

20 IRAS No, you shall paint when you are old.

CHARMIAN Wrinkles forbid!

ALEXAS Vex not his prescience; be attentive.

CHARMIAN Hush!

SOOTHSAYER

You shall be more beloving than beloved.

CHARMIAN I had rather heat my liver with drinking.

ALEXAS Nay, hear him.

CHARMIAN Good now, some excellent fortune! Let me be married to three kings in a forenoon and widow them all. Let me have a child at fifty, to whom Herod of

Jewry may do homage. Find me to marry me with 30
Octavius Caesar, and companion me with my mistress.

SOOTHSAYER
 You shall outlive the lady whom you serve.

CHARMIAN O, excellent! I love long life better than figs.

SOOTHSAYER
 You have seen and proved a fairer former fortune
 Than that which is to approach.

CHARMIAN Then belike my children shall have no
 names. Prithee, how many boys and wenches must I
 have?

SOOTHSAYER
 If every of your wishes had a womb,
 And fertile every wish, a million.   40

CHARMIAN Out, fool, I forgive thee for a witch.

ALEXAS You think none but your sheets are privy to your
 wishes.

CHARMIAN Nay, come, tell Iras hers.

ALEXAS We'll know all our fortunes.

ENOBARBUS Mine, and most of our fortunes, tonight
 shall be drunk to bed.

IRAS There's a palm presages chastity, if nothing else.

CHARMIAN E'en as the o'erflowing Nilus presageth
 famine.   50

IRAS (to Charmian) Go, you wild bedfellow, you cannot
 soothsay.

CHARMIAN Nay, if an oily palm be not a fruitful prognostication, I cannot scratch mine ear. Prithee, tell her
 but a workyday fortune.

SOOTHSAYER Your fortunes are alike.

IRAS But how, but how? Give me particulars.

SOOTHSAYER I have said.

IRAS Am I not an inch of fortune better than she?

60 CHARMIAN Well, if you were but an inch of fortune
better than I, where would you choose it?

IRAS Not in my husband's nose.

CHARMIAN Our worser thoughts heavens mend! Alexas –
come, his fortune, his fortune! O, let him marry a
woman that cannot go, sweet Isis, I beseech thee, and
let her die too, and give him a worse, and let worse
follow worse till the worst of all follow him laughing to
his grave, fiftyfold a cuckold! Good Isis, hear me this
prayer, though thou deny me a matter of more weight;
70 good Isis, I beseech thee!

IRAS Amen. Dear goddess, hear that prayer of the people!
For, as it is a heart-breaking to see a handsome man
loose-wived, so it is a deadly sorrow to behold a foul
knave uncuckolded. Therefore, dear Isis, keep decorum,
and fortune him accordingly!

CHARMIAN Amen.

ALEXAS Lo now, if it lay in their hands to make me a
cuckold, they would make themselves whores but
they'd do't.

ENOBARBUS

80 Hush! Here comes Antony.

CHARMIAN   Not he; the Queen.
            Enter Cleopatra

CLEOPATRA
Saw you my lord?

ENOBARBUS   No, lady.

CLEOPATRA   Was he not here?

CHARMIAN
No, madam.

CLEOPATRA
He was disposed to mirth; but on the sudden
A Roman thought hath struck him. Enobarbus!

ENOBARBUS
Madam?

CLEOPATRA
Seek him, and bring him hither. Where's Alexas?

ALEXAS
Here at your service. My lord approaches.
Enter Antony with a Messenger and Attendants

CLEOPATRA
We will not look upon him. Go with us.
Exeunt all but Antony, Messenger, and Attendants

MESSENGER
Fulvia thy wife first came into the field.

ANTONY
Against my brother Lucius?   90

MESSENGER
Ay.
But soon that war had end, and the time's state
Made friends of them, jointing their force 'gainst
    Caesar,
Whose better issue in the war from Italy
Upon the first encounter drave them.

ANTONY   Well, what worst?

MESSENGER
The nature of bad news infects the teller.

ANTONY
When it concerns the fool or coward. On.
Things that are past are done, with me. 'Tis thus:
Who tells me true, though in his tale lie death,
I hear him as he flattered.

MESSENGER   Labienus –   100
This is stiff news – hath with his Parthian force
Extended Asia; from Euphrates
His conquering banner shook, from Syria

> To Lydia and to Ionia,
> Whilst –

ANTONY Antony, thou wouldst say –

MESSENGER   O, my lord.

ANTONY

> Speak to me home; mince not the general tongue.
> Name Cleopatra as she is called in Rome.
> Rail thou in Fulvia's phrase, and taunt my faults
> With such full licence as both truth and malice
110 Have power to utter. O, then we bring forth weeds
> When our quick winds lie still, and our ills told us
> Is as our earing. Fare thee well awhile.

MESSENGER

> At your noble pleasure.   *Exit*

ANTONY

> From Sicyon, ho, the news? Speak there!

FIRST ATTENDANT

> The man from Sicyon – is there such an one?

SECOND ATTENDANT

> He stays upon your will.

ANTONY   Let him appear.

> (*aside*) These strong Egyptian fetters I must break,
> Or lose myself in dotage.

> > *Enter another Messenger, with a letter*
> >   What are you?

MESSENGER

> Fulvia thy wife is dead.

ANTONY   Where died she?

MESSENGER

120 In Sicyon.

> Her length of sickness, with what else more serious
> Importeth thee to know, this bears.

> > *He gives him the letter*

ANTONY   Forbear me.

Exit Messenger

There's a great spirit gone! Thus did I desire it.
What our contempts doth often hurl from us,
We wish it ours again. The present pleasure,
By revolution lowering, does become
The opposite of itself. She's good, being gone;
The hand could pluck her back that shoved her on.
I must from this enchanting queen break off.
Ten thousand harms, more than the ills I know,   130
My idleness doth hatch. How now, Enobarbus!

Enter Enobarbus

ENOBARBUS What's your pleasure, sir?

ANTONY I must with haste from hence.

ENOBARBUS Why, then we kill all our women. We see
how mortal an unkindness is to them. If they suffer
our departure, death's the word.

ANTONY I must be gone.

ENOBARBUS Under a compelling occasion, let women die.
It were pity to cast them away for nothing, though
between them and a great cause they should be esteemed   140
nothing. Cleopatra, catching but the least noise of this,
dies instantly. I have seen her die twenty times upon
far poorer moment. I do think there is mettle in death,
which commits some loving act upon her, she hath such
a celerity in dying.

ANTONY She is cunning past man's thought.

ENOBARBUS Alack, sir, no; her passions are made of
nothing but the finest part of pure love. We cannot call
her winds and waters sighs and tears; they are greater
storms and tempests than almanacs can report. This   150
cannot be cunning in her; if it be, she makes a shower
of rain as well as Jove.

ANTONY Would I had never seen her!

ENOBARBUS O, sir, you had then left unseen a wonderful
piece of work, which not to have been blessed withal
would have discredited your travel.

ANTONY Fulvia is dead.

ENOBARBUS Sir?

ANTONY Fulvia is dead.

160 ENOBARBUS Fulvia?

ANTONY Dead.

ENOBARBUS Why, sir, give the gods a thankful sacrifice.
When it pleaseth their deities to take the wife of a man
from him, it shows to man the tailors of the earth;
comforting therein that when old robes are worn out
there are members to make new. If there were no more
women but Fulvia, then had you indeed a cut, and the
case to be lamented. This grief is crowned with con-
solation: your old smock brings forth a new petticoat;
170 and indeed the tears live in an onion that should water
this sorrow.

ANTONY
   The business she hath broachèd in the state
   Cannot endure my absence.

ENOBARBUS And the business you have broached here
cannot be without you; especially that of Cleopatra's,
which wholly depends on your abode.

ANTONY
   No more light answers. Let our officers
   Have notice what we purpose. I shall break
   The cause of our expedience to the Queen
180 And get her leave to part. For not alone
   The death of Fulvia, with more urgent touches,
   Do strongly speak to us, but the letters too
   Of many our contriving friends in Rome

68

Petition us at home. Sextus Pompeius
Hath given the dare to Caesar and commands
The empire of the sea. Our slippery people,
Whose love is never linked to the deserver
Till his deserts are past, begin to throw
Pompey the Great and all his dignities
Upon his son; who, high in name and power, 190
Higher than both in blood and life, stands up
For the main soldier; whose quality, going on,
The sides o'th'world may danger. Much is breeding
Which, like the courser's hair, hath yet but life
And not a serpent's poison. Say our pleasure,
To such whose place is under us, requires
Our quick remove from hence.

ENOBARBUS I shall do't.   *Exeunt*

Enter Cleopatra, Charmian, Alexas, and Iras   I.3

CLEOPATRA
  Where is he?
CHARMIAN   I did not see him since.
CLEOPATRA *(to Alexas)*
  See where he is, who's with him, what he does.
  I did not send you. If you find him sad,
  Say I am dancing; if in mirth, report
  That I am sudden sick. Quick, and return.
                              Exit Alexas
CHARMIAN
  Madam, methinks, if you did love him dearly,
  You do not hold the method to enforce
  The like from him.
CLEOPATRA   What should I do I do not?

CHARMIAN

In each thing give him way. Cross him in nothing.

CLEOPATRA

10 Thou teachest like a fool: the way to lose him.

CHARMIAN

Tempt him not so too far. I wish, forbear.
In time we hate that which we often fear.

Enter Antony

But here comes Antony.

CLEOPATRA   I am sick and sullen.

ANTONY

I am sorry to give breathing to my purpose –

CLEOPATRA

Help me away, dear Charmian! I shall fall.
It cannot be thus long; the sides of nature
Will not sustain it.

ANTONY   Now, my dearest queen –

CLEOPATRA

Pray you, stand farther from me.

ANTONY   What's the matter?

CLEOPATRA

I know by that same eye there's some good news.
20 What says the married woman – you may go?
Would she had never given you leave to come!
Let her not say 'tis I that keep you here.
I have no power upon you. Hers you are.

ANTONY

The gods best know –

CLEOPATRA   O, never was there queen
So mightily betrayed! Yet at the first
I saw the treasons planted.

ANTONY   Cleopatra –

CLEOPATRA

Why should I think you can be mine, and true –

Though you in swearing shake the thronèd gods —
Who have been false to Fulvia? Riotous madness,
To be entangled with those mouth-made vows   30
Which break themselves in swearing!

ANTONY   Most sweet queen —

CLEOPATRA

Nay, pray you seek no colour for your going,
But bid farewell, and go. When you sued staying,
Then was the time for words. No going then!
Eternity was in our lips and eyes,
Bliss in our brows' bent; none our parts so poor
But was a race of heaven. They are so still,
Or thou, the greatest soldier of the world,
Art turned the greatest liar.

ANTONY   How now, lady!

CLEOPATRA

I would I had thy inches. Thou shouldst know   40
There were a heart in Egypt.

ANTONY   Hear me, Queen.
The strong necessity of time commands
Our services awhile; but my full heart
Remains in use with you. Our Italy
Shines o'er with civil swords. Sextus Pompeius
Makes his approaches to the port of Rome.
Equality of two domestic powers
Breed scrupulous faction; the hated, grown to strength,
Are newly grown to love. The condemned Pompey,
Rich in his father's honour, creeps apace   50
Into the hearts of such as have not thrived
Upon the present state, whose numbers threaten;
And quietness, grown sick of rest, would purge
By any desperate change. My more particular,
And that which most with you should safe my going,
Is Fulvia's death.

CLEOPATRA

Though age from folly could not give me freedom,
It does from childishness. Can Fulvia die?

ANTONY

She's dead, my queen.
60 Look here,
(*He gives her the letter*)
and at thy sovereign leisure read
The garboils she awaked. At the last, best,
See when and where she died.

CLEOPATRA   O most false love!

Where be the sacred vials thou shouldst fill
With sorrowful water? Now I see, I see,
In Fulvia's death, how mine received shall be.

ANTONY

Quarrel no more, but be prepared to know
The purposes I bear; which are, or cease,
As you shall give th'advice. By the fire
That quickens Nilus' slime, I go from hence
70 Thy soldier-servant, making peace or war
As thou affects.

CLEOPATRA   Cut my lace, Charmian, come.

But let it be. I am quickly ill and well,
So Antony loves.

ANTONY   My precious queen, forbear,

And give true evidence to his love, which stands
An honourable trial.

CLEOPATRA   So Fulvia told me.

I prithee turn aside and weep for her;
Then bid adieu to me, and say the tears
Belong to Egypt. Good now, play one scene
Of excellent dissembling, and let it look
80 Like perfect honour.

ANTONY   You'll heat my blood; no more.

CLEOPATRA
  You can do better yet; but this is meetly.
ANTONY
  Now by my sword –
CLEOPATRA   And target. Still he mends.
  But this is not the best. Look, prithee, Charmian,
  How this Herculean Roman does become
  The carriage of his chafe.
ANTONY   I'll leave you, lady.
CLEOPATRA
  Courteous lord, one word.
  Sir, you and I must part, but that's not it.
  Sir, you and I have loved, but there's not it.
  That you know well. Something it is I would –
  O, my oblivion is a very Antony,   90
  And I am all forgotten.
ANTONY   But that your royalty
  Holds idleness your subject, I should take you
  For idleness itself.
CLEOPATRA   'Tis sweating labour
  To bear such idleness so near the heart
  As Cleopatra this. But, sir, forgive me,
  Since my becomings kill me when they do not
  Eye well to you. Your honour calls you hence.
  Therefore be deaf to my unpitied folly,
  And all the gods go with you! Upon your sword
  Sit laurel victory, and smooth success   100
  Be strewed before your feet!
ANTONY   Let us go. Come.
  Our separation so abides and flies
  That thou residing here goes yet with me,
  And I hence fleeting here remain with thee.
  Away!   *Exeunt*

Enter Octavius Caesar, reading a letter, Lepidus, and
        their train

CAESAR

    You may see, Lepidus, and henceforth know
    It is not Caesar's natural vice to hate
    Our great competitor. From Alexandria
    This is the news: he fishes, drinks, and wastes
    The lamps of night in revel; is not more manlike
    Than Cleopatra, nor the queen of Ptolemy
    More womanly than he; hardly gave audience, or
    Vouchsafed to think he had partners. You shall find
        there
    A man who is the abstract of all faults

10 That all men follow.

LEPIDUS   I must not think there are
    Evils enow to darken all his goodness.
    His faults, in him, seem as the spots of heaven,
    More fiery by night's blackness, hereditary
    Rather than purchased, what he cannot change
    Than what he chooses.

CAESAR

    You are too indulgent. Let's grant it is not
    Amiss to tumble on the bed of Ptolemy,
    To give a kingdom for a mirth, to sit
    And keep the turn of tippling with a slave,

20 To reel the streets at noon, and stand the buffet
    With knaves that smells of sweat. Say this becomes him –
    As his composure must be rare indeed
    Whom these things cannot blemish – yet must Antony
    No way excuse his foils when we do bear
    So great weight in his lightness. If he filled
    His vacancy with his voluptuousness,
    Full surfeits and the dryness of his bones
    Call on him for't. But to confound such time

That drums him from his sport and speaks as loud
As his own state and ours, 'tis to be chid   30
As we rate boys who, being mature in knowledge,
Pawn their experience to their present pleasure
And so rebel to judgement.

Enter a Messenger

LEPIDUS   Here's more news.

MESSENGER
Thy biddings have been done; and every hour,
Most noble Caesar, shalt thou have report
How 'tis abroad. Pompey is strong at sea,
And it appears he is beloved of those
That only have feared Caesar; to the ports
The discontents repair, and men's reports
Give him much wronged.

CAESAR   I should have known no less.   40
It hath been taught us from the primal state
That he which is was wished until he were;
And the ebbed man, ne'er loved till ne'er worth love,
Comes deared by being lacked. This common body,
Like to a vagabond flag upon the stream,
Goes to and back, lackeying the varying tide,
To rot itself with motion.

MESSENGER   Caesar, I bring thee word
Menecrates and Menas, famous pirates,
Makes the sea serve them, which they ear and wound
With keels of every kind. Many hot inroads   50
They make in Italy. The borders maritime
Lack blood to think on't, and flush youth revolt.
No vessel can peep forth but 'tis as soon
Taken as seen; for Pompey's name strikes more
Than could his war resisted.

CAESAR   Antony,
Leave thy lascivious wassails. When thou once

Was beaten from Modena, where thou slew'st
Hirtius and Pansa, consuls, at thy heel
Did famine follow, whom thou fought'st against,
60 Though daintily brought up, with patience more
Than savages could suffer. Thou didst drink
The stale of horses and the gilded puddle
Which beasts would cough at. Thy palate then did
    deign
The roughest berry on the rudest hedge.
Yea, like the stag when snow the pasture sheets,
The barks of trees thou browsèd'st. On the Alps
It is reported thou didst eat strange flesh,
Which some did die to look on. And all this –
It wounds thine honour that I speak it now –
70 Was borne so like a soldier that thy cheek
So much as lanked not.

LEPIDUS   'Tis pity of him.

CAESAR
Let his shames quickly
Drive him to Rome. 'Tis time we twain
Did show ourselves i'th'field; and to that end
Assemble we immediate council. Pompey
Thrives in our idleness.

LEPIDUS   Tomorrow, Caesar,
I shall be furnished to inform you rightly
Both what by sea and land I can be able
To front this present time.

CAESAR   Till which encounter,
80 It is my business too. Farewell.

LEPIDUS
Farewell, my lord. What you shall know meantime
Of stirs abroad, I shall beseech you, sir,
To let me be partaker.

CAESAR   Doubt not, sir;
  I knew it for my bond.   *Exeunt*

    Enter Cleopatra, Charmian, Iras, and Mardian   I.5
CLEOPATRA
  Charmian!
CHARMIAN
  Madam?
CLEOPATRA (*yawning*)
  Ha, ha.
  Give me to drink mandragora.
CHARMIAN   Why, madam?
CLEOPATRA
  That I might sleep out this great gap of time
  My Antony is away.
CHARMIAN   You think of him too much.
CLEOPATRA
  O, 'tis treason!
CHARMIAN   Madam, I trust, not so.
CLEOPATRA
  Thou, eunuch Mardian!
MARDIAN   What's your highness' pleasure?
CLEOPATRA
  Not now to hear thee sing. I take no pleasure
  In aught an eunuch has. 'Tis well for thee   10
  That, being unseminared, thy freer thoughts
  May not fly forth of Egypt. Hast thou affections?
MARDIAN
  Yes, gracious madam.
CLEOPATRA
  Indeed?
MARDIAN
  Not in deed, madam; for I can do nothing

77

But what indeed is honest to be done.
Yet have I fierce affections, and think
What Venus did with Mars.

CLEOPATRA   O, Charmian,
Where think'st thou he is now? Stands he, or sits he?
20 Or does he walk? Or is he on his horse?
O happy horse, to bear the weight of Antony!
Do bravely, horse, for wot'st thou whom thou mov'st?
The demi-Atlas of this earth, the arm
And burgonet of men. He's speaking now,
Or murmuring 'Where's my serpent of old Nile?'
For so he calls me. Now I feed myself
With most delicious poison. Think on me,
That am with Phoebus' amorous pinches black
And wrinkled deep in time. Broad-fronted Caesar,
30 When thou wast here above the ground, I was
A morsel for a monarch; and great Pompey
Would stand and make his eyes grow in my brow;
There would he anchor his aspect, and die
With looking on his life.

          Enter Alexas

ALEXAS   Sovereign of Egypt, hail!

CLEOPATRA
How much unlike art thou Mark Antony!
Yet, coming from him, that great medicine hath
With his tinct gilded thee.
How goes it with my brave Mark Antony?

ALEXAS
Last thing he did, dear Queen,
40 He kissed – the last of many doubled kisses –
This orient pearl. His speech sticks in my heart.

CLEOPATRA
Mine ear must pluck it thence.

ALEXAS   'Good friend,' quoth he,

'Say the firm Roman to great Egypt sends
This treasure of an oyster; at whose foot,
To mend the petty present, I will piece
Her opulent throne with kingdoms. All the East,
Say thou, shall call her mistress.' So he nodded,
And soberly did mount an arrogant steed,
Who neighed so high that what I would have spoke
Was beastly dumbed by him.

CLEOPATRA   What was he, sad or merry? 50

ALEXAS

Like to the time o'th'year between the extremes
Of hot and cold, he was nor sad nor merry.

CLEOPATRA

O well-divided disposition! Note him,
Note him, good Charmian, 'tis the man; but note him!
He was not sad, for he would shine on those
That make their looks by his; he was not merry,
Which seemed to tell them his remembrance lay
In Egypt with his joy; but between both.
O heavenly mingle! Be'st thou sad or merry,
The violence of either thee becomes,   60
So does it no man else. Met'st thou my posts?

ALEXAS

Ay, madam, twenty several messengers.
Why do you send so thick?

CLEOPATRA   Who's born that day
When I forget to send to Antony
Shall die a beggar. Ink and paper, Charmian.
Welcome, my good Alexas. Did I, Charmian,
Ever love Caesar so?

CHARMIAN   O, that brave Caesar!

CLEOPATRA

Be choked with such another emphasis!
Say 'the brave Antony'.

CHARMIAN   The valiant Caesar!
CLEOPATRA
70   By Isis, I will give thee bloody teeth
     If thou with Caesar paragon again
     My man of men.
CHARMIAN   By your most gracious pardon,
     I sing but after you.
CLEOPATRA   My salad days,
     When I was green in judgement, cold in blood,
     To say as I said then. But come, away,
     Get me ink and paper.
     He shall have every day a several greeting,
     Or I'll unpeople Egypt.   *Exeunt*

*

II.1   *Enter Pompey, Menecrates, and Menas, in warlike*
              manner

POMPEY
     If the great gods be just, they shall assist
     The deeds of justest men.
MENECRATES   Know, worthy Pompey,
     That what they do delay they not deny.
POMPEY
     Whiles we are suitors to their throne, decays
     The thing we sue for.
MENECRATES   We, ignorant of ourselves,
     Beg often our own harms, which the wise powers
     Deny us for our good; so find we profit
     By losing of our prayers.
POMPEY   I shall do well.
     The people love me, and the sea is mine;
10   My powers are crescent, and my auguring hope

Says it will come to th'full. Mark Antony
In Egypt sits at dinner, and will make
No wars without doors. Caesar gets money where
He loses hearts. Lepidus flatters both,
Of both is flattered; but he neither loves,
Nor either cares for him.

MENAS   Caesar and Lepidus
Are in the field. A mighty strength they carry.

POMPEY
Where have you this? 'Tis false.

MENAS   From Silvius, sir.

POMPEY
He dreams. I know they are in Rome together,
Looking for Antony. But all the charms of love,   20
Salt Cleopatra, soften thy waned lip!
Let witchcraft join with beauty, lust with both!
Tie up the libertine in a field of feasts;
Keep his brain fuming. Epicurean cooks
Sharpen with cloyless sauce his appetite,
That sleep and feeding may prorogue his honour
Even till a Lethe'd dullness –

> *Enter Varrius*

                              How now, Varrius?

VARRIUS
This is most certain that I shall deliver:
Mark Antony is every hour in Rome
Expected. Since he went from Egypt 'tis   30
A space for farther travel.

POMPEY   I could have given less matter
A better ear. Menas, I did not think
This amorous surfeiter would have donned his helm
For such a petty war. His soldiership
Is twice the other twain. But let us rear
The higher our opinion, that our stirring

Can from the lap of Egypt's widow pluck
The ne'er lust-wearied Antony.

MENAS   I cannot hope
Caesar and Antony shall well greet together.
40   His wife that's dead did trespasses to Caesar.
His brother warred upon him – although, I think,
Not moved by Antony.

POMPEY   I know not, Menas,
How lesser enmities may give way to greater.
Were't not that we stand up against them all,
'Twere pregnant they should square between them-
          selves,
For they have entertainèd cause enough
To draw their swords. But how the fear of us
May cement their divisions and bind up
The petty difference, we yet not know.
50   Be't as our gods will have't! It only stands
Our lives upon to use our strongest hands.
Come, Menas.   *Exeunt*

II.2   *Enter Enobarbus and Lepidus*

LEPIDUS
Good Enobarbus, 'tis a worthy deed,
And shall become you well, to entreat your captain
To soft and gentle speech.

ENOBARBUS   I shall entreat him
To answer like himself. If Caesar move him,
Let Antony look over Caesar's head
And speak as loud as Mars. By Jupiter,
Were I the wearer of Antonio's beard,
I would not shave't today.

LEPIDUS   'Tis not a time
For private stomaching.

ENOBARBUS   Every time
  Serves for the matter that is then born in't.   10
LEPIDUS
  But small to greater matters must give way.
ENOBARBUS
  Not if the small come first.
LEPIDUS   Your speech is passion;
  But pray you stir no embers up. Here comes
  The noble Antony.
        Enter Antony and Ventidius
ENOBARBUS   And yonder Caesar.
        Enter Caesar, Maecenas, and Agrippa
ANTONY
  If we compose well here, to Parthia.
  Hark, Ventidius.
CAESAR   I do not know,
  Maecenas; ask Agrippa.
LEPIDUS (*to Caesar and Antony*) Noble friends,
  That which combined us was most great, and let not
  A leaner action rend us. What's amiss,
  May it be gently heard. When we debate   20
  Our trivial difference loud, we do commit
  Murder in healing wounds. Then, noble partners,
  The rather for I earnestly beseech,
  Touch you the sourest points with sweetest terms,
  Nor curstness grow to th'matter.
ANTONY   'Tis spoken well.
  Were we before our armies, and to fight,
  I should do thus.
        Flourish
CAESAR
  Welcome to Rome.
ANTONY
  Thank you.

83

CAESAR

30   Sit.

ANTONY

Sit, sir.

CAESAR

Nay then.

    They sit

ANTONY

I learn you take things ill which are not so,
Or, being, concern you not.

CAESAR   I must be laughed at
If, or for nothing or a little, I
Should say myself offended, and with you
Chiefly i'th'world; more laughed at that I should
Once name you derogately, when to sound your name
It not concerned me.

ANTONY   My being in Egypt, Caesar,
40   What was't to you?

CAESAR

No more than my residing here at Rome
Might be to you in Egypt. Yet if you there
Did practise on my state, your being in Egypt
Might be my question.

ANTONY   How intend you – practised?

CAESAR

You may be pleased to catch at mine intent
By what did here befall me. Your wife and brother
Made wars upon me, and their contestation
Was theme for you. You were the word of war.

ANTONY

You do mistake your business. My brother never
50   Did urge me in his act. I did inquire it,
And have my learning from some true reports
That drew their swords with you. Did he not rather

84

Discredit my authority with yours,
And make the wars alike against my stomach,
Having alike your cause? Of this, my letters
Before did satisfy you. If you'll patch a quarrel,
As matter whole you have to make it with,
It must not be with this.

CAESAR   You praise yourself
By laying defects of judgement to me, but
You patched up your excuses.

ANTONY   Not so, not so;   60
I know you could not lack, I am certain on't,
Very necessity of this thought, that I,
Your partner in the cause 'gainst which he fought,
Could not with graceful eyes attend those wars
Which fronted mine own peace. As for my wife,
I would you had her spirit in such another;
The third o'th'world is yours, which with a snaffle
You may pace easy, but not such a wife.

ENOBARBUS Would we had all such wives, that the men
might go to wars with the women.   70

ANTONY

So much uncurbable, her garboils, Caesar,
Made out of her impatience – which not wanted
Shrewdness of policy too – I grieving grant
Did you too much disquiet. For that you must
But say I could not help it.

CAESAR   I wrote to you
When, rioting in Alexandria, you
Did pocket up my letters, and with taunts
Did gibe my missive out of audience.

ANTONY   Sir,
He fell upon me, ere admitted, then.
Three kings I had newly feasted, and did want   80
Of what I was i'th'morning; but next day

I told him of myself, which was as much
As to have asked him pardon. Let this fellow
Be nothing of our strife; if we contend,
Out of our question wipe him.

CAESAR   You have broken
The article of your oath, which you shall never
Have tongue to charge me with.

LEPIDUS   Soft, Caesar!

ANTONY
No, Lepidus; let him speak.
The honour is sacred which he talks on now,
90 Supposing that I lacked it. But on, Caesar:
The article of my oath –

CAESAR
To lend me arms and aid when I required them,
The which you both denied.

ANTONY   Neglected rather;
And then when poisoned hours had bound me up
From mine own knowledge. As nearly as I may,
I'll play the penitent to you; but mine honesty
Shall not make poor my greatness, nor my power
Work without it. Truth is that Fulvia,
To have me out of Egypt, made wars here,
100 For which myself, the ignorant motive, do
So far ask pardon as befits mine honour
To stoop in such a case.

LEPIDUS   'Tis noble spoken.

MAECENAS
If it might please you to enforce no further
The griefs between ye: to forget them quite
Were to remember that the present need
Speaks to atone you.

LEPIDUS   Worthily spoken, Maecenas.

ENOBARBUS Or, if you borrow one another's love for the

instant, you may, when you hear no more words of
Pompey, return it again: you shall have time to wrangle
in when you have nothing else to do.   110

ANTONY

Thou art a soldier only. Speak no more.

ENOBARBUS That truth should be silent I had almost
forgot.

ANTONY

You wrong this presence; therefore speak no more.

ENOBARBUS Go to, then; your considerate stone.

CAESAR

I do not much dislike the matter, but
The manner of his speech; for't cannot be
We shall remain in friendship, our conditions
So diff'ring in their acts. Yet if I knew
What hoop should hold us staunch, from edge to edge   120
O'th'world I would pursue it.

AGRIPPA   Give me leave, Caesar.

CAESAR

Speak, Agrippa.

AGRIPPA

Thou hast a sister by the mother's side,
Admired Octavia. Great Mark Antony
Is now a widower.

CAESAR   Say not so, Agrippa.
If Cleopatra heard you, your reproof
Were well deserved of rashness.

ANTONY

I am not married, Caesar. Let me hear
Agrippa further speak.

AGRIPPA

To hold you in perpetual amity,   130
To make you brothers, and to knit your hearts
With an unslipping knot, take Antony

87

Octavia to his wife; whose beauty claims
No worse a husband than the best of men;
Whose virtue and whose general graces speak
That which none else can utter. By this marriage
All little jealousies, which now seem great,
And all great fears, which now import their dangers,
Would then be nothing. Truths would be tales,
140   Where now half-tales be truths. Her love to both
Would each to other, and all loves to both,
Draw after her. Pardon what I have spoke,
For 'tis a studied, not a present thought,
By duty ruminated.

ANTONY   Will Caesar speak?

CAESAR

Not till he hears how Antony is touched
With what is spoke already.

ANTONY   What power is in Agrippa,
If I would say 'Agrippa, be it so',
To make this good?

CAESAR   The power of Caesar, and
His power unto Octavia.

ANTONY   May I never
150   To this good purpose, that so fairly shows,
Dream of impediment! Let me have thy hand.
Further this act of grace, and from this hour
The heart of brothers govern in our loves
And sway our great designs.

CAESAR   There's my hand.
A sister I bequeath you whom no brother
Did ever love so dearly. Let her live
To join our kingdoms and our hearts; and never
Fly off our loves again.

LEPIDUS   Happily, amen.

ANTONY
  I did not think to draw my sword 'gainst Pompey,
  For he hath laid strange courtesies and great   160
  Of late upon me. I must thank him only,
  Lest my remembrance suffer ill report;
  At heel of that, defy him.

LEPIDUS   Time calls upon's.
  Of us must Pompey presently be sought,
  Or else he seeks out us.

ANTONY   Where lies he?

CAESAR
  About the Mount Misena.

ANTONY   What is his strength?

CAESAR
  By land, great and increasing; but by sea
  He is an absolute master.

ANTONY   So is the fame.
  Would we had spoke together! Haste we for it.
  Yet, ere we put ourselves in arms, dispatch we   170
  The business we have talked of.

CAESAR   With most gladness;
  And do invite you to my sister's view,
  Whither straight I'll lead you.

ANTONY   Let us, Lepidus,
  Not lack your company.

LEPIDUS   Noble Antony,
  Not sickness should detain me.

                 Flourish. Exeunt all but Enobarbus,
                        Agrippa, and Maecenas

MAECENAS Welcome from Egypt, sir.

ENOBARBUS Half the heart of Caesar, worthy Maecenas.
  My honourable friend, Agrippa.

AGRIPPA Good Enobarbus.

180 MAECENAS We have cause to be glad that matters are so
well disgested. You stayed well by't in Egypt.

ENOBARBUS Ay, sir, we did sleep day out of countenance
and made the night light with drinking.

MAECENAS Eight wild boars roasted whole at a breakfast,
and but twelve persons there. Is this true?

ENOBARBUS This was but as a fly by an eagle. We had
much more monstrous matter of feast, which worthily
deserved noting.

MAECENAS She's a most triumphant lady, if report be
190 square to her.

ENOBARBUS When she first met Mark Antony, she
pursed up his heart, upon the river of Cydnus.

AGRIPPA There she appeared indeed! Or my reporter
devised well for her.

ENOBARBUS
I will tell you.
The barge she sat in, like a burnished throne,
Burned on the water. The poop was beaten gold;
Purple the sails, and so perfumèd that
The winds were lovesick with them. The oars were
        silver,
200 Which to the tune of flutes kept stroke and made
The water which they beat to follow faster,
As amorous of their strokes. For her own person,
It beggared all description. She did lie
In her pavilion, cloth-of-gold of tissue,
O'erpicturing that Venus where we see
The fancy outwork nature. On each side her
Stood pretty dimpled boys, like smiling cupids,
With divers-coloured fans, whose wind did seem
To glow the delicate cheeks which they did cool,
210 And what they undid did.

AGRIPPA   O, rare for Antony!

ENOBARBUS

Her gentlewomen, like the Nereides,
So many mermaids, tended her i'th'eyes,
And made their bends adornings. At the helm
A seeming mermaid steers. The silken tackle
Swell with the touches of those flower-soft hands,
That yarely frame the office. From the barge
A strange invisible perfume hits the sense
Of the adjacent wharfs. The city cast
Her people out upon her; and Antony,
Enthroned i'th'market-place, did sit alone,   220
Whistling to th'air; which, but for vacancy,
Had gone to gaze on Cleopatra too,
And made a gap in nature.

AGRIPPA   Rare Egyptian!

ENOBARBUS

Upon her landing, Antony sent to her,
Invited her to supper. She replied
It should be better he became her guest;
Which she entreated. Our courteous Antony,
Whom ne'er the word of 'No' woman heard speak,
Being barbered ten times o'er, goes to the feast,
And, for his ordinary, pays his heart   230
For what his eyes eat only.

AGRIPPA   Royal wench!
She made great Caesar lay his sword to bed.
He ploughed her, and she cropped.

ENOBARBUS   I saw her once
Hop forty paces through the public street;
And, having lost her breath, she spoke, and panted,
That she did make defect perfection,
And, breathless, power breathe forth.

MAECENAS

Now Antony must leave her utterly.

ENOBARBUS
 Never; he will not.
240 Age cannot wither her, nor custom stale
  Her infinite variety. Other women cloy
  The appetites they feed, but she makes hungry
  Where most she satisfies; for vilest things
  Become themselves in her, that the holy priests
  Bless her when she is riggish.

MAECENAS
 If beauty, wisdom, modesty, can settle
  The heart of Antony, Octavia is
  A blessèd lottery to him.

AGRIPPA   Let us go.
 Good Enobarbus, make yourself my guest
250 Whilst you abide here.

ENOBARBUS   Humbly, sir, I thank you.

             Exeunt

II.3   *Enter Antony and Caesar, with Octavia between them*

ANTONY
 The world and my great office will sometimes
  Divide me from your bosom.

OCTAVIA   All which time,
 Before the gods my knee shall bow my prayers
  To them for you.

ANTONY   Good night, sir. My Octavia,
 Read not my blemishes in the world's report.
  I have not kept my square, but that to come
  Shall all be done by th'rule. Good night, dear lady.
  Good night, sir.

CAESAR Good night.   *Exeunt Caesar and Octavia*
    Enter the Soothsayer

10 ANTONY Now, sirrah: you do wish yourself in Egypt?

SOOTHSAYER Would I had never come from thence, nor
  you thither.

ANTONY If you can, your reason?

SOOTHSAYER I see it in my motion, have it not in my
  tongue; but yet hie you to Egypt again.

ANTONY
  Say to me, whose fortunes shall rise higher,
  Caesar's, or mine?

SOOTHSAYER
  Caesar's.
  Therefore, O Antony, stay not by his side.
  Thy daemon – that thy spirit which keeps thee – is   20
  Noble, courageous, high, unmatchable,
  Where Caesar's is not. But near him thy angel
  Becomes afeard, as being o'erpowered. Therefore
  Make space enough between you.

ANTONY   Speak this no more.

SOOTHSAYER
  To none but thee; no more but when to thee.
  If thou dost play with him at any game,
  Thou art sure to lose; and of that natural luck
  He beats thee 'gainst the odds. Thy lustre thickens
  When he shines by. I say again, thy spirit
  Is all afraid to govern thee near him;   30
  But, he away, 'tis noble.

ANTONY   Get thee gone.
  Say to Ventidius I would speak with him.
  He shall to Parthia.

                                        Exit Soothsayer

              Be it art or hap,
  He hath spoken true. The very dice obey him,
  And in our sports my better cunning faints
  Under his chance. If we draw lots, he speeds;
  His cocks do win the battle still of mine

II.3–4–5

When it is all to nought, and his quails ever
Beat mine, inhooped, at odds. I will to Egypt;
40 And though I make this marriage for my peace,
I'th'East my pleasure lies.

> *Enter Ventidius*

                              O, come, Ventidius.
You must to Parthia. Your commission's ready;
Follow me, and receive't.   *Exeunt*

II.4   *Enter Lepidus, Maecenas, and Agrippa*

LEPIDUS
Trouble yourselves no further. Pray you, hasten
Your generals after.

AGRIPPA   Sir, Mark Antony
Will e'en but kiss Octavia, and we'll follow.

LEPIDUS
Till I shall see you in your soldier's dress,
Which will become you both, farewell.

MAECENAS   We shall,
As I conceive the journey, be at th'Mount
Before you, Lepidus.

LEPIDUS   Your way is shorter.
My purposes do draw me much about.
You'll win two days upon me.

MAECENAS *and* AGRIPPA   Sir, good success.

LEPIDUS
10 Farewell.   *Exeunt*

II.5   *Enter Cleopatra, Charmian, Iras, and Alexas*

CLEOPATRA
Give me some music – music, moody food
Of us that trade in love.

94

ALL   The music, ho!
    Enter Mardian the eunuch

CLEOPATRA
  Let it alone! Let's to billiards. Come, Charmian.

CHARMIAN
  My arm is sore; best play with Mardian.

CLEOPATRA
  As well a woman with an eunuch played
  As with a woman. Come, you'll play with me, sir?

MARDIAN
  As well as I can, madam.

CLEOPATRA
  And when good will is showed, though't come too short,
  The actor may plead pardon. I'll none now.
  Give me mine angle. We'll to th'river; there,   10
  My music playing far off, I will betray
  Tawny-finned fishes. My bended hook shall pierce
  Their slimy jaws; and as I draw them up,
  I'll think them every one an Antony,
  And say 'Ah, ha! Y'are caught!'

CHARMIAN   'Twas merry when
  You wagered on your angling; when your diver
  Did hang a salt fish on his hook, which he
  With fervency drew up.

CLEOPATRA   That time – O times! –
  I laughed him out of patience; and that night
  I laughed him into patience; and next morn,   20
  Ere the ninth hour, I drunk him to his bed;
  Then put my tires and mantles on him, whilst
  I wore his sword Philippan.
    Enter a Messenger

                     O, from Italy!
  Ram thou thy fruitful tidings in mine ears,
  That long time have been barren.

MESSENGER   Madam, madam –

CLEOPATRA

    Antonio's dead! If thou say so, villain,
    Thou kill'st thy mistress; but well and free,
    If thou so yield him, there is gold and here
    My bluest veins to kiss, a hand that kings
30   Have lipped, and trembled kissing.

MESSENGER

    First, madam, he is well.

CLEOPATRA   Why, there's more gold.

    But, sirrah, mark, we use
    To say the dead are well. Bring it to that,
    The gold I give thee will I melt and pour
    Down thy ill-uttering throat.

MESSENGER

    Good madam, hear me.

CLEOPATRA   Well, go to, I will.

    But there's no goodness in thy face if Antony
    Be free and healthful; so tart a favour
    To trumpet such good tidings? If not well,
40   Thou shouldst come like a Fury crowned with snakes,
    Not like a formal man.

MESSENGER   Will't please you hear me?

CLEOPATRA

    I have a mind to strike thee ere thou speak'st.
    Yet, if thou say Antony lives, is well,
    Or friends with Caesar, or not captive to him,
    I'll set thee in a shower of gold, and hail
    Rich pearls upon thee.

MESSENGER   Madam, he's well.

CLEOPATRA   Well said.

MESSENGER

    And friends with Caesar.

CLEOPATRA   Th' art an honest man.

MESSENGER

Caesar and he are greater friends than ever.

CLEOPATRA

Make thee a fortune from me.

MESSENGER   But yet, madam –

CLEOPATRA

I do not like 'But yet'; it does allay   50
The good precedence. Fie upon 'But yet'!
'But yet' is as a gaoler to bring forth
Some monstrous malefactor. Prithee, friend,
Pour out the pack of matter to mine ear,
The good and bad together. He's friends with Caesar,
In state of health, thou sayst, and, thou sayst, free.

MESSENGER

Free, madam! No; I made no such report.
He's bound unto Octavia.

CLEOPATRA   For what good turn?

MESSENGER

For the best turn i'th'bed.

CLEOPATRA   I am pale, Charmian.

MESSENGER

Madam, he's married to Octavia.   60

CLEOPATRA

The most infectious pestilence upon thee!
    She strikes him down

MESSENGER

Good madam, patience.

CLEOPATRA   What say you?
    She strikes him

                                        Hence,
Horrible villain, or I'll spurn thine eyes
Like balls before me! I'll unhair thy head!
    She hales him up and down
Thou shalt be whipped with wire and stewed in brine,

97

Smarting in lingering pickle!

MESSENGER   Gracious madam,
I that do bring the news made not the match.

CLEOPATRA
Say 'tis not so, a province I will give thee,
And make thy fortunes proud. The blow thou hadst
70 Shall make thy peace for moving me to rage,
And I will boot thee with what gift beside
Thy modesty can beg.

MESSENGER   He's married, madam.

CLEOPATRA
Rogue, thou hast lived too long.
       She draws a knife

MESSENGER   Nay, then I'll run.
What mean you, madam? I have made no fault.
                                             Exit

CHARMIAN
Good madam, keep yourself within yourself.
The man is innocent.

CLEOPATRA
Some innocents 'scape not the thunderbolt.
Melt Egypt into Nile, and kindly creatures
Turn all to serpents! Call the slave again.
80 Though I am mad, I will not bite him. Call!

CHARMIAN
He is afeard to come.

CLEOPATRA   I will not hurt him.
                                    Exit Charmian
These hands do lack nobility, that they strike
A meaner than myself; since I myself
Have given myself the cause.
       Enter Charmian and the Messenger
                          Come hither, sir.
Though it be honest, it is never good

To bring bad news. Give to a gracious message
An host of tongues, but let ill tidings tell
Themselves when they be felt.

MESSENGER   I have done my duty.

CLEOPATRA

Is he married?
I cannot hate thee worser than I do   90
If thou again say 'Yes'.

MESSENGER   He's married, madam.

CLEOPATRA

The gods confound thee! Dost thou hold there still?

MESSENGER

Should I lie, madam?

CLEOPATRA   O, I would thou didst,
So half my Egypt were submerged and made
A cistern for scaled snakes! Go get thee hence.
Hadst thou Narcissus in thy face, to me
Thou wouldst appear most ugly. He is married?

MESSENGER

I crave your highness' pardon.

CLEOPATRA   He is married?

MESSENGER

Take no offence that I would not offend you;
To punish me for what you make me do   100
Seems much unequal. He's married to Octavia.

CLEOPATRA

O, that his fault should make a knave of thee,
That art not what th' art sure of! Get thee hence.
The merchandise which thou hast brought from Rome
Are all too dear for me. Lie they upon thy hand,
And be undone by 'em.   *Exit Messenger*

CHARMIAN   Good your highness, patience.

CLEOPATRA

In praising Antony I have dispraised Caesar.

99

CHARMIAN
Many times, madam.

CLEOPATRA   I am paid for't now.
Lead me from hence;
110 I faint. O, Iras, Charmian! 'Tis no matter.
Go to the fellow, good Alexas; bid him
Report the feature of Octavia, her years,
Her inclination. Let him not leave out
The colour of her hair. Bring me word quickly.

Exit Alexas

Let him for ever go – let him not, Charmian.
Though he be painted one way like a Gorgon,
The other way's a Mars. (*To Mardian*) Bid you Alexas
Bring me word how tall she is. – Pity me, Charmian,
But do not speak to me. Lead me to my chamber.

Exeunt

II.6   *Flourish. Enter Pompey and Menas at one door,
              with drum and trumpet; at another, Caesar, Lepidus,
              Antony, Enobarbus, Maecenas, Agrippa, with soldiers
              marching*

POMPEY
Your hostages I have; so have you mine;
And we shall talk before we fight.

CAESAR   Most meet
That first we come to words; and therefore have we
Our written purposes before us sent;
Which if thou hast considered, let us know
If 'twill tie up thy discontented sword
And carry back to Sicily much tall youth
That else must perish here.

POMPEY   To you all three,
The senators alone of this great world,

Chief factors for the gods: I do not know   10
Wherefore my father should revengers want,
Having a son and friends, since Julius Caesar,
Who at Philippi the good Brutus ghosted,
There saw you labouring for him. What was't
That moved pale Cassius to conspire? And what
Made the all-honoured, honest, Roman Brutus,
With the armed rest, courtiers of beauteous freedom,
To drench the Capitol, but that they would
Have one man but a man? And that is it
Hath made me rig my navy, at whose burden   20
The angered ocean foams; with which I meant
To scourge th'ingratitude that despiteful Rome
Cast on my noble father.

CAESAR   Take your time.

ANTONY
Thou canst not fear us, Pompey, with thy sails.
We'll speak with thee at sea. At land thou know'st
How much we do o'ercount thee.

POMPEY   At land indeed
Thou dost o'ercount me of my father's house;
But since the cuckoo builds not for himself,
Remain in't as thou mayst.

LEPIDUS   Be pleased to tell us –
For this is from the present – how you take   30
The offers we have sent you.

CAESAR   There's the point.

ANTONY
Which do not be entreated to, but weigh
What it is worth embraced.

CAESAR   And what may follow,
To try a larger fortune.

POMPEY   You have made me offer
Of Sicily, Sardinia; and I must

Rid all the sea of pirates; then, to send
Measures of wheat to Rome; this 'greed upon,
To part with unhacked edges and bear back
Our targes undinted.

ALL THE TRIUMVIRS That's our offer.

POMPEY   Know, then,
40 I came before you here a man prepared
To take this offer. But Mark Antony
Put me to some impatience. Though I lose
The praise of it by telling, you must know,
When Caesar and your brother were at blows,
Your mother came to Sicily and did find
Her welcome friendly.

ANTONY   I have heard it, Pompey,
And am well studied for a liberal thanks,
Which I do owe you.

POMPEY   Let me have your hand.
I did not think, sir, to have met you here.

ANTONY
50 The beds i'th'East are soft; and thanks to you,
That called me timelier than my purpose hither;
For I have gained by't.

CAESAR (to Pompey)   Since I saw you last
There is a change upon you.

POMPEY   Well, I know not
What counts harsh Fortune casts upon my face,
But in my bosom shall she never come
To make my heart her vassal.

LEPIDUS   Well met here.

POMPEY
I hope so, Lepidus. Thus we are agreed.
I crave our composition may be written,
And sealed between us.

CAESAR   That's the next to do.

POMPEY

We'll feast each other ere we part, and let's   60
Draw lots who shall begin.

ANTONY   That will I, Pompey.

POMPEY

No, Antony, take the lot.
But, first or last, your fine Egyptian cookery
Shall have the fame. I have heard that Julius Caesar
Grew fat with feasting there.

ANTONY   You have heard much.

POMPEY

I have fair meanings, sir.

ANTONY   And fair words to them.

POMPEY

Then so much have I heard.
And I have heard Apollodorus carried –

ENOBARBUS

No more of that: he did so.

POMPEY   What, I pray you?

ENOBARBUS

A certain queen to Caesar in a mattress.   70

POMPEY

I know thee now. How far'st thou, soldier?

ENOBARBUS   Well;
And well am like to do, for I perceive
Four feasts are toward.

POMPEY   Let me shake thy hand.
I never hated thee; I have seen thee fight
When I have envied thy behaviour.

ENOBARBUS   Sir,
I never loved you much; but I ha' praised ye
When you have well deserved ten times as much
As I have said you did.

POMPEY   Enjoy thy plainness;

103

It nothing ill becomes thee.
80 Aboard my galley I invite you all.
Will you lead, lords?

ALL   Show's the way, sir.

POMPEY   Come.

Exeunt all but Enobarbus and Menas

MENAS (*aside*) Thy father, Pompey, would ne'er have
made this treaty. – You and I have known, sir.

ENOBARBUS At sea, I think.

MENAS We have, sir.

ENOBARBUS You have done well by water.

MENAS And you by land.

ENOBARBUS I will praise any man that will praise me;
though it cannot be denied what I have done by land.

90 MENAS Nor what I have done by water.

ENOBARBUS Yes, something you can deny for your own
safety: you have been a great thief by sea.

MENAS And you by land.

ENOBARBUS There I deny my land service. But give me
your hand, Menas. If our eyes had authority, here they
might take two thieves kissing.

MENAS All men's faces are true, whatsome'er their hands
are.

ENOBARBUS But there is never a fair woman has a true
100 face.

MENAS No slander; they steal hearts.

ENOBARBUS We came hither to fight with you.

MENAS For my part, I am sorry it is turned to a drinking.
Pompey doth this day laugh away his fortune.

ENOBARBUS If he do, sure he cannot weep't back again.

MENAS Y'have said, sir. We looked not for Mark Antony
here. Pray you, is he married to Cleopatra?

ENOBARBUS Caesar's sister is called Octavia.

MENAS True, sir; she was the wife of Caius Marcellus.

ENOBARBUS But she is now the wife of Marcus Antonius. 110
MENAS Pray ye, sir?
ENOBARBUS 'Tis true.
MENAS Then is Caesar and he for ever knit together.
ENOBARBUS If I were bound to divine of this unity, I
would not prophesy so.
MENAS I think the policy of that purpose made more in
the marriage than the love of the parties.
ENOBARBUS I think so too. But you shall find the band
that seems to tie their friendship together will be the
very strangler of their amity. Octavia is of a holy, cold, 120
and still conversation.
MENAS Who would not have his wife so?
ENOBARBUS Not he that himself is not so; which is Mark
Antony. He will to his Egyptian dish again. Then shall
the sighs of Octavia blow the fire up in Caesar, and, as
I said before, that which is the strength of their amity
shall prove the immediate author of their variance.
Antony will use his affection where it is. He married but
his occasion here.
MENAS And thus it may be. Come, sir, will you aboard? 130
I have a health for you.
ENOBARBUS I shall take it, sir. We have used our throats
in Egypt.
MENAS Come, let's away.   *Exeunt*

Music plays. Enter two or three Servants, with a banquet II.7
FIRST SERVANT Here they'll be, man. Some o'their
plants are ill-rooted already; the least wind i'th'world
will blow them down.
SECOND SERVANT Lepidus is high-coloured.
FIRST SERVANT They have made him drink alms drink.
SECOND SERVANT As they pinch one another by the

disposition, he cries out 'No more'; reconciles them
to his entreaty, and himself to th'drink.

FIRST SERVANT But it raises the greater war between
10   him and his discretion.

SECOND SERVANT Why, this it is to have a name in great
men's fellowship. I had as lief have a reed that will do
me no service as a partisan I could not heave.

FIRST SERVANT To be called into a huge sphere, and
not to be seen to move in't, are the holes where eyes
should be, which pitifully disaster the cheeks.

*A sennet sounded. Enter Caesar, Antony, Pompey,
Lepidus, Agrippa, Maecenas, Enobarbus, Menas, with
other captains, and a Boy*

ANTONY (*to Lepidus*)

Thus do they, sir: they take the flow o'th'Nile
By certain scales i'th'pyramid. They know
By th'height, the lowness, or the mean if dearth
20 Or foison follow. The higher Nilus swells,
The more it promises; as it ebbs, the seedsman
Upon the slime and ooze scatters his grain,
And shortly comes to harvest.

LEPIDUS Y'have strange serpents there.

ANTONY Ay, Lepidus.

LEPIDUS Your serpent of Egypt is bred now of your mud
by the operation of your sun; so is your crocodile.

ANTONY They are so.

POMPEY Sit – and some wine! A health to Lepidus!

30 LEPIDUS I am not so well as I should be, but I'll ne'er
out.

ENOBARBUS Not till you have slept; I fear me you'll be
in till then.

LEPIDUS Nay, certainly, I have heard the Ptolemies'
pyramises are very goodly things; without contradiction
I have heard that.

MENAS *(aside to Pompey)*
  Pompey, a word.
POMPEY *(aside to Menas)* Say in mine ear; what is't?
MENAS *(aside to Pompey)*
  Forsake thy seat, I do beseech thee, captain,
  And hear me speak a word.
POMPEY *(aside to Menas)*   Forbear me till anon.
  (aloud) This wine for Lepidus!   40
LEPIDUS What manner o'thing is your crocodile?
ANTONY It is shaped, sir, like itself, and it is as broad
  as it has breadth. It is just so high as it is, and moves
  with it own organs. It lives by that which nourisheth it,
  and the elements once out of it, it transmigrates.
LEPIDUS What colour is it of?
ANTONY Of it own colour too.
LEPIDUS 'Tis a strange serpent.
ANTONY 'Tis so; and the tears of it are wet.
CAESAR Will this description satisfy him?   50
ANTONY With the health that Pompey gives him; else he
  is a very epicure.
    Menas whispers to Pompey
POMPEY *(aside to Menas)*
  Go hang, sir, hang! Tell me of that? Away!
  Do as I bid you. – Where's this cup I called for?
MENAS *(aside to Pompey)*
  If for the sake of merit thou wilt hear me,
  Rise from thy stool.
POMPEY *(aside to Menas)* I think th' art mad. The matter?
    He rises and they walk aside
MENAS
  I have ever held my cap off to thy fortunes.
POMPEY
  Thou hast served me with much faith. What's else to
      say? –

Be jolly, lords.

ANTONY   These quicksands, Lepidus,

60   Keep off them, for you sink.

MENAS

Wilt thou be lord of all the world?

POMPEY   What sayst thou?

MENAS

Wilt thou be lord of the whole world? That's twice.

POMPEY

How should that be?

MENAS   But entertain it,

And though thou think me poor, I am the man

Will give thee all the world.

POMPEY   Hast thou drunk well?

MENAS

No, Pompey, I have kept me from the cup.

Thou art, if thou dar'st be, the earthly Jove;

Whate'er the ocean pales, or sky inclips,

Is thine, if thou wilt ha't.

POMPEY   Show me which way.

MENAS

70   These three world-sharers, these competitors,

Are in thy vessel. Let me cut the cable;

And when we are put off, fall to their throats.

All there is thine.

POMPEY   Ah, this thou shouldst have done,

And not have spoke on't. In me 'tis villainy;

In thee't had been good service. Thou must know

'Tis not my profit that does lead mine honour;

Mine honour, it. Repent that e'er thy tongue

Hath so betrayed thine act. Being done unknown,

I should have found it afterwards well done,

80   But must condemn it now. Desist, and drink.

MENAS (*aside*)
 For this I'll never follow thy palled fortunes more.
 Who seeks, and will not take when once 'tis offered,
 Shall never find it more.

POMPEY   This health to Lepidus!

ANTONY
 Bear him ashore. – I'll pledge it for him, Pompey.

ENOBARBUS
 Here's to thee, Menas!

MENAS   Enobarbus, welcome.

POMPEY
 Fill till the cup be hid.

ENOBARBUS (*pointing to the servant who is carrying off
          Lepidus*)
 There's a strong fellow, Menas.

MENAS
 Why?

ENOBARBUS
 'A bears the third part of the world, man; seest not?

MENAS
 The third part then is drunk. Would it were all,   90
 That it might go on wheels!

ENOBARBUS
 Drink thou; increase the reels.

MENAS
 Come.

POMPEY
 This is not yet an Alexandrian feast.

ANTONY
 It ripens towards it. Strike the vessels, ho!
 Here's to Caesar!

CAESAR   I could well forbear't.
 It's monstrous labour when I wash my brain

And it grows fouler.

ANTONY   Be a child o'th'time.

CAESAR

Possess it, I'll make answer.

100 But I had rather fast from all, four days,
Than drink so much in one.

ENOBARBUS (to Antony)   Ha, my brave emperor!
Shall we dance now the Egyptian bacchanals
And celebrate our drink?

POMPEY   Let's ha't, good soldier.

ANTONY

Come, let's all take hands
Till that the conquering wine hath steeped our sense
In soft and delicate Lethe.

ENOBARBUS   All take hands.

Make battery to our ears with the loud music;
The while I'll place you; then the boy shall sing.
The holding every man shall beat as loud
110 As his strong sides can volley.

Music plays. Enobarbus places them hand in hand

BOY (*sings*)

        Come, thou monarch of the vine,
        Plumpy Bacchus with pink eyne!
        In thy fats our cares be drowned;
        With thy grapes our hairs be crowned.
            Cup us till the world go round,
            Cup us till the world go round!

CAESAR

What would you more? Pompey, good night. (*To
        Antony*) Good brother,
Let me request you off. Our graver business
Frowns at this levity. Gentle lords, let's part.
120 You see we have burnt our cheeks. Strong Enobarb
Is weaker than the wine, and mine own tongue

Spleets what it speaks. The wild disguise hath almost
Anticked us all. What needs more words? Good night.
Good Antony, your hand.

POMPEY   I'll try you on the shore.

ANTONY

And shall, sir. Give's your hand.

POMPEY   O, Antony,
You have my father's house. But what, we are friends!
Come down into the boat.

                Exeunt all but Enobarbus and Menas

ENOBARBUS   Take heed you fall not.
Menas, I'll not on shore.

MENAS   No, to my cabin.
These drums! These trumpets, flutes! What!
Let Neptune hear we bid a loud farewell   130
To these great fellows. Sound and be hanged, sound
    out!

    Sound a flourish, with drums

ENOBARBUS Hoo, says 'a. There's my cap.

    He throws his cap in the air

MENAS Hoa! Noble captain, come.   *Exeunt*

                 *

    Enter Ventidius, as it were in triumph, with Silius and III.1
    other officers and soldiers. Before Ventidius is borne
    the dead body of Pacorus

VENTIDIUS

Now, darting Parthia, art thou struck; and now
Pleased Fortune does of Marcus Crassus' death
Make me revenger. Bear the King's son's body
Before our army. Thy Pacorus, Orodes,
Pays this for Marcus Crassus.

SILIUS   Noble Ventidius,

Whilst yet with Parthian blood thy sword is warm,
The fugitive Parthians follow. Spur through Media,
Mesopotamia, and the shelters whither
The routed fly. So thy grand captain, Antony,
Shall set thee on triumphant chariots, and
Put garlands on thy head.

VENTIDIUS   O Silius, Silius,
I have done enough. A lower place, note well,
May make too great an act. For learn this, Silius:
Better to leave undone than by our deed
Acquire too high a fame when him we serve's away.
Caesar and Antony have ever won
More in their officer than person. Sossius,
One of my place in Syria, his lieutenant,
For quick accumulation of renown,
Which he achieved by th'minute, lost his favour.
Who does i'th'wars more than his captain can
Becomes his captain's captain; and ambition,
The soldier's virtue, rather makes choice of loss
Than gain which darkens him.
I could do more to do Antonius good,
But 'twould offend him, and in his offence
Should my performance perish.

SILIUS   Thou hast, Ventidius, that
Without the which a soldier and his sword
Grants scarce distinction. Thou wilt write to Antony?

VENTIDIUS
I'll humbly signify what in his name,
That magical word of war, we have effected;
How, with his banners and his well-paid ranks,
The ne'er-yet-beaten horse of Parthia
We have jaded out o'th'field.

SILIUS   Where is he now?

VENTIDIUS

  He purposeth to Athens; whither, with what haste
  The weight we must convey with's will permit,
  We shall appear before him. – On, there. Pass along.

                               Exeunt

    Enter Agrippa at one door, Enobarbus at another   III.2

AGRIPPA

  What, are the brothers parted?

ENOBARBUS

  They have dispatched with Pompey; he is gone.
  The other three are sealing. Octavia weeps
  To part from Rome; Caesar is sad, and Lepidus
  Since Pompey's feast, as Menas says, is troubled
  With the green-sickness.

AGRIPPA   'Tis a noble Lepidus.

ENOBARBUS

  A very fine one. O, how he loves Caesar!

AGRIPPA

  Nay, but how dearly he adores Mark Antony!

ENOBARBUS

  Caesar? Why, he's the Jupiter of men.

AGRIPPA

  What's Antony? The god of Jupiter.   10

ENOBARBUS

  Spake you of Caesar? How! The nonpareil!

AGRIPPA

  O Antony! O thou Arabian bird!

ENOBARBUS

  Would you praise Caesar, say 'Caesar' – go no further.

AGRIPPA

  Indeed, he plied them both with excellent praises.

ENOBARBUS

But he loves Caesar best, yet he loves Antony –
Hoo! Hearts, tongues, figures, scribes, bards, poets,
    cannot
Think, speak, cast, write, sing, number – hoo! –
His love to Antony. But as for Caesar,
Kneel down, kneel down, and wonder.

AGRIPPA   Both he loves.

ENOBARBUS

20   They are his shards, and he their beetle. So –
        (*Trumpet within*)
    This is to horse. Adieu, noble Agrippa.

AGRIPPA

Good fortune, worthy soldier, and farewell!
        Enter Caesar, Antony, Lepidus, and Octavia

ANTONY

No further, sir.

CAESAR

You take from me a great part of myself;
Use me well in't. Sister, prove such a wife
As my thoughts make thee, and as my farthest band
Shall pass on thy approof. Most noble Antony,
Let not the piece of virtue which is set
Betwixt us as the cement of our love,
30 To keep it builded, be the ram to batter
The fortress of it; for better might we
Have loved without this mean, if on both parts
This be not cherished.

ANTONY   Make me not offended
In your distrust.

CAESAR   I have said.

ANTONY   You shall not find,
Though you be therein curious, the least cause
For what you seem to fear. So, the gods keep you,

And make the hearts of Romans serve your ends!
We will here part.

CAESAR
  Farewell, my dearest sister, fare thee well.
  The elements be kind to thee, and make   40
  Thy spirits all of comfort. Fare thee well.

OCTAVIA (*weeping*)
  My noble brother!

ANTONY
  The April's in her eyes; it is love's spring,
  And these the showers to bring it on. Be cheerful.

OCTAVIA
  Sir, look well to my husband's house; and –

CAESAR   What,
  Octavia?

OCTAVIA I'll tell you in your ear.

ANTONY
  Her tongue will not obey her heart, nor can
  Her heart inform her tongue – the swan's-down feather
  That stands upon the swell at the full of tide,
  And neither way inclines.

ENOBARBUS (*aside to Agrippa*) Will Caesar weep?   50

AGRIPPA (*aside to Enobarbus*)
  He has a cloud in's face.

ENOBARBUS (*aside to Agrippa*)
  He were the worse for that, were he a horse;
  So is he, being a man.

AGRIPPA (*aside to Enobarbus*) Why, Enobarbus,
  When Antony found Julius Caesar dead,
  He cried almost to roaring; and he wept
  When at Philippi he found Brutus slain.

ENOBARBUS (*aside to Agrippa*)
  That year indeed he was troubled with a rheum.
  What willingly he did confound he wailed,

Believe't, till I wept too.

CAESAR   No, sweet Octavia,
60 You shall hear from me still; the time shall not
    Outgo my thinking on you.

ANTONY   Come, sir, come,
    I'll wrestle with you in my strength of love.
    Look, here I have you; thus I let you go,
    And give you to the gods.

CAESAR   Adieu; be happy!

LEPIDUS (*to Octavia*)
    Let all the number of the stars give light
    To thy fair way!

CAESAR   Farewell, farewell!
        He kisses Octavia

ANTONY   Farewell!
                                Trumpets sound. Exeunt

III.3   *Enter Cleopatra, Charmian, Iras, and Alexas*

CLEOPATRA
    Where is the fellow?

ALEXAS   Half afeard to come.

CLEOPATRA
    Go to, go to.
        Enter the Messenger as before
            Come hither, sir.

ALEXAS   Good majesty,
    Herod of Jewry dare not look upon you
    But when you are well pleased.

CLEOPATRA   That Herod's head
    I'll have; but how, when Antony is gone,
    Through whom I might command it? – Come thou
        near.

MESSENGER
  Most gracious majesty!
CLEOPATRA   Didst thou behold Octavia?
MESSENGER
  Ay, dread queen.
CLEOPATRA   Where?
MESSENGER   Madam, in Rome.
  I looked her in the face, and saw her led
  Between her brother and Mark Antony.   10
CLEOPATRA
  Is she as tall as me?
MESSENGER   She is not, madam.
CLEOPATRA
  Didst hear her speak? Is she shrill-tongued or low?
MESSENGER
  Madam, I heard her speak; she is low-voiced.
CLEOPATRA
  That's not so good. He cannot like her long.
CHARMIAN
  Like her? O Isis! 'Tis impossible.
CLEOPATRA
  I think so, Charmian. Dull of tongue, and dwarfish.
  What majesty is in her gait? Remember,
  If e'er thou look'st on majesty.
MESSENGER   She creeps;
  Her motion and her station are as one.
  She shows a body rather than a life,   20
  A statue than a breather.
CLEOPATRA   Is this certain?
MESSENGER
  Or I have no observance.
CHARMIAN   Three in Egypt
  Cannot make better note.

CLEOPATRA   He's very knowing,
  I do perceive't. There's nothing in her yet.
  The fellow has good judgement.
CHARMIAN   Excellent.
CLEOPATRA
  Guess at her years, I prithee.
MESSENGER   Madam,
  She was a widow –
CLEOPATRA   Widow? Charmian, hark.
MESSENGER
  And I do think she's thirty.
CLEOPATRA
  Bear'st thou her face in mind? Is't long or round?
MESSENGER
30 Round, even to faultiness.
CLEOPATRA
  For the most part, too, they are foolish that are so.
  Her hair, what colour?
MESSENGER   Brown, madam; and her forehead
  As low as she would wish it.
CLEOPATRA   There's gold for thee.
  Thou must not take my former sharpness ill.
  I will employ thee back again. I find thee
  Most fit for business. Go, make thee ready.
  Our letters are prepared.   *Exit Messenger*
CHARMIAN   A proper man.
CLEOPATRA
  Indeed he is so: I repent me much
  That so I harried him. Why, methinks, by him,
40 This creature's no such thing.
CHARMIAN   Nothing, madam.
CLEOPATRA
  The man hath seen some majesty, and should know.

CHARMIAN

Hath he seen majesty? Isis else defend,
And serving you so long!

CLEOPATRA

I have one thing more to ask him yet, good Charmian.
But 'tis no matter; thou shalt bring him to me
Where I will write. All may be well enough.

CHARMIAN

I warrant you, madam. *Exeunt*

Enter Antony and Octavia III.4

ANTONY

Nay, nay, Octavia, not only that;
That were excusable, that and thousands more
Of semblable import – but he hath waged
New wars 'gainst Pompey; made his will, and read it
To public ear;
Spoke scantly of me; when perforce he could not
But pay me terms of honour, cold and sickly
He vented them, most narrow measure lent me;
When the best hint was given him, he not took't,
Or did it from his teeth.

OCTAVIA   O, my good lord,   10
Believe not all; or, if you must believe,
Stomach not all. A mere unhappy lady,
If this division chance, ne'er stood between,
Praying for both parts.
The good gods will mock me presently
When I shall pray 'O, bless my lord and husband!';
Undo that prayer by crying out as loud
'O, bless my brother!' Husband win, win brother,
Prays, and destroys the prayer; no midway

20 'Twixt these extremes at all.

ANTONY   Gentle Octavia,
Let your best love draw to that point which seeks
Best to preserve it. If I lose mine honour,
I lose myself; better I were not yours
Than yours so branchless. But, as you requested,
Yourself shall go between's. The meantime, lady,
I'll raise the preparation of a war
Shall stain your brother. Make your soonest haste;
So your desires are yours.

OCTAVIA   Thanks to my lord.
The Jove of power make me, most weak, most weak,
30 Your reconciler! Wars 'twixt you twain would be
As if the world should cleave, and that slain men
Should solder up the rift.

ANTONY
When it appears to you where this begins,
Turn your displeasure that way, for our faults
Can never be so equal that your love
Can equally move with them. Provide your going;
Choose your own company, and command what cost
Your heart has mind to.   *Exeunt*

III.5   *Enter Enobarbus and Eros*

ENOBARBUS How now, friend Eros?

EROS There's strange news come, sir.

ENOBARBUS What, man?

EROS Caesar and Lepidus have made wars upon Pompey.

ENOBARBUS This is old. What is the success?

EROS Caesar, having made use of him in the wars 'gainst
 Pompey, presently denied him rivality, would not let
 him partake in the glory of the action; and, not resting
 here, accuses him of letters he had formerly wrote to

Pompey; upon his own appeal, seizes him; so the poor 10
third is up, till death enlarge his confine.

ENOBARBUS
Then, world, thou hast a pair of chaps, no more;
And throw between them all the food thou hast,
They'll grind the one the other. Where's Antony?

EROS
He's walking in the garden – thus, and spurns
The rush that lies before him; cries 'Fool Lepidus!'
And threats the throat of that his officer
That murdered Pompey.

ENOBARBUS   Our great navy's rigged.

EROS
For Italy and Caesar. More, Domitius:
My lord desires you presently. My news   20
I might have told hereafter.

ENOBARBUS   'Twill be naught;
But let it be. Bring me to Antony.

EROS   Come, sir.   *Exeunt*

          Enter Agrippa, Maecenas, and Caesar   III.6
CAESAR
Contemning Rome, he has done all this and more
In Alexandria. Here's the manner of't:
I'th'market-place on a tribunal silvered,
Cleopatra and himself in chairs of gold
Were publicly enthroned; at the feet sat
Caesarion, whom they call my father's son,
And all the unlawful issue that their lust
Since then hath made between them. Unto her
He gave the stablishment of Egypt; made her
Of lower Syria, Cyprus, Lydia,   10
Absolute queen.

MAECENAS   This in the public eye?

CAESAR

I'th'common showplace, where they exercise.
His sons he there proclaimed the kings of kings;
Great Media, Parthia, and Armenia
He gave to Alexander; to Ptolemy he assigned
Syria, Cilicia, and Phoenicia. She
In th'habiliments of the goddess Isis
That day appeared, and oft before gave audience,
As 'tis reported, so.

MAECENAS   Let Rome be thus informed.

AGRIPPA

Who, queasy with his insolence already,
Will their good thoughts call from him.

CAESAR

The people knows it, and have now received
His accusations.

AGRIPPA   Who does he accuse?

CAESAR

Caesar; and that, having in Sicily
Sextus Pompeius spoiled, we had not rated him
His part o'th'isle. Then does he say he lent me
Some shipping, unrestored. Lastly, he frets
That Lepidus of the triumvirate
Should be deposed; and, being, that we detain
All his revenue.

AGRIPPA   Sir, this should be answered.

CAESAR

'Tis done already, and the messenger gone.
I have told him Lepidus was grown too cruel,
That he his high authority abused,
And did deserve his change. For what I have conquered,
I grant him part; but then in his Armenia,
And other of his conquered kingdoms, I

Demand the like.

MAECENAS   He'll never yield to that.

CAESAR

Nor must not then be yielded to in this.
    Enter Octavia with her train

OCTAVIA

Hail, Caesar and my lord! Hail, most dear Caesar!

CAESAR

That ever I should call thee castaway!   40

OCTAVIA

You have not called me so, nor have you cause.

CAESAR

Why have you stol'n upon us thus? You come not
Like Caesar's sister. The wife of Antony
Should have an army for an usher, and
The neighs of horse to tell of her approach
Long ere she did appear. The trees by th'way
Should have borne men, and expectation fainted,
Longing for what it had not. Nay, the dust
Should have ascended to the roof of heaven,
Raised by your populous troops. But you are come   50
A market maid to Rome, and have prevented
The ostentation of our love; which, left unshown,
Is often left unloved. We should have met you
By sea and land, supplying every stage
With an augmented greeting.

OCTAVIA   Good my lord,
To come thus was I not constrained, but did it
On my free will. My lord, Mark Antony,
Hearing that you prepared for war, acquainted
My grievèd ear withal; whereon I begged
His pardon for return.

CAESAR   Which soon he granted,   60
Being an obstruct 'tween his lust and him.

123

OCTAVIA
Do not say so, my lord.

CAESAR I have eyes upon him,
And his affairs come to me on the wind.
Where is he now?

OCTAVIA My lord, in Athens.

CAESAR
No, my most wrongèd sister; Cleopatra
Hath nodded him to her. He hath given his empire
Up to a whore; who now are levying
The kings o'th'earth for war. He hath assembled
Bocchus, the King of Libya; Archelaus,
70 Of Cappadocia; Philadelphos, King
Of Paphlagonia; the Thracian king, Adallas;
King Mauchus of Arabia; King of Pont;
Herod of Jewry; Mithridates, King
Of Comagene; Polemon and Amyntas,
The Kings of Mede and Lycaonia;
With a more larger list of sceptres.

OCTAVIA Ay me most wretched,
That have my heart parted betwixt two friends
That does afflict each other!

CAESAR Welcome hither.
Your letters did withhold our breaking forth,
80 Till we perceived both how you were wrong led
And we in negligent danger. Cheer your heart;
Be you not troubled with the time, which drives
O'er your content these strong necessities;
But let determined things to destiny
Hold unbewailed their way. Welcome to Rome;
Nothing more dear to me. You are abused
Beyond the mark of thought, and the high gods,
To do you justice, makes his ministers
Of us and those that love you. Best of comfort,

And ever welcome to us.

AGRIPPA   Welcome, lady.   90

MAECENAS

Welcome, dear madam.

Each heart in Rome does love and pity you.

Only th'adulterous Antony, most large

In his abominations, turns you off

And gives his potent regiment to a trull

That noises it against us.

OCTAVIA   Is it so, sir?

CAESAR

Most certain. Sister, welcome. Pray you

Be ever known to patience. My dear'st sister!   *Exeunt*

Enter Cleopatra and Enobarbus   III.7

CLEOPATRA

I will be even with thee, doubt it not.

ENOBARBUS

But why, why, why?

CLEOPATRA

Thou hast forspoke my being in these wars,

And sayst it is not fit.

ENOBARBUS   Well, is it, is it?

CLEOPATRA

Is't not denounced against us? Why should not we

Be there in person?

ENOBARBUS (*aside*)   Well, I could reply:

If we should serve with horse and mares together,

The horse were merely lost; the mares would bear

A soldier and his horse.

CLEOPATRA   What is't you say?

ENOBARBUS

Your presence needs must puzzle Antony,   10

Take from his heart, take from his brain, from's time,
What should not then be spared. He is already
Traduced for levity; and 'tis said in Rome
That Photinus, an eunuch, and your maids
Manage this war.

CLEOPATRA   Sink Rome, and their tongues rot
That speak against us! A charge we bear i'th'war,
And as the president of my kingdom will
Appear there for a man. Speak not against it;
I will not stay behind.

       Enter Antony and Canidius

ENOBARBUS   Nay, I have done.
80   Here comes the Emperor.

ANTONY   Is it not strange, Canidius,
That from Tarentum and Brundisium
He could so quickly cut the Ionian sea
And take in Toryne? – You have heard on't, sweet?

CLEOPATRA
Celerity is never more admired
Than by the negligent.

ANTONY   A good rebuke,
Which might have well becomed the best of men
To taunt at slackness. Canidius, we
Will fight with him by sea.

CLEOPATRA   By sea; what else?

CANIDIUS
Why will my lord do so?

ANTONY   For that he dares us to't.

ENOBARBUS
90   So hath my lord dared him to single fight.

CANIDIUS
Ay, and to wage this battle at Pharsalia,
Where Caesar fought with Pompey. But these offers,
Which serve not for his vantage, he shakes off;

And so should you.

ENOBARBUS   Your ships are not well manned.
  Your mariners are muleters, reapers, people
  Engrossed by swift impress. In Caesar's fleet
  Are those that often have 'gainst Pompey fought;
  Their ships are yare; yours, heavy. No disgrace
  Shall fall you for refusing him at sea,
  Being prepared for land.

ANTONY   By sea, by sea.   40

ENOBARBUS
  Most worthy sir, you therein throw away
  The absolute soldiership you have by land,
  Distract your army, which doth most consist
  Of war-marked footmen, leave unexecuted
  Your own renownèd knowledge, quite forgo
  The way which promises assurance, and
  Give up yourself merely to chance and hazard
  From firm security.

ANTONY   I'll fight at sea.

CLEOPATRA
  I have sixty sails, Caesar none better.

ANTONY
  Our overplus of shipping will we burn,   50
  And with the rest full-manned, from th'head of Actium
  Beat th'approaching Caesar. But if we fail,
  We then can do't at land.

    Enter a Messenger

                Thy business?

MESSENGER
  The news is true, my lord; he is descried.
  Caesar has taken Toryne.

ANTONY
  Can he be there in person? 'Tis impossible;
  Strange that his power should be. Canidius,

Our nineteen legions thou shalt hold by land
And our twelve thousand horse. We'll to our ship.
60 Away, my Thetis!

Enter a Soldier

               How now, worthy soldier?

SOLDIER
O noble emperor, do not fight by sea.
Trust not to rotten planks. Do you misdoubt
This sword and these my wounds? Let th'Egyptians
And the Phoenicians go a-ducking; we
Have used to conquer standing on the earth
And fighting foot to foot.

ANTONY   Well, well; away!

Exeunt Antony, Cleopatra, and Enobarbus

SOLDIER
By Hercules, I think I am i'th'right.

CANIDIUS
Soldier, thou art; but his whole action grows
Not in the power on't. So our leader's led,
70 And we are women's men.

SOLDIER   You keep by land
The legions and the horse whole, do you not?

C NIDIUS
Marcus Octavius, Marcus Justeius,
Publicola, and Caelius are for sea;
But we keep whole by land. This speed of Caesar's
Carries beyond belief.

SOLDIER   While he was yet in Rome,
His power went out in such distractions as
Beguiled all spies.

CANIDIUS   Who's his lieutenant, hear you?

SOLDIER
They say one Taurus.

CANIDIUS   Well I know the man.

Enter a Messenger

MESSENGER
  The Emperor calls Canidius.

CANIDIUS
  With news the time's with labour and throes forth   80
  Each minute some.   *Exeunt*

Enter Caesar and Taurus, with their army, marching   III.8

CAESAR
  Taurus!

TAURUS
  My lord?

CAESAR
  Strike not by land; keep whole; provoke not battle
  Till we have done at sea. Do not exceed
  The prescript of this scroll. Our fortune lies
  Upon this jump.   *Exeunt*

Enter Antony and Enobarbus   III.9

ANTONY
  Set we our squadrons on yond side o'th'hill
  In eye of Caesar's battle; from which place
  We may the number of the ships behold,
  And so proceed accordingly.   *Exeunt*

*Canidius marcheth with his land army one way over
the stage, and Taurus, the lieutenant of Caesar, with
his army, the other way. After their going in is heard
the noise of a sea fight*
Alarum. Enter Enobarbus

ENOBARBUS
Naught, naught, all naught! I can behold no longer.
Th'*Antoniad*, the Egyptian admiral,
With all their sixty, fly and turn the rudder.
To see't mine eyes are blasted.
Enter Scarus

SCARUS   Gods and goddesses,
All the whole synod of them!

ENOBARBUS   What's thy passion?

SCARUS
The greater cantle of the world is lost
With very ignorance. We have kissed away
Kingdoms and provinces.

ENOBARBUS   How appears the fight?

SCARUS
On our side like the tokened pestilence,
10   Where death is sure. Yon ribaudred nag of Egypt –
Whom leprosy o'ertake! – i'th'midst o'th'fight,
When vantage like a pair of twins appeared,
Both as the same, or rather ours the elder,
The breese upon her, like a cow in June,
Hoists sails and flies.

ENOBARBUS   That I beheld.
Mine eyes did sicken at the sight, and could not
Endure a further view.

SCARUS   She once being loofed,
The noble ruin of her magic, Antony,
Claps on his sea wing and, like a doting mallard,
20   Leaving the fight in height, flies after her.

130

I never saw an action of such shame.
Experience, manhood, honour, ne'er before
Did violate so itself.

ENOBARBUS   Alack, alack!

    Enter Canidius

CANIDIUS

Our fortune on the sea is out of breath,
And sinks most lamentably. Had our general
Been what he knew himself, it had gone well.
O, he has given example for our flight
Most grossly by his own.

ENOBARBUS

Ay, are you thereabouts? Why then, good night indeed.

CANIDIUS

Toward Peloponnesus are they fled.   30

SCARUS

'Tis easy to't; and there I will attend
What further comes.

CANIDIUS   To Caesar will I render
My legions and my horse. Six kings already
Show me the way of yielding.

ENOBARBUS   I'll yet follow
The wounded chance of Antony, though my reason
Sits in the wind against me.   *Exeunt*

    Enter Antony with attendants   III.11

ANTONY

Hark! The land bids me tread no more upon't;
It is ashamed to bear me. Friends, come hither.
I am so lated in the world that I
Have lost my way for ever. I have a ship
Laden with gold; take that; divide it. Fly,
And make your peace with Caesar.

131

ALL   Fly? Not we.

ANTONY

    I have fled myself, and have instructed cowards
    To run and show their shoulders. Friends, be gone.
    I have myself resolved upon a course

10   Which has no need of you. Be gone.
    My treasure's in the harbour. Take it. O,
    I followed that I blush to look upon.
    My very hairs do mutiny, for the white
    Reprove the brown for rashness, and they them
    For fear and doting. Friends, be gone; you shall
    Have letters from me to some friends that will
    Sweep your way for you. Pray you, look not sad,
    Nor make replies of loathness; take the hint
    Which my despair proclaims. Let that be left

20   Which leaves itself. To the seaside straightway!
    I will possess you of that ship and treasure.
    Leave me, I pray, a little. Pray you now,
    Nay, do so; for indeed I have lost command.
    Therefore I pray you. I'll see you by and by.

Exeunt attendants. Antony
sits down

Enter Cleopatra, led by Charmian, Iras, and Eros

EROS

    Nay, gentle madam, to him, comfort him.

IRAS Do, most dear queen.

CHARMIAN Do; why, what else?

CLEOPATRA Let me sit down. O, Juno!

ANTONY No, no, no, no, no.

30 **EROS** See you here, sir?

ANTONY O, fie, fie, fie!

CHARMIAN Madam!

IRAS Madam, O, good empress!

EROS Sir, sir!

ANTONY
    Yes, my lord, yes. He at Philippi kept
    His sword e'en like a dancer, while I struck
    The lean and wrinkled Cassius; and 'twas I
    That the mad Brutus ended. He alone
    Dealt on lieutenantry, and no practice had
    In the brave squares of war. Yet now – no matter.   40
CLEOPATRA Ah, stand by.
EROS The Queen, my lord, the Queen.
IRAS
    Go to him, madam, speak to him;
    He's unqualitied with very shame.
CLEOPATRA Well then, sustain me. O!
EROS
    Most noble sir, arise. The Queen approaches.
    Her head's declined, and death will seize her but
    Your comfort makes the rescue.
ANTONY
    I have offended reputation,
    A most unnoble swerving.
EROS   Sir, the Queen.   50
ANTONY
    O, whither hast thou led me, Egypt? See
    How I convey my shame out of thine eyes
    By looking back what I have left behind
    'Stroyed in dishonour.
CLEOPATRA   O my lord, my lord,
    Forgive my fearful sails! I little thought
    You would have followed.
ANTONY   Egypt, thou knew'st too well
    My heart was to thy rudder tied by th'strings,
    And thou shouldst tow me after. O'er my spirit
    Thy full supremacy thou knew'st, and that
    Thy beck might from the bidding of the gods   60

Command me.

CLEOPATRA   O, my pardon!

ANTONY   Now I must
To the young man send humble treaties, dodge
And palter in the shifts of lowness, who
With half the bulk o'th'world played as I pleased,
Making and marring fortunes. You did know
How much you were my conqueror, and that
My sword, made weak by my affection, would
Obey it on all cause.

CLEOPATRA   Pardon, pardon!

ANTONY
Fall not a tear, I say; one of them rates
70 All that is won and lost. Give me a kiss.
Even this repays me. – We sent our schoolmaster;
Is 'a come back? – Love, I am full of lead.
Some wine, within there, and our viands! Fortune
        knows
We scorn her most when most she offers blows.

                                    Exeunt

III.12   *Enter Caesar, Agrippa, Dolabella, and Thidias, with
              others*

CAESAR
Let him appear that's come from Antony.
Know you him?

DOLABELLA   Caesar, 'tis his schoolmaster:
An argument that he is plucked, when hither
He sends so poor a pinion of his wing,
Which had superfluous kings for messengers
Not many moons gone by.

        Enter Ambassador from Antony

CAESAR   Approach and speak.

AMBASSADOR

Such as I am, I come from Antony.
I was of late as petty to his ends
As is the morn-dew on the myrtle leaf
10   To his grand sea.

CAESAR   Be't so. Declare thine office.

AMBASSADOR

Lord of his fortunes he salutes thee, and
Requires to live in Egypt; which not granted,
He lessons his requests, and to thee sues
To let him breathe between the heavens and earth,
A private man in Athens. This for him.
Next, Cleopatra does confess thy greatness,
Submits her to thy might, and of thee craves
The circle of the Ptolemies for her heirs,
Now hazarded to thy grace.

CAESAR   For Antony,
20   I have no ears to his request. The Queen
Of audience nor desire shall fail, so she
From Egypt drive her all-disgracèd friend
Or take his life there. This if she perform,
She shall not sue unheard. So to them both.

AMBASSADOR

Fortune pursue thee!

CAESAR   Bring him through the bands.

                              Exit Ambassador

(*To Thidias*) To try thy eloquence now 'tis time.
        Dispatch.
From Antony win Cleopatra. Promise,
And in our name, what she requires; add more,
From thine invention, offers. Women are not
30   In their best fortunes strong, but want will perjure
The ne'er-touched vestal. Try thy cunning, Thidias.
Make thine own edict for thy pains, which we

Will answer as a law.

THIDIAS   Caesar, I go.

CAESAR

  Observe how Antony becomes his flaw,
  And what thou think'st his very action speaks
  In every power that moves.

THIDIAS   Caesar, I shall.

                            Exeunt

III.13   *Enter Cleopatra, Enobarbus, Charmian, and Iras*

CLEOPATRA

  What shall we do, Enobarbus?

ENOBARBUS   Think, and die.

CLEOPATRA

  Is Antony or we in fault for this?

ENOBARBUS

  Antony only, that would make his will
  Lord of his reason. What though you fled
  From that great face of war, whose several ranges
  Frighted each other? Why should he follow?
  The itch of his affection should not then
  Have nicked his captainship, at such a point,
  When half to half the world opposed, he being
10 The merèd question. 'Twas a shame no less
  Than was his loss, to course your flying flags
  And leave his navy gazing.

CLEOPATRA   Prithee, peace.

      Enter the Ambassador, with Antony

ANTONY

  Is that his answer?

AMBASSADOR

  Ay, my lord.

ANTONY
  The Queen shall then have courtesy, so she
  Will yield us up.
AMBASSADOR   He says so.
ANTONY   Let her know't. –
  To the boy Caesar send this grizzled head,
  And he will fill thy wishes to the brim
  With principalities.
CLEOPATRA   That head, my lord?
ANTONY (to Ambassador)
  To him again! Tell him he wears the rose   20
  Of youth upon him; from which the world should note
  Something particular. His coin, ships, legions,
  May be a coward's, whose ministers would prevail
  Under the service of a child as soon
  As i'th'command of Caesar. I dare him therefore
  To lay his gay comparisons apart,
  And answer me declined, sword against sword,
  Ourselves alone. I'll write it. Follow me.
                              Exeunt Antony and Ambassador
ENOBARBUS (aside)
  Yes, like enough, high-battled Caesar will
  Unstate his happiness and be staged to th'show   30
  Against a sworder! I see men's judgements are
  A parcel of their fortunes, and things outward
  Do draw the inward quality after them
  To suffer all alike. That he should dream,
  Knowing all measures, the full Caesar will
  Answer his emptiness! Caesar, thou hast subdued
  His judgement too.
          Enter a Servant
SERVANT   A messenger from Caesar.
CLEOPATRA
  What, no more ceremony? See, my women,

137

Against the blown rose may they stop their nose
40   That kneeled unto the buds. Admit him, sir.

Exit Servant

ENOBARBUS *(aside)*
   Mine honesty and I begin to square.
   The loyalty well held to fools does make
   Our faith mere folly. Yet he that can endure
   To follow with allegiance a fallen lord
   Does conquer him that did his master conquer
   And earns a place i'th'story.

   Enter Thidias

CLEOPATRA   Caesar's will?
THIDIAS
   Hear it apart.
CLEOPATRA   None but friends; say boldly.
THIDIAS
   So, haply, are they friends to Antony.
ENOBARBUS
   He needs as many, sir, as Caesar has,
50   Or needs not us. If Caesar please, our master
   Will leap to be his friend; for us, you know,
   Whose he is we are, and that is Caesar's.
THIDIAS   So.
   Thus then, thou most renowned: Caesar entreats
   Not to consider in what case thou stand'st
   Further than he is Caesar.
CLEOPATRA   Go on; right royal.
THIDIAS
   He knows that you embraced not Antony
   As you did love, but as you feared him.
CLEOPATRA   O!
THIDIAS
   The scars upon your honour therefore he
   Does pity, as constrainèd blemishes,

Not as deserved.

CLEOPATRA   He is a god, and knows   60
What is most right. Mine honour was not yielded,
But conquered merely.

ENOBARBUS (*aside*)   To be sure of that,
I will ask Antony. Sir, sir, thou art so leaky
That we must leave thee to thy sinking, for
Thy dearest quit thee.   *Exit*

THIDIAS   Shall I say to Caesar
What you require of him? For he partly begs
To be desired to give. It much would please him
That of his fortunes you should make a staff
To lean upon. But it would warm his spirits
To hear from me you had left Antony,   70
And put yourself under his shroud,
The universal landlord.

CLEOPATRA   What's your name?

THIDIAS
My name is Thidias.

CLEOPATRA   Most kind messenger,
Say to great Caesar this: in deputation
I kiss his conquering hand. Tell him I am prompt
To lay my crown at's feet, and there to kneel,
Till from his all-obeying breath I hear
The doom of Egypt.

THIDIAS   'Tis your noblest course.
Wisdom and fortune combating together,
If that the former dare but what it can,   80
No chance may shake it. Give me grace to lay
My duty on your hand.

         She gives him her hand

CLEOPATRA   Your Caesar's father oft,
When he hath mused of taking kingdoms in,
Bestowed his lips on that unworthy place,

139

As it rained kisses.

Enter Antony and Enobarbus

ANTONY   Favours, by Jove that thunders!
What art thou, fellow?

THIDIAS   One that but performs
The bidding of the fullest man, and worthiest
To have command obeyed.

ENOBARBUS *(aside)*   You will be whipped.

ANTONY
Approach there! – Ah, you kite! Now, gods and devils!
90 Authority melts from me. Of late, when I cried 'Ho!',
Like boys unto a muss, kings would start forth
And cry 'Your will?' Have you no ears? I am
Antony yet.

Enter servants

               Take hence this Jack and whip him.

ENOBARBUS *(aside)*
'Tis better playing with a lion's whelp
Than with an old one dying.

ANTONY   Moon and stars!
Whip him! Were't twenty of the greatest tributaries
That do acknowledge Caesar, should I find them
So saucy with the hand of she here – what's her name
Since she was Cleopatra? Whip him, fellows,
100 Till like a boy you see him cringe his face
And whine aloud for mercy. Take him hence.

THIDIAS
Mark Antony –

ANTONY   Tug him away. Being whipped,
Bring him again. The Jack of Caesar's shall
Bear us an errand to him. *Exeunt servants with Thidias*
You were half blasted ere I knew you. Ha!
Have I my pillow left unpressed in Rome,
Forborne the getting of a lawful race,

And by a gem of women, to be abused
By one that looks on feeders?

CLEOPATRA   Good my lord –

ANTONY

You have been a boggler ever.   110
But when we in our viciousness grow hard –
O, misery on't! – the wise gods seel our eyes,
In our own filth drop our clear judgements, make us
Adore our errors, laugh at's while we strut
To our confusion.

CLEOPATRA   O, is't come to this?

ANTONY

I found you as a morsel cold upon
Dead Caesar's trencher. Nay, you were a fragment
Of Gnaeus Pompey's, besides what hotter hours,
Unregistered in vulgar fame, you have
Luxuriously picked out. For I am sure,   120
Though you can guess what temperance should be,
You know not what it is.

CLEOPATRA   Wherefore is this?

ANTONY

To let a fellow that will take rewards
And say 'God quit you!' be familiar with
My playfellow, your hand, this kingly seal
And plighter of high hearts! O that I were
Upon the hill of Basan to outroar
The hornèd herd! For I have savage cause,
And to proclaim it civilly were like
A haltered neck which does the hangman thank   130
For being yare about him.

       Enter a Servant with Thidias
                          Is he whipped?

SERVANT
Soundly, my lord.

ANTONY   Cried he? And begged 'a pardon?

SERVANT

He did ask favour.

ANTONY

If that thy father live, let him repent
Thou wast not made his daughter; and be thou sorry
To follow Caesar in his triumph, since
Thou hast been whipped for following him. Henceforth
The white hand of a lady fever thee;
Shake thou to look on't. Get thee back to Caesar.
140 Tell him thy entertainment. Look thou say
He makes me angry with him; for he seems
Proud and disdainful, harping on what I am,
Not what he knew I was. He makes me angry,
And at this time most easy 'tis to do't,
When my good stars that were my former guides
Have empty left their orbs and shot their fires
Into th'abysm of hell. If he mislike
My speech and what is done, tell him he has
Hipparchus, my enfranchèd bondman, whom
150 He may at pleasure whip, or hang, or torture,
As he shall like, to quit me. Urge it thou.
Hence with thy stripes, be gone!   *Exit Thidias*

CLEOPATRA

Have you done yet?

ANTONY   Alack, our terrene moon
Is now eclipsed, and it portends alone
The fall of Antony.

CLEOPATRA   I must stay his time.

ANTONY

To flatter Caesar, would you mingle eyes
With one that ties his points?

CLEOPATRA   Not know me yet?

ANTONY
   Cold-hearted toward me?
CLEOPATRA   Ah, dear, if I be so,
   From my cold heart let heaven engender hail,
   And poison it in the source, and the first stone   160
   Drop in my neck: as it determines, so
   Dissolve my life! The next Caesarion smite,
   Till by degrees the memory of my womb,
   Together with my brave Egyptians all,
   By the discandying of this pelleted storm,
   Lie graveless, till the flies and gnats of Nile
   Have buried them for prey!
ANTONY   I am satisfied.
   Caesar sits down in Alexandria, where
   I will oppose his fate. Our force by land
   Hath nobly held; our severed navy too   170
   Have knit again, and fleet, threatening most sea-like.
   Where hast thou been, my heart? Dost thou hear, lady?
   If from the field I shall return once more
   To kiss these lips, I will appear in blood.
   I and my sword will earn our chronicle.
   There's hope in't yet.
CLEOPATRA   That's my brave lord!
ANTONY
   I will be treble-sinewed, hearted, breathed,
   And fight maliciously. For when mine hours
   Were nice and lucky, men did ransom lives
   Of me for jests; but now I'll set my teeth   180
   And send to darkness all that stop me. Come,
   Let's have one other gaudy night. Call to me
   All my sad captains. Fill our bowls once more.
   Let's mock the midnight bell.
CLEOPATRA   It is my birthday.

I had thought t'have held it poor. But since my lord
Is Antony again, I will be Cleopatra.

ANTONY

We will yet do well.

CLEOPATRA

Call all his noble captains to my lord.

ANTONY

Do so, we'll speak to them; and tonight I'll force

190   The wine peep through their scars. Come on, my
          queen,
There's sap in't yet! The next time I do fight,
I'll make death love me, for I will contend
Even with his pestilent scythe.

Exeunt all but Enobarbus

ENOBARBUS

Now he'll outstare the lightning. To be furious
Is to be frighted out of fear, and in that mood
The dove will peck the estridge; and I see still
A diminution in our captain's brain
Restores his heart. When valour preys on reason,
It eats the sword it fights with. I will seek

200   Some way to leave him.   *Exit*

*

IV.1   *Enter Caesar, Agrippa, and Maecenas, with their
            army, Caesar reading a letter*

CAESAR

He calls me boy, and chides as he had power
To beat me out of Egypt. My messenger
He hath whipped with rods; dares me to personal
          combat,
Caesar to Antony. Let the old ruffian know

I have many other ways to die; meantime
Laugh at his challenge.

MAECENAS   Caesar must think,
When one so great begins to rage, he's hunted
Even to falling. Give him no breath, but now
Make boot of his distraction. Never anger
Made good guard for itself.

CAESAR   Let our best heads   10
Know that tomorrow the last of many battles
We mean to fight. Within our files there are,
Of those that served Mark Antony but late,
Enough to fetch him in. See it done,
And feast the army; we have store to do't,
And they have earned the waste. Poor Antony!

                                        Exeunt

Enter Antony, Cleopatra, Enobarbus, Charmian, Iras,   IV.2
Alexas, with others

ANTONY
He will not fight with me, Domitius?

ENOBARBUS   No.

ANTONY
Why should he not?

ENOBARBUS
He thinks, being twenty times of better fortune,
He is twenty men to one.

ANTONY   Tomorrow, soldier,
By sea and land I'll fight. Or I will live
Or bathe my dying honour in the blood
Shall make it live again. Woo't thou fight well?

ENOBARBUS
I'll strike, and cry 'Take all.'

ANTONY   Well said; come on.

Call forth my household servants. Let's tonight
10   Be bounteous at our meal.
> *Enter three or four servitors*
                             Give me thy hand.
Thou hast been rightly honest. So hast thou;
Thou, and thou, and thou. You have served me well,
And kings have been your fellows.

CLEOPATRA (*aside to Enobarbus*)   What means this?

ENOBARBUS (*aside to Cleopatra*)
  'Tis one of those odd tricks which sorrow shoots
Out of the mind.

ANTONY   And thou art honest too.
I wish I could be made so many men,
And all of you clapped up together in
An Antony, that I might do you service
So good as you have done.

ALL THE SERVANTS   The gods forbid!

ANTONY
20   Well, my good fellows, wait on me tonight.
Scant not my cups, and make as much of me
As when mine empire was your fellow too
And suffered my command.

CLEOPATRA (*aside to Enobarbus*) What does he mean?

ENOBARBUS (*aside to Cleopatra*)
  To make his followers weep.

ANTONY   Tend me tonight.
May be it is the period of your duty.
Haply you shall not see me more; or if,
A mangled shadow. Perchance tomorrow
You'll serve another master. I look on you
As one that takes his leave. Mine honest friends,
30   I turn you not away, but, like a master
Married to your good service, stay till death.
Tend me tonight two hours, I ask no more,

And the gods yield you for't!

ENOBARBUS   What mean you, sir,
To give them this discomfort? Look, they weep,
And I, an ass, am onion-eyed. For shame,
Transform us not to women.

ANTONY   Ho, ho, ho!
Now the witch take me if I meant it thus!
Grace grow where those drops fall! My hearty friends,
You take me in too dolorous a sense,
For I spake to you for your comfort, did desire you   40
To burn this night with torches. Know, my hearts,
I hope well of tomorrow, and will lead you
Where rather I'll expect victorious life
Than death and honour. Let's to supper, come,
And drown consideration.   *Exeunt*

Enter a company of Soldiers   IV.3

FIRST SOLDIER
Brother, good night. Tomorrow is the day.

SECOND SOLDIER
It will determine one way. Fare you well.
Heard you of nothing strange about the streets?

FIRST SOLDIER Nothing. What news?

SECOND SOLDIER Belike 'tis but a rumour. Good night
to you.

FIRST SOLDIER Well, sir, good night.
            They meet other Soldiers

SECOND SOLDIER Soldiers, have careful watch.

THIRD SOLDIER And you. Good night, good night.
            They place themselves in every corner of the stage

SECOND SOLDIER
Here we. An if tomorrow   10
Our navy thrive, I have an absolute hope

Our landmen will stand up.

FIRST SOLDIER   'Tis a brave army,
And full of purpose.

Music of hautboys under the stage

SECOND SOLDIER   Peace! What noise?

FIRST SOLDIER   List, list!

SECOND SOLDIER
Hark!

FIRST SOLDIER Music i'th'air.

THIRD SOLDIER   Under the earth.

FOURTH SOLDIER
It signs well, does it not?

THIRD SOLDIER   No.

FIRST SOLDIER   Peace, I say!
What should this mean?

SECOND SOLDIER
'Tis the god Hercules, whom Antony loved,
Now leaves him.

FIRST SOLDIER Walk; let's see if other watchmen
Do hear what we do.

80 SECOND SOLDIER How now, masters?

ALL (*speaking together*) How now? How now? Do you
hear this?

FIRST SOLDIER Ay. Is't not strange?

THIRD SOLDIER Do you hear, masters? Do you hear?

FIRST SOLDIER
Follow the noise so far as we have quarter.
Let's see how it will give off.

ALL Content. 'Tis strange.   *Exeunt*

ANTONY

Eros! Mine armour, Eros!

CLEOPATRA   Sleep a little.

ANTONY

No, my chuck. Eros! Come, mine armour, Eros!

Enter Eros with armour

Come, good fellow, put thine iron on.

If fortune be not ours today, it is

Because we brave her. Come.

CLEOPATRA   Nay, I'll help too.

What's this for?

ANTONY   Ah, let be, let be! Thou art

The armourer of my heart. False, false; this, this.

CLEOPATRA

Sooth, la, I'll help; thus it must be.

ANTONY   Well, well,

We shall thrive now. Seest thou, my good fellow?

Go put on thy defences.

EROS   Briefly, sir.   10

CLEOPATRA

Is not this buckled well?

ANTONY   Rarely, rarely.

He that unbuckles this, till we do please

To daff't for our repose, shall hear a storm.

Thou fumblest, Eros, and my queen's a squire

More tight at this than thou. Dispatch. O, love,

That thou couldst see my wars today, and knew'st

The royal occupation; thou shouldst see

A workman in't.

Enter an armed Soldier

                  Good morrow to thee. Welcome.

Thou look'st like him that knows a warlike charge.

20 To business that we love we rise betime
And go to't with delight.

SOLDIER   A thousand, sir,
Early though't be, have on their riveted trim,
And at the port expect you.

     Shout. Trumpets flourish. Enter Captains and
     soldiers

CAPTAIN
The morn is fair. Good morrow, General.

ALL THE SOLDIERS
Good morrow, General.

ANTONY   'Tis well blown, lads.
This morning, like the spirit of a youth
That means to be of note, begins betimes.
So, so. Come, give me that; this way; well said.
Fare thee well, dame. Whate'er becomes of me,
30 This is a soldier's kiss. Rebukeable
And worthy shameful check it were to stand
On more mechanic compliment. I'll leave thee
Now like a man of steel. You that will fight,
Follow me close; I'll bring you to't. Adieu.

     Exeunt all but Cleopatra and Charmian

CHARMIAN
Please you retire to your chamber?

CLEOPATRA   Lead me.
He goes forth gallantly. That he and Caesar might
Determine this great war in single fight!
Then Antony – but now. Well, on.   *Exeunt*

IV.5   *Trumpets sound. Enter Antony and Eros, a Soldier*
     meeting them

SOLDIER
The gods make this a happy day to Antony!

ANTONY

Would thou and those thy scars had once prevailed
To make me fight at land!

SOLDIER   Hadst thou done so,
The kings that have revolted, and the soldier
That has this morning left thee, would have still
Followed thy heels.

ANTONY   Who's gone this morning?

SOLDIER   Who?
One ever near thee; call for Enobarbus,
He shall not hear thee, or from Caesar's camp
Say 'I am none of thine.'

ANTONY   What sayst thou?

SOLDIER   Sir,
He is with Caesar.

EROS   Sir, his chests and treasure   10
He has not with him.

ANTONY   Is he gone?

SOLDIER   Most certain.

ANTONY

Go, Eros, send his treasure after; do it.
Detain no jot, I charge thee. Write to him –
I will subscribe – gentle adieus and greetings.
Say that I wish he never find more cause
To change a master. O, my fortunes have
Corrupted honest men! Dispatch. Enobarbus!

                                        Exeunt

Flourish. Enter Agrippa and Caesar, with Eno-   IV.6
barbus, and Dolabella

CAESAR

Go forth, Agrippa, and begin the fight.
Our will is Antony be took alive;

Make it so known.

AGRIPPA Caesar, I shall. *Exit*

CAESAR
The time of universal peace is near.
Prove this a prosperous day, the three-nooked world
Shall bear the olive freely.

Enter a Messenger

MESSENGER Antony
Is come into the field.

CAESAR Go charge Agrippa
Plant those that have revolted in the vant,

10 That Antony may seem to spend his fury
Upon himself. *Exeunt all but Enobarbus*

ENOBARBUS
Alexas did revolt and went to Jewry on
Affairs of Antony; there did dissuade
Great Herod to incline himself to Caesar
And leave his master Antony. For this pains
Caesar hath hanged him. Canidius and the rest
That fell away have entertainment, but
No honourable trust. I have done ill,
Of which I do accuse myself so sorely

20 That I will joy no more.

Enter a Soldier of Caesar's

SOLDIER Enobarbus, Antony
Hath after thee sent all thy treasure, with
His bounty overplus. The messenger
Came on my guard, and at thy tent is now
Unloading of his mules.

ENOBARBUS I give it you.

SOLDIER
Mock not, Enobarbus.
I tell you true. Best you safed the bringer
Out of the host. I must attend mine office

Or would have done't myself. Your emperor
Continues still a Jove.   *Exit*

ENOBARBUS

I am alone the villain of the earth,   30
And feel I am so most. O Antony,
Thou mine of bounty, how wouldst thou have paid
My better service, when my turpitude
Thou dost so crown with gold! This blows my heart.
If swift thought break it not, a swifter mean
Shall outstrike thought; but thought will do't, I feel.
I fight against thee? No, I will go seek
Some ditch wherein to die; the foul'st best fits
My latter part of life.   *Exit*

Alarum. Drums and trumpets. Enter Agrippa and   IV.7
others

AGRIPPA

Retire! We have engaged ourselves too far.
Caesar himself has work, and our oppression
Exceeds what we expected.   *Exeunt*
    Alarums. Enter Antony, and Scarus wounded

SCARUS

O my brave emperor, this is fought indeed!
Had we done so at first, we had droven them home
With clouts about their heads.

ANTONY   Thou bleed'st apace.

SCARUS

I had a wound here that was like a T,
But now 'tis made an H.
    Retreat sounded far off

ANTONY   They do retire.

SCARUS

We'll beat 'em into bench-holes. I have yet

10 Room for six scotches more.

    Enter Eros

EROS

  They are beaten, sir, and our advantage serves
  For a fair victory.

SCARUS   Let us score their backs

  And snatch 'em up, as we take hares, behind.
  'Tis sport to maul a runner.

ANTONY   I will reward thee

  Once for thy sprightly comfort, and tenfold
  For thy good valour. Come thee on.

SCARUS   I'll halt after.

                                    Exeunt

IV.8   *Alarum. Enter Antony, with Scarus and others,*
             marching

ANTONY

  We have beat him to his camp. Run one before
  And let the Queen know of our gests. Tomorrow,
  Before the sun shall see's, we'll spill the blood
  That has today escaped. I thank you all,
  For doughty-handed are you, and have fought
  Not as you served the cause, but as't had been
  Each man's like mine; you have shown all Hectors.
  Enter the city, clip your wives, your friends,
  Tell them your feats, whilst they with joyful tears
10 Wash the congealment from your wounds, and kiss
  The honoured gashes whole.

    Enter Cleopatra

              (*To Scarus*) Give me thy hand.

  To this great fairy I'll commend thy acts,
  Make her thanks bless thee. – O thou day o'th'world,
  Chain mine armed neck; leap thou, attire and all,

Through proof of harness to my heart, and there
Ride on the pants triumphing.

CLEOPATRA   Lord of lords!
O infinite virtue, com'st thou smiling from
The world's great snare uncaught?

ANTONY   My nightingale,
We have beat them to their beds. What, girl! Though
    grey
Do something mingle with our younger brown, yet ha'   20
    we
A brain that nourishes our nerves, and can
Get goal for goal of youth. Behold this man.
Commend unto his lips thy favouring hand. –
Kiss it, my warrior. – He hath fought today
As if a god in hate of mankind had
Destroyed in such a shape.

CLEOPATRA   I'll give thee, friend,
An armour all of gold; it was a king's.

ANTONY
He has deserved it, were it carbuncled
Like holy Phoebus' car. Give me thy hand.
Through Alexandria make a jolly march.   30
Bear our hacked targets like the men that owe them.
Had our great palace the capacity
To camp this host, we all would sup together
And drink carouses to the next day's fate,
Which promises royal peril. Trumpeters,
With brazen din blast you the city's ear;
Make mingle with our rattling tabourines,
That heaven and earth may strike their sounds together,
Applauding our approach.

                       Trumpets sound. Exeunt

Enter a Sentry and his company, the watch. Enobar-
      bus follows

SENTRY
   If we be not relieved within this hour,
   We must return to th'court of guard. The night
   Is shiny, and they say we shall embattle
   By th'second hour i'th'morn.
FIRST WATCH   This last day was
   A shrewd one to's.
ENOBARBUS   O, bear me witness, night –
SECOND WATCH
   What man is this?
FIRST WATCH   Stand close, and list him.
ENOBARBUS
   Be witness to me, O thou blessèd moon,
   When men revolted shall upon record
   Bear hateful memory, poor Enobarbus did
10 Before thy face repent!
SENTRY   Enobarbus?
SECOND WATCH   Peace;
   Hark further.
ENOBARBUS
   O sovereign mistress of true melancholy,
   The poisonous damp of night disponge upon me,
   That life, a very rebel to my will,
   May hang no longer on me. Throw my heart
   Against the flint and hardness of my fault,
   Which, being dried with grief, will break to powder,
   And finish all foul thoughts. O Antony,
   Nobler than my revolt is infamous,
20 Forgive me in thine own particular,
   But let the world rank me in register
   A master-leaver and a fugitive.
   O Antony! O Antony!   *He dies*

FIRST WATCH   Let's speak to him.
SENTRY

Let's hear him, for the things he speaks
May concern Caesar.
SECOND WATCH   Let's do so. But he sleeps.
SENTRY

Swoons rather, for so bad a prayer as his
Was never yet for sleep.
FIRST WATCH   Go we to him.
SECOND WATCH

Awake, sir, awake; speak to us.
FIRST WATCH   Hear you, sir?
SENTRY

The hand of death hath raught him.
          Drums afar off

                              Hark! The drums
Demurely wake the sleepers. Let us bear him   30
To th'court of guard; he is of note. Our hour
Is fully out.
SECOND WATCH

Come on then; he may recover yet.

                              Exeunt with the body

          Enter Antony and Scarus, with their army   IV.10
ANTONY

Their preparation is today by sea;
We please them not by land.
SCARUS   For both, my lord.
ANTONY

I would they'd fight i'th'fire or i'th'air;
We'd fight there too. But this it is: our foot
Upon the hills adjoining to the city
Shall stay with us. Order for sea is given;

They have put forth the haven –
Where their appointment we may best discover
And look on their endeavour.   *Exeunt*

IV.11   *Enter Caesar and his army*

CAESAR
But being charged, we will be still by land –
Which, as I take't, we shall, for his best force
Is forth to man his galleys. To the vales,
And hold our best advantage.   *Exeunt*

IV.12   *Alarum afar off, as at a sea fight*
              Enter Antony and Scarus

ANTONY
Yet they are not joined. Where yond pine does stand
I shall discover all. I'll bring thee word
Straight how 'tis like to go.   *Exit*
SCARUS   Swallows have built
In Cleopatra's sails their nests. The augurers
Say they know not, they cannot tell, look grimly,
And dare not speak their knowledge. Antony
Is valiant, and dejected, and by starts
His fretted fortunes give him hope and fear
Of what he has and has not.
         Enter Antony
ANTONY   All is lost!
10   This foul Egyptian hath betrayèd me.
My fleet hath yielded to the foe, and yonder
They cast their caps up and carouse together
Like friends long lost. Triple-turned whore! 'Tis thou
Hast sold me to this novice, and my heart
Makes only wars on thee. Bid them all fly;

158

For when I am revenged upon my charm,
I have done all. Bid them all fly, begone!

Exit Scarus

O sun, thy uprise shall I see no more.
Fortune and Antony part here; even here
Do we shake hands. All come to this? The hearts   20
That spanieled me at heels, to whom I gave
Their wishes, do discandy, melt their sweets
On blossoming Caesar; and this pine is barked
That overtopped them all. Betrayed I am.
O this false soul of Egypt! This grave charm,
Whose eye becked forth my wars, and called them
      home,
Whose bosom was my crownet, my chief end,
Like a right gypsy hath at fast and loose
Beguiled me to the very heart of loss.
What, Eros, Eros!

    Enter Cleopatra

              Ah, thou spell! Avaunt!   30

CLEOPATRA
Why is my lord enraged against his love?

ANTONY
Vanish, or I shall give thee thy deserving
And blemish Caesar's triumph. Let him take thee
And hoist thee up to the shouting plebeians;
Follow his chariot, like the greatest spot
Of all thy sex; most monster-like be shown
For poor'st diminutives, for doits, and let
Patient Octavia plough thy visage up
With her preparèd nails.   *Exit Cleopatra*

            'Tis well th' art gone,
If it be well to live; but better 'twere   40
Thou fell'st into my fury, for one death
Might have prevented many. Eros, ho!

The shirt of Nessus is upon me. Teach me,
Alcides, thou mine ancestor, thy rage.
Let me lodge Lichas on the horns o'th'moon,
And with those hands that grasped the heaviest club
Subdue my worthiest self. The witch shall die.
To the young Roman boy she hath sold me, and I fall
Under this plot; she dies for't. Eros, ho!   *Exit*

IV.13   *Enter Cleopatra, Charmian, Iras, and Mardian*

CLEOPATRA
  Help me, my women! O, he's more mad
  Than Telamon for his shield; the boar of Thessaly
  Was never so embossed.

CHARMIAN   To th'monument!
  There lock yourself, and send him word you are dead.
  The soul and body rive not more in parting
  Than greatness going off.

CLEOPATRA   To th'monument!
  Mardian, go tell him I have slain myself;
  Say that the last I spoke was 'Antony',
  And word it, prithee, piteously. Hence, Mardian,
10 And bring me how he takes my death to the monument.
                                    Exeunt

IV.14   *Enter Antony and Eros*

ANTONY
  Eros, thou yet behold'st me?

EROS   Ay, noble lord.

ANTONY
  Sometime we see a cloud that's dragonish,
  A vapour sometime like a bear or lion,
  A towered citadel, a pendent rock,

A forkèd mountain, or blue promontory
With trees upon't that nod unto the world
And mock our eyes with air. Thou hast seen these signs;
They are black vesper's pageants.

EROS   Ay, my lord.

ANTONY

That which is now a horse, even with a thought
The rack dislimns, and makes it indistinct   10
As water is in water.

EROS   It does, my lord.

ANTONY

My good knave Eros, now thy captain is
Even such a body. Here I am Antony,
Yet cannot hold this visible shape, my knave.
I made these wars for Egypt; and the Queen –
Whose heart I thought I had, for she had mine,
Which, whilst it was mine, had annexed unto't
A million more, now lost – she, Eros, has
Packed cards with Caesar, and false-played my glory
Unto an enemy's triumph.   20
Nay, weep not, gentle Eros, there is left us
Ourselves to end ourselves.

    Enter Mardian

                              O, thy vile lady!
She has robbed me of my sword.

MARDIAN   No, Antony;
My mistress loved thee, and her fortunes mingled
With thine entirely.

ANTONY   Hence, saucy eunuch, peace!
She hath betrayed me and shall die the death.

MARDIAN

Death of one person can be paid but once,
And that she has discharged. What thou wouldst do
Is done unto thy hand. The last she spake

161

30 Was 'Antony! Most noble Antony!'
    Then in the midst a tearing groan did break
    The name of Antony; it was divided
    Between her heart and lips. She rendered life,
    Thy name so buried in her.

ANTONY   Dead, then?

MARDIAN   Dead.

ANTONY
    Unarm, Eros. The long day's task is done,
    And we must sleep. (*To Mardian*) That thou depart'st
        hence safe
    Does pay thy labour richly. Go.   *Exit Mardian*
                              Off, pluck off!
    The sevenfold shield of Ajax cannot keep
    The battery from my heart. O, cleave, my sides!
40 Heart, once be stronger than thy continent,
    Crack thy frail case! Apace, Eros, apace!
    No more a soldier. Bruisèd pieces, go;
    You have been nobly borne. – From me awhile.
                                        Exit Eros

    I will o'ertake thee, Cleopatra, and
    Weep for my pardon. So it must be, for now
    All length is torture; since the torch is out,
    Lie down, and stray no farther. Now all labour
    Mars what it does; yea, very force entangles
    Itself with strength. Seal then, and all is done.
50 Eros! – I come, my queen – Eros! Stay for me.
    Where souls do couch on flowers, we'll hand in hand,
    And with our sprightly port make the ghosts gaze:
    Dido and her Aeneas shall want troops,
    And all the haunt be ours. – Come, Eros, Eros!
            Enter Eros

EROS
    What would my lord?

162

ANTONY   Since Cleopatra died,
I have lived in such dishonour that the gods
Detest my baseness. I, that with my sword
Quartered the world, and o'er green Neptune's back
With ships made cities, condemn myself to lack
The courage of a woman; less noble mind   60
Than she which by her death our Caesar tells
'I am conqueror of myself.' Thou art sworn, Eros,
That, when the exigent should come, which now
Is come indeed, when I should see behind me
Th'inevitable prosecution of
Disgrace and horror, that on my command
Thou then wouldst kill me. Do't; the time is come.
Thou strik'st not me; 'tis Caesar thou defeat'st.
Put colour in thy cheek.

EROS   The gods withhold me!
Shall I do that which all the Parthian darts,   70
Though enemy, lost aim and could not?

ANTONY   Eros,
Wouldst thou be windowed in great Rome and see
Thy master thus: with pleached arms, bending down
His corrigible neck, his face subdued
To penetrative shame, whilst the wheeled seat
Of fortunate Caesar, drawn before him, branded
His baseness that ensued?

EROS   I would not see't.

ANTONY
Come then; for with a wound I must be cured.
Draw that thy honest sword, which thou hast worn
Most useful for thy country.

EROS   O, sir, pardon me.   80

ANTONY
When I did make thee free, swor'st thou not then
To do this when I bade thee? Do it at once,

Or thy precedent services are all
But accidents unpurposed. Draw, and come.

EROS
Turn from me then that noble countenance
Wherein the worship of the whole world lies.

ANTONY
Lo thee!

He turns from him

EROS
My sword is drawn.

ANTONY   Then let it do at once
The thing why thou hast drawn it.

EROS   My dear master,
90 My captain, and my emperor, let me say,
Before I strike this bloody stroke, farewell.

ANTONY
'Tis said, man, and farewell.

EROS
Farewell, great chief. Shall I strike now?

ANTONY   Now, Eros.

EROS
Why, there then! Thus I do escape the sorrow
Of Antony's death.   *He kills himself*

ANTONY   Thrice nobler than myself,
Thou teachest me, O valiant Eros, what
I should, and thou couldst not. My queen and Eros
Have by their brave instruction got upon me
A nobleness in record. But I will be
100 A bridegroom in my death, and run into't
As to a lover's bed. Come then; and, Eros,
Thy master dies thy scholar. To do thus
I learned of thee.

He falls on his sword

                    How? Not dead? Not dead?

The guard, ho! O, dispatch me!

Enter Decretas and a company of the Guard

FIRST GUARD   What's the noise?

ANTONY

I have done my work ill, friends. O, make an end
Of what I have begun.

SECOND GUARD   The star is fallen.

FIRST GUARD

And time is at his period.

ALL THE GUARDS   Alas, and woe!

ANTONY

Let him that loves me strike me dead.

FIRST GUARD   Not I.

SECOND GUARD

Nor I.

THIRD GUARD

Nor anyone.   *Exeunt Guard* 110

DECRETAS

Thy death and fortunes bid thy followers fly.
This sword but shown to Caesar, with this tidings,
Shall enter me with him.

        Enter Diomedes

DIOMEDES

Where's Antony?

DECRETAS   There, Diomed, there.

DIOMEDES   Lives he?

Wilt thou not answer, man?   *Exit Decretas*

ANTONY

Art thou there, Diomed? Draw thy sword, and give me
Sufficing strokes for death.

DIOMEDES   Most absolute lord,
My mistress Cleopatra sent me to thee.

ANTONY

When did she send thee?

DIOMEDES   Now, my lord.
ANTONY   Where is she?
DIOMEDES
120   Locked in her monument. She had a prophesying fear
       Of what hath come to pass; for when she saw –
       Which never shall be found – you did suspect
       She had disposed with Caesar, and that your rage
       Would not be purged, she sent you word she was dead;
       But, fearing since how it might work, hath sent
       Me to proclaim the truth, and I am come,
       I dread, too late.
ANTONY
       Too late, good Diomed. Call my guard, I prithee.
DIOMEDES
       What ho! The Emperor's guard! The guard, what ho!
130   Come, your lord calls!
            Enter four or five of the Guard of Antony
ANTONY
       Bear me, good friends, where Cleopatra bides.
       'Tis the last service that I shall command you.
FIRST GUARD
       Woe, woe are we, sir, you may not live to wear
       All your true followers out.
ALL THE GUARDS   Most heavy day!
ANTONY
       Nay, good my fellows, do not please sharp fate
       To grace it with your sorrows. Bid that welcome
       Which comes to punish us, and we punish it,
       Seeming to bear it lightly. Take me up.
       I have led you oft; carry me now, good friends,
140   And have my thanks for all.
                              Exeunt, bearing Antony

Enter Cleopatra and her maids, aloft, with Charmian IV.15
and Iras

CLEOPATRA
O, Charmian, I will never go from hence.

CHARMIAN
Be comforted, dear madam.

CLEOPATRA   No, I will not.
All strange and terrible events are welcome,
But comforts we despise. Our size of sorrow,
Proportioned to our cause, must be as great
As that which makes it.

          Enter Diomedes below

                              How now? Is he dead?

DIOMEDES
His death's upon him, but not dead.
Look out o'th'other side your monument;
His guard have brought him thither.

          Enter, below, the Guard, bearing Antony

CLEOPATRA   O sun,
Burn the great sphere thou mov'st in; darkling stand   10
The varying shore o'th'world! O Antony,
Antony, Antony! Help, Charmian, help, Iras, help!
Help, friends below! Let's draw him hither.

ANTONY   Peace!
Not Caesar's valour hath o'erthrown Antony,
But Antony's hath triumphed on itself.

CLEOPATRA
So it should be, that none but Antony
Should conquer Antony, but woe 'tis so!

ANTONY
I am dying, Egypt, dying; only
I here importune death awhile, until
Of many thousand kisses the poor last   20
I lay upon thy lips.

CLEOPATRA   I dare not, dear;
　　Dear my lord, pardon. I dare not,
　　Lest I be taken. Not th'imperious show
　　Of the full-fortuned Caesar ever shall
　　Be brooched with me. If knife, drugs, serpents, have
　　Edge, sting, or operation, I am safe.
　　Your wife Octavia, with her modest eyes
　　And still conclusion, shall acquire no honour
　　Demuring upon me. But come, come, Antony –
30　Help me, my women – we must draw thee up.
　　Assist, good friends.
ANTONY   O, quick, or I am gone.
CLEOPATRA
　　Here's sport indeed! How heavy weighs my lord!
　　Our strength is all gone into heaviness,
　　That makes the weight. Had I great Juno's power,
　　The strong-winged Mercury should fetch thee up
　　And set thee by Jove's side. Yet come a little;
　　Wishers were ever fools. O, come, come, come.
　　　　They heave Antony aloft to Cleopatra
　　And welcome, welcome! Die when thou hast lived;
　　Quicken with kissing. Had my lips that power,
40　Thus would I wear them out.
ALL THE GUARDS   A heavy sight!
ANTONY
　　I am dying, Egypt, dying.
　　Give me some wine, and let me speak a little.
CLEOPATRA
　　No, let me speak, and let me rail so high
　　That the false housewife Fortune break her wheel,
　　Provoked by my offence.
ANTONY   One word, sweet queen.
　　Of Caesar seek your honour, with your safety. O!

CLEOPATRA

    They do not go together.

ANTONY   Gentle, hear me:

    None about Caesar trust but Proculeius.

CLEOPATRA

    My resolution and my hands I'll trust,

    None about Caesar.   50

ANTONY

    The miserable change now at my end

    Lament nor sorrow at, but please your thoughts

    In feeding them with those my former fortunes,

    Wherein I lived; the greatest prince o'th'world,

    The noblest; and do now not basely die,

    Not cowardly put off my helmet to

    My countryman; a Roman, by a Roman

    Valiantly vanquished. Now my spirit is going;

    I can no more.

CLEOPATRA   Noblest of men, woo't die?

    Hast thou no care of me? Shall I abide   60

    In this dull world, which in thy absence is

    No better than a sty? O, see, my women,

Antony dies

    The crown o'th'earth doth melt. My lord!

    O, withered is the garland of the war,

    The soldier's pole is fall'n; young boys and girls

    Are level now with men. The odds is gone,

    And there is nothing left remarkable

    Beneath the visiting moon.

    She faints

CHARMIAN   O, quietness, lady!

IRAS

    She's dead too, our sovereign.

CHARMIAN   Lady!

IRAS   Madam!

CHARMIAN

70   O madam, madam, madam!

IRAS

Royal Egypt! Empress!

CHARMIAN   Peace, peace, Iras!

CLEOPATRA

No more but e'en a woman, and commanded
By such poor passion as the maid that milks
And does the meanest chares. It were for me
To throw my sceptre at the injurious gods,
To tell them that this world did equal theirs
Till they had stolen our jewel. All's but naught.
Patience is sottish, and impatience does
Become a dog that's mad; then is it sin
80   To rush into the secret house of death
Ere death dare come to us? How do you, women?
What, what, good cheer! Why, how now, Charmian?
My noble girls! Ah, women, women, look,
Our lamp is spent, it's out. Good sirs, take heart.
We'll bury him; and then, what's brave, what's noble,
Let's do't after the high Roman fashion,
And make death proud to take us. Come, away.
This case of that huge spirit now is cold.
Ah, women, women! Come; we have no friend
90   But resolution, and the briefest end.

Exeunt, bearing off Antony's body

*

V.1   *Enter Caesar, Agrippa, Dolabella, Maecenas,*
             Gallus, Proculeius, with his council of war

CAESAR

Go to him, Dolabella, bid him yield.

Being so frustrate, tell him, he mocks
The pauses that he makes.
DOLABELLA   Caesar, I shall.   *Exit*
    Enter Decretas, with the sword of Antony
CAESAR
  Wherefore is that? And what art thou that dar'st
  Appear thus to us?
DECRETAS   I am called Decretas.
  Mark Antony I served, who best was worthy
  Best to be served. Whilst he stood up and spoke,
  He was my master, and I wore my life
  To spend upon his haters. If thou please
  To take me to thee, as I was to him   10
  I'll be to Caesar; if thou pleasest not,
  I yield thee up my life.
CAESAR   What is't thou sayst?
DECRETAS
  I say, O Caesar, Antony is dead.
CAESAR
  The breaking of so great a thing should make
  A greater crack. The round world
  Should have shook lions into civil streets
  And citizens to their dens. The death of Antony
  Is not a single doom; in the name lay
  A moiety of the world.
DECRETAS   He is dead, Caesar,
  Not by a public minister of justice   20
  Nor by a hirèd knife; but that self hand
  Which writ his honour in the acts it did
  Hath, with the courage which the heart did lend it,
  Splitted the heart. This is his sword;
  I robbed his wound of it. Behold it stained
  With his most noble blood.
CAESAR   Look you, sad friends.

The gods rebuke me, but it is tidings
To wash the eyes of kings.

AGRIPPA   And strange it is
That nature must compel us to lament
80 Our most persisted deeds.

MAECENAS   His taints and honours
Waged equal with him.

AGRIPPA   A rarer spirit never
Did steer humanity. But you gods will give us
Some faults to make us men. Caesar is touched.

MAECENAS
When such a spacious mirror's set before him,
He needs must see himself.

CAESAR   O Antony,
I have followed thee to this. But we do launch
Diseases in our bodies. I must perforce
Have shown to thee such a declining day
Or look on thine. We could not stall together
40 In the whole world. But yet let me lament
With tears as sovereign as the blood of hearts
That thou, my brother, my competitor
In top of all design, my mate in empire,
Friend and companion in the front of war,
The arm of mine own body, and the heart
Where mine his thoughts did kindle – that our stars,
Unreconciliable, should divide
Our equalness to this. Hear me, good friends –
       (*Enter an Egyptian*)
But I will tell you at some meeter season.
50 The business of this man looks out of him;
We'll hear him what he says. Whence are you?

EGYPTIAN
A poor Egyptian yet. The Queen my mistress,
Confined in all she has, her monument,

Of thy intents desires instruction,
That she preparèdly may frame herself
To th'way she's forced to.

CAESAR   Bid her have good heart.
She soon shall know of us, by some of ours,
How honourable and how kindly we
Determine for her. For Caesar cannot live
To be ungentle.

EGYPTIAN   So the gods preserve thee!   *Exit* 60

CAESAR
Come hither, Proculeius. Go and say
We purpose her no shame. Give her what comforts
The quality of her passion shall require,
Lest in her greatness, by some mortal stroke,
She do defeat us. For her life in Rome
Would be eternal in our triumph. Go,
And with your speediest bring us what she says
And how you find her.

PROCULEIUS   Caesar, I shall.   *Exit*

CAESAR
Gallus, go you along.   *Exit Gallus*
                    Where's Dolabella,
To second Proculeius?

ALL CAESAR'S ATTENDANTS Dolabella!   70

CAESAR
Let him alone, for I remember now
How he's employed. He shall in time be ready.
Go with me to my tent, where you shall see
How hardly I was drawn into this war,
How calm and gentle I proceeded still
In all my writings. Go with me, and see
What I can show in this.   *Exeunt*

CLEOPATRA

> My desolation does begin to make
> A better life. 'Tis paltry to be Caesar:
> Not being Fortune, he's but Fortune's knave,
> A minister of her will. And it is great
> To do that thing that ends all other deeds,
> Which shackles accidents and bolts up change;
> Which sleeps, and never palates more the dung,
> The beggar's nurse and Caesar's.

> > *Enter, to the gates of the monument, Proculeius,*
> > *Gallus, and soldiers*

PROCULEIUS

> Caesar sends greeting to the Queen of Egypt,
10 And bids thee study on what fair demands
> Thou mean'st to have him grant thee.

CLEOPATRA   What's thy name?

PROCULEIUS

> My name is Proculeius.

CLEOPATRA   Antony

> Did tell me of you, bade me trust you, but
> I do not greatly care to be deceived,
> That have no use for trusting. If your master
> Would have a queen his beggar, you must tell him
> That majesty, to keep decorum, must
> No less beg than a kingdom. If he please
> To give me conquered Egypt for my son,
20 He gives me so much of mine own as I
> Will kneel to him with thanks.

PROCULEIUS   Be of good cheer;

> Y'are fall'n into a princely hand; fear nothing.
> Make your full reference freely to my lord,
> Who is so full of grace that it flows over
> On all that need. Let me report to him

Your sweet dependency, and you shall find
A conqueror that will pray in aid for kindness,
Where he for grace is kneeled to.

CLEOPATRA   Pray you, tell him
I am his fortune's vassal, and I send him
The greatness he has got. I hourly learn   30
A doctrine of obedience, and would gladly
Look him i'th'face.

PROCULEIUS   This I'll report, dear lady.
Have comfort, for I know your plight is pitied
Of him that caused it.

    The soldiers approach Cleopatra from behind

GALLUS
You see how easily she may be surprised.
    They seize Cleopatra
Guard her till Caesar come.   *Exit Gallus*

IRAS
Royal queen!

CHARMIAN
O Cleopatra! Thou art taken, queen.

CLEOPATRA
Quick, quick, good hands!
    She draws a dagger

PROCULEIUS   Hold, worthy lady, hold!
    He disarms her
Do not yourself such wrong, who are in this   40
Relieved, but not betrayed.

CLEOPATRA   What, of death too,
That rids our dogs of languish?

PROCULEIUS   Cleopatra,
Do not abuse my master's bounty by
Th'undoing of yourself. Let the world see
His nobleness well acted, which your death
Will never let come forth.

CLEOPATRA   Where art thou, death?
Come hither, come! Come, come, and take a queen
Worth many babes and beggars!
PROCULEIUS   O, temperance, lady!
CLEOPATRA
Sir, I will eat no meat, I'll not drink, sir –
50   If idle talk will once be necessary –
I'll not sleep neither. This mortal house I'll ruin,
Do Caesar what he can. Know, sir, that I
Will not wait pinioned at your master's court,
Nor once be chastised with the sober eye
Of dull Octavia. Shall they hoist me up
And show me to the shouting varletry
Of censuring Rome? Rather a ditch in Egypt
Be gentle grave unto me! Rather on Nilus' mud
Lay me stark nak'd and let the waterflies
60   Blow me into abhorring! Rather make
My country's high pyramides my gibbet
And hang me up in chains!
PROCULEIUS   You do extend
These thoughts of horror further than you shall
Find cause in Caesar.
        Enter Dolabella
DOLABELLA   Proculeius,
What thou hast done thy master Caesar knows,
And he hath sent for thee. For the Queen,
I'll take her to my guard.
PROCULEIUS   So, Dolabella,
It shall content me best. Be gentle to her.
(To Cleopatra) To Caesar I will speak what you shall
        please,
70   If you'll employ me to him.
CLEOPATRA   Say I would die.
                Exeunt Proculeius and soldiers

DOLABELLA
  Most noble empress, you have heard of me?
CLEOPATRA
  I cannot tell.
DOLABELLA   Assuredly you know me.
CLEOPATRA
  No matter, sir, what I have heard or known.
  You laugh when boys or women tell their dreams;
  Is't not your trick?
DOLABELLA   I understand not, madam.
CLEOPATRA
  I dreamt there was an emperor Antony.
  O, such another sleep, that I might see
  But such another man!
DOLABELLA   If it might please ye –
CLEOPATRA
  His face was as the heavens, and therein stuck
  A sun and moon, which kept their course and lighted   80
  The little O o'th'earth.
DOLABELLA   Most sovereign creature –
CLEOPATRA
  His legs bestrid the ocean; his reared arm
  Crested the world; his voice was propertied
  As all the tunèd spheres, and that to friends;
  But when he meant to quail and shake the orb,
  He was as rattling thunder. For his bounty,
  There was no winter in't; an Antony it was
  That grew the more by reaping. His delights
  Were dolphin-like; they showed his back above
  The element they lived in. In his livery   90
  Walked crowns and crownets; realms and islands were
  As plates dropped from his pocket.
DOLABELLA   Cleopatra –

CLEOPATRA

Think you there was or might be such a man
As this I dreamt of?

DOLABELLA   Gentle madam, no.

CLEOPATRA

You lie, up to the hearing of the gods.
But if there be nor ever were one such,
It's past the size of dreaming. Nature wants stuff
To vie strange forms with fancy, yet t'imagine
An Antony were nature's piece 'gainst fancy,
100 Condemning shadows quite.

DOLABELLA   Hear me, good madam.

Your loss is as yourself, great; and you bear it
As answering to the weight. Would I might never
O'ertake pursued success but I do feel,
By the rebound of yours, a grief that smites
My very heart at root.

CLEOPATRA   I thank you, sir.

Know you what Caesar means to do with me?

DOLABELLA

I am loath to tell you what I would you knew.

CLEOPATRA

Nay, pray you, sir.

DOLABELLA   Though he be honourable –

CLEOPATRA

He'll lead me, then, in triumph?

DOLABELLA

110 Madam, he will. I know't.

          Flourish. Enter Proculeius, Caesar, Gallus, Maecenas,
          and others of Caesar's train

ALL

Make way there! Caesar!

CAESAR

Which is the Queen of Egypt?

DOLABELLA

It is the Emperor, madam.
Cleopatra kneels

CAESAR

Arise! You shall not kneel.
I pray you rise; rise, Egypt.

CLEOPATRA   Sir, the gods
Will have it thus. My master and my lord
I must obey.

CAESAR   Take to you no hard thoughts.
The record of what injuries you did us,
Though written in our flesh, we shall remember
As things but done by chance.

CLEOPATRA   Sole sir o'th'world,   120
I cannot project mine own cause so well
To make it clear, but do confess I have
Been laden with like frailties which before
Have often shamed our sex.

CAESAR   Cleopatra, know,
We will extenuate rather than enforce.
If you apply yourself to our intents,
Which towards you are most gentle, you shall find
A benefit in this change; but if you seek
To lay on me a cruelty by taking
Antony's course, you shall bereave yourself   130
Of my good purposes, and put your children
To that destruction which I'll guard them from
If thereon you rely. I'll take my leave.

CLEOPATRA

And may, through all the world; 'tis yours, and we,
Your scutcheons and your signs of conquest, shall
Hang in what place you please. Here, my good lord.
She gives him a paper

CAESAR

  You shall advise me in all for Cleopatra.

CLEOPATRA

  This is the brief of money, plate, and jewels
  I am possessed of. 'Tis exactly valued,
140 Not petty things admitted. Where's Seleucus?

    Enter Seleucus

SELEUCUS

  Here, madam.

CLEOPATRA

  This is my treasurer. Let him speak, my lord,
  Upon his peril, that I have reserved
  To myself nothing. Speak the truth, Seleucus.

SELEUCUS

  Madam,
  I had rather seel my lips than to my peril
  Speak that which is not.

CLEOPATRA   What have I kept back?

SELEUCUS

  Enough to purchase what you have made known.

CAESAR

  Nay, blush not, Cleopatra. I approve
150 Your wisdom in the deed.

CLEOPATRA   See, Caesar; O behold,
  How pomp is followed! Mine will now be yours,
  And should we shift estates, yours would be mine.
  The ingratitude of this Seleucus does
  Even make me wild. O slave, of no more trust
  Than love that's hired! What, goest thou back? Thou
      shalt
  Go back, I warrant thee; but I'll catch thine eyes,
  Though they had wings. Slave, soulless villain, dog!
  O rarely base!

CAESAR   Good queen, let us entreat you.

CLEOPATRA

  O Caesar, what a wounding shame is this,
  That thou vouchsafing here to visit me,   160
  Doing the honour of thy lordliness
  To one so meek, that mine own servant should
  Parcel the sum of my disgraces by
  Addition of his envy. Say, good Caesar,
  That I some lady trifles have reserved,
  Immoment toys, things of such dignity
  As we greet modern friends withal; and say
  Some nobler token I have kept apart
  For Livia and Octavia, to induce
  Their mediation – must I be unfolded   170
  With one that I have bred? The gods! It smites me
  Beneath the fall I have. (*To Seleucus*) Prithee go hence,
  Or I shall show the cinders of my spirits
  Through th'ashes of my chance. Wert thou a man,
  Thou wouldst have mercy on me.

CAESAR   Forbear, Seleucus.
                              Exit Seleucus

CLEOPATRA

  Be it known that we, the greatest, are misthought
  For things that others do; and when we fall,
  We answer others' merits in our name,
  Are therefore to be pitied.

CAESAR   Cleopatra,
  Not what you have reserved nor what acknowledged   180
  Put we i'th'roll of conquest. Still be't yours;
  Bestow it at your pleasure, and believe
  Caesar's no merchant, to make prize with you
  Of things that merchants sold. Therefore be cheered.
  Make not your thoughts your prisons. No, dear queen,
  For we intend so to dispose you as
  Yourself shall give us counsel. Feed and sleep.

Our care and pity is so much upon you
That we remain your friend; and so adieu.

CLEOPATRA

190 My master, and my lord!

CAESAR   Not so. Adieu.

        Flourish. Exeunt Caesar, Dolabella, Proculeius,
       Gallus, Maecenas, and Caesar's other attendants

CLEOPATRA

He words me, girls, he words me, that I should not
Be noble to myself. But hark thee, Charmian.
    She whispers to Charmian

IRAS

Finish, good lady; the bright day is done,
And we are for the dark.

CLEOPATRA   Hie thee again.
I have spoke already, and it is provided;
Go put it to the haste.

CHARMIAN   Madam, I will.

    Enter Dolabella

DOLABELLA

Where's the Queen?

CHARMIAN   Behold, sir.   *Exit*

CLEOPATRA   Dolabella!

DOLABELLA

Madam, as thereto sworn, by your command,
Which my love makes religion to obey,
200 I tell you this: Caesar through Syria
Intends his journey, and within three days
You with your children will he send before.
Make your best use of this. I have performed
Your pleasure and my promise.

CLEOPATRA   Dolabella,
I shall remain your debtor.

DOLABELLA   I, your servant.

Adieu, good queen; I must attend on Caesar.

CLEOPATRA

Farewell, and thanks.   *Exit Dolabella*
                 Now, Iras, what think'st thou?
Thou, an Egyptian puppet, shall be shown
In Rome as well as I. Mechanic slaves
With greasy aprons, rules, and hammers shall   210
Uplift us to the view. In their thick breaths,
Rank of gross diet, shall we be enclouded,
And forced to drink their vapour.

IRAS   The gods forbid!

CLEOPATRA

Nay, 'tis most certain, Iras. Saucy lictors
Will catch at us like strumpets, and scald rhymers
Ballad us out o'tune. The quick comedians
Extemporally will stage us, and present
Our Alexandrian revels. Antony
Shall be brought drunken forth, and I shall see
Some squeaking Cleopatra boy my greatness   220
I'th'posture of a whore.

IRAS   O, the good gods!

CLEOPATRA

Nay that's certain.

IRAS

I'll never see't! For I am sure my nails
Are stronger than mine eyes.

CLEOPATRA   Why, that's the way
To fool their preparation, and to conquer
Their most absurd intents.
    Enter Charmian
                 Now, Charmian!
Show me, my women, like a queen. Go fetch
My best attires. I am again for Cydnus,
To meet Mark Antony. Sirrah Iras, go.

230　Now, noble Charmian, we'll dispatch indeed,
　　And when thou hast done this chare, I'll give thee leave
　　To play till doomsday. – Bring our crown and all.

Exit Iras

　　　A noise within
　　Wherefore's this noise?
　　　Enter a Guardsman
GUARDSMAN　　　　　　　Here is a rural fellow
　　That will not be denied your highness' presence.
　　He brings you figs.
CLEOPATRA
　　Let him come in.　　　　　　　　*Exit Guardsman*
　　　　　　What poor an instrument
　　May do a noble deed! He brings me liberty.
　　My resolution's placed, and I have nothing
　　Of woman in me. Now from head to foot
240'　I am marble-constant; now the fleeting moon
　　No planet is of mine.
　　　Enter Guardsman and Clown with a basket
GUARDSMAN　　　　　　This is the man.
CLEOPATRA
　　Avoid, and leave him.　　　　　　*Exit Guardsman*
　　Hast thou the pretty worm of Nilus there,
　　That kills and pains not?
CLOWN Truly I have him; but I would not be the party
　　that should desire you to touch him, for his biting is
　　immortal. Those that do die of it do seldom or never
　　recover.
CLEOPATRA Remember'st thou any that have died on't?
250 CLOWN Very many, men and women too. I heard of one
　　　of them no longer than yesterday; a very honest
　　　woman, but something given to lie, as a woman should
　　　not do but in the way of honesty; how she died of the
　　　biting of it, what pain she felt; truly, she makes a very

good report o'th'worm. But he that will believe all that they say shall never be saved by half that they do. But this is most falliable, the worm's an odd worm.

CLEOPATRA Get thee hence, farewell.

CLOWN I wish you all joy of the worm.

He sets down the basket

CLEOPATRA Farewell. 260

CLOWN You must think this, look you, that the worm will do his kind.

CLEOPATRA Ay, ay, farewell.

CLOWN Look you, the worm is not to be trusted but in the keeping of wise people; for indeed there is no goodness in the worm.

CLEOPATRA Take thou no care; it shall be heeded.

CLOWN·Very good. Give it nothing, I pray you, for it is not worth the feeding.

CLEOPATRA Will it eat me? 270

CLOWN You must not think I am so simple but I know the devil himself will not eat a woman. I know that a woman is a dish for the gods, if the devil dress her not. But truly, these same whoreson devils do the gods great harm in their women; for in every ten that they make, the devils mar five.

CLEOPATRA Well, get thee gone, farewell.

CLOWN Yes, forsooth. I wish you joy o'th'worm. *Exit*

Enter Iras with a robe, crown, sceptre, and other regalia

CLEOPATRA

Give me my robe; put on my crown; I have
Immortal longings in me. Now no more 280
The juice of Egypt's grape shall moist this lip.
Yare, yare, good Iras; quick – methinks I hear
Antony call. I see him rouse himself
To praise my noble act. I hear him mock

185

The luck of Caesar, which the gods give men
To excuse their after wrath. Husband, I come.
Now to that name my courage prove my title!
I am fire and air; my other elements
I give to baser life. So, have you done?
290   Come then, and take the last warmth of my lips.
Farewell, kind Charmian, Iras, long farewell.

> *She kisses them. Iras falls and dies*

Have I the aspic in my lips? Dost fall?
If thou and nature can so gently part,
The stroke of death is as a lover's pinch,
Which hurts, and is desired. Dost thou lie still?
If thus thou vanishest, thou tell'st the world
It is not worth leave-taking.

CHARMIAN

Dissolve, thick cloud, and rain, that I may say
The gods themselves do weep.

CLEOPATRA   This proves me base;
300   If she first meet the curlèd Antony,
He'll make demand of her, and spend that kiss
Which is my heaven to have. (*To an asp*) Come, thou
                mortal wretch,
With thy sharp teeth this knot intrinsicate
Of life at once untie. Poor venomous fool,
Be angry, and dispatch. O, couldst thou speak,
That I might hear thee call great Caesar ass
Unpolicied!

CHARMIAN   O eastern star!

CLEOPATRA   Peace, peace!
Dost thou not see my baby at my breast,
That sucks the nurse asleep?

CHARMIAN   O, break! O, break!

CLEOPATRA

310   As sweet as balm, as soft as air, as gentle –

O, Antony! Nay, I will take thee too.
    She applies another asp to her arm
  What should I stay –   *She dies*

CHARMIAN
  In this vile world? So, fare thee well.
  Now boast thee, death, in thy possession lies
  A lass unparalleled. Downy windows, close;
  And golden Phoebus never be beheld
  Of eyes again so royal! Your crown's awry;
  I'll mend it, and then play –
    Enter the Guard, rustling in

FIRST GUARD
  Where's the Queen?

CHARMIAN   Speak softly, wake her not.

FIRST GUARD
  Caesar hath sent –

CHARMIAN   Too slow a messenger.   320
    She applies an asp to herself
  O, come apace, dispatch. I partly feel thee.

FIRST GUARD
  Approach, ho! All's not well; Caesar's beguiled.

SECOND GUARD
  There's Dolabella sent from Caesar; call him.

FIRST GUARD
  What work is here, Charmian? Is this well done?

CHARMIAN
  It is well done, and fitting for a princess
  Descended of so many royal kings.
  Ah, soldier!   *Charmian dies*
    Enter Dolabella

DOLABELLA
  How goes it here?

SECOND GUARD   All dead.

DOLABELLA   Caesar, thy thoughts

Touch their effects in this. Thyself art coming
330   To see performed the dreaded act which thou
So sought'st to hinder.

Enter Caesar, and all his train, marching

ALL   A way there, a way for Caesar!

DOLABELLA
O, sir, you are too sure an augurer;
That you did fear is done.

CAESAR   Bravest at the last,
She levelled at our purposes and, being royal,
Took her own way. The manner of their deaths?
I do not see them bleed.

DOLABELLA   Who was last with them?

FIRST GUARD
A simple countryman, that brought her figs.
This was his basket.

CAESAR   Poisoned, then.

FIRST GUARD   O, Caesar,
This Charmian lived but now; she stood and spake.
340   I found her trimming up the diadem
On her dead mistress. Tremblingly she stood,
And on the sudden dropped.

CAESAR   O, noble weakness!
If they had swallowed poison, 'twould appear
By external swelling; but she looks like sleep,
As she would catch another Antony
In her strong toil of grace.

DOLABELLA   Here, on her breast,
There is a vent of blood, and something blown;
The like is on her arm.

FIRST GUARD
This is an aspic's trail; and these fig leaves
350   Have slime upon them, such as th'aspic leaves
Upon the caves of Nile.

CAESAR   Most probable
That so she died; for her physician tells me
She hath pursued conclusions infinite
Of easy ways to die. Take up her bed,
And bear her women from the monument.
She shall be buried by her Antony.
No grave upon the earth shall clip in it
A pair so famous. High events as these
Strike those that make them; and their story is
No less in pity than his glory which   360
Brought them to be lamented. Our army shall
In solemn show attend this funeral,
And then to Rome. Come, Dolabella, see
High order in this great solemnity.   *Exeunt*

COMMENTARY

ACT and scene divisions are those of Peter Alexander's edition of the *Complete Works* (London, 1951). 'F' refers to the first Folio of Shakespeare's plays (1623). Biblical quotations are from the Bishops' Bible (1568 etc.), the one most likely to have been read by Shakespeare. Quotations from North's Plutarch are from *Shakespeare's Plutarch*, edited by T. J. B. Spencer (Penguin Books, 1964).

Historical Note

Shakespeare probably assumes a general knowledge of the historical events which form the subject of the play. The action covers the ten years preceding the deaths of Antony and Cleopatra in 30 B.C. The earliest event dramatized is Antony's departure from Alexandria (40 B.C.). The treaty of Misenum between the second triumvirate (Antony, Octavius, and Lepidus) and Sextus Pompeius belonged to 39 B.C., the defeat of the Parthians by Ventidius to 38 B.C., the deposition of Lepidus to 36 B.C., the Roman Senate's declaration of war on Cleopatra to 32 B.C., and the Battle of Actium to 31 B.C. A few other events which took place before the play opens are occasionally alluded to; these include the Battle of Pharsalus between Julius Caesar and Pompey the Great (48 B.C.), the assassination of Julius Caesar (44 B.C.), and the Battle of Philippi in which Brutus and Cassius were defeated by Antony and Octavius (42 B.C.). (The last two were dramatized by Shakespeare in *Julius Caesar*, to which *Antony and Cleopatra* is something of a sequel.)

I.1   The first appearance of Antony and Cleopatra forms a tableau: Antony rejects Empire for Love. The 'presenters' of the tableau are the disapproving pair

Demetrius and Philo, through whose eyes we are invited to view Antony's degeneration. The mutual antipathy of Roman and Egyptian values is at once established.

1   *our general* (Antony)

2   *O'erflows the measure* exceeds the limit. But the expression suggests abundance as well as a culpable prodigality.

3   *files and musters* ordered formations

4   *plated* armoured

5   *office* service

6   *tawny front* dark face

     captain's captain-like (*captain* meaning 'military commander')

8   *reneges all temper* renounces all self-control. *Reneges* is pronounced as two syllables, with a hard 'g'.

10   *gypsy's.* Since gypsies were thought to be Egyptian in origin, qualities popularly associated with them such as lasciviousness and duplicity could be given to Cleopatra. In the next scene her maids are given another gypsy-like trait – an interest in fortune-telling.

     (stage direction) *Flourish* fanfare of trumpets

     train body of attendants, retinue

12   *The triple pillar of the world* (one of the triumvirs, who between them ruled the Roman Empire)

13   *fool* dupe

15   *There's beggary in the love that can be reckoned* the love that can be computed or assessed is less than infinite, and therefore contemptible (beggarly)

16   *bourn* limit

18   *Grates me! The sum* it irks me (but) tell it in brief

20   *Fulvia* (Antony's wife)

21   *the scarce-bearded Caesar* (that is, Octavius). Octavius was Julius Caesar's great-nephew; Caesar made him his adopted son and his heir. At the time of the opening of the play Octavius was aged twenty-three; Antony was nearly twenty years older.

23   *Take in* conquer
      enfranchise liberate
24   *How* what?
25   *Perchance?* She refers back to her earlier words,
      Fulvia perchance is angry.
      like likely
26   *dismission* discharge from service
28   *Where's Fulvia's process? ... Both!* Cleopatra makes,
      or pretends to make, a slip of the tongue – she meant
      Caesar, but says *Fulvia* by mistake, and then adds that
      Both might have their reasons for wanting Antony in
      Rome.
      process legal summons (to appear in court)
31   *homager* vassal
      else so or else
33   *arch.* A triumphal arch is probably imagined. In
      pageants and civic festivities a triumphal arch was con-
      ventionally used to represent a city or realm. (See
      G. R. Kernodle, *From Art to Theatre* (Chicago, 1944),
      page 90.) Shakespeare extends it to signify an empire.
34   *ranged* (1) ordered; (2) spacious
      Here is my space my wide-stretching empire is here (in
      Cleopatra)
36–40 *The nobleness ... peerless.* These lines dramatize
      Plutarch's account of the way of life adopted by An-
      tony and Cleopatra after their first meeting: 'For they
      made an order between them which they called
      Amimetobion (as much to say, "no life comparable
      and matchable with it"), one feasting each other by
      turns, and in cost exceeding all measure and reason'
      (*Shakespeare's Plutarch*, page 204). After the words
      to do thus the lovers may embrace; or perhaps these
      words refer more generally to their present style of
      life.
37   *such a mutual pair* a pair so perfectly matched
38–9 *in which I bind ... weet.* Antony uses the style of a
      public proclamation.

39   *weet* know

42–3   *Antony | Will be himself.* Antony will be the fool he is (while Cleopatra will *seem the fool I am not*).

43   *stirred* roused, excited

45   *confound* waste

         conference conversation

46–7   *There's not a minute . . . pleasure now.* The suggestion is that every moment is capable of containing a wealth of present pleasure. The word *now* is stressed. Some editors unnecessarily emend to 'new'.

49–51   *Whom everything . . . admired.* Compare Cleopatra's tribute to Antony at I.5.59–61 and Enobarbus's tribute to Cleopatra at II.2.240–45.

52–4   *and all alone . . . qualities of people.* Plutarch writes: 'And sometime also when he would go up and down the city disguised like a slave in the night, and would peer into poor men's windows and their shops, and scold and brawl with them within the house, Cleopatra would be also in a chambermaid's array, and amble up and down the streets with him, so that oftentimes Antonius bare away both mocks and blows' (pages 205–6).

56   *with* by

58   *that great property* that peculiar greatness

59   *still* always

60   *approves the common liar* proves that what the malicious gossips say is true. The suggestion of paradox (what the *liar* says is true) is one of many such in the play.

62   *Of* for

I.2   This and the next scene establish the atmosphere of Cleopatra's Egypt, one of sex-talk, idleness, and languor out of which Antony has to extricate himself. His reception of the news from Rome and his decision to leave Egypt mark the first move in the action of the

play. Plutarch writes: 'Now Antonius delighting in
these fond and childish pastimes, very ill news were
brought him from two places. The first from Rome:
that his brother Lucius and Fulvia his wife fell out
first between themselves, and afterwards fell to open
war with Caesar, and had brought all to nought, that
they were both driven to fly out of Italy. The second
news, as bad as the first: that Labienus conquered all
Asia with the army of the Parthians, from the river
of Euphrates and from Syria unto the countries of
Lydia and Ionia. Then began Antonius with much ado
a little to rouse himself, as if he had been wakened out
of a deep sleep and, as a man may say, coming out of a
great drunkenness' (pages 207–8).

4–5   *charge his horns with garlands* be a contented cuckold.
He will load (*charge*) his (emblematic) cuckold's horns
with the bridegroom's floral chaplet. Alexas has
apparently been referring to the man (*this husband*)
whom Charmian is destined to marry.

10–11   The Soothsayer speaks in dignified blank verse.

12   *banquet* (a light refreshment of fruit and wine)

16   *make* cause (to happen)

18   *fairer* more fortunate. In the following lines Charmian
takes it to mean 'more plump', 'in better condition',
while Iras takes it as 'more beautiful'. The solemn
utterances of the Soothsayer serve momentarily to
throw our minds forward to the end of the play,
since everything he so ambiguously prophesies seems
to come true. By saying that Charmian will be *far
fairer* than she is, he may mean simply that she is
going to die (the dead being, according to this point of
view, more fortunate than the living.) Similarly
Charmian's reference to *figs* (line 33) will remind
anyone who knows Cleopatra's story of the way she
met her death.

25   *liver* (when someone was in love, his liver was thought
to be inflamed)

27   *Good now* come on!

29–30   *Herod of Jewry* (who martyred the Holy Innocents in his attempt to kill the infant Christ; Charmian is being extravagantly ambitious in hoping for his homage)

30   *Find me* discover (in my palm)

33   *figs* (a phallic allusion; figs were thought to look like the male sexual organs, and were also used as an aphrodisiac)

34   *proved* experienced

36   *belike* probably

36–7   *shall have no names* will be bastards

41   *I forgive thee for a witch* you are no prophet (and so can be acquitted of the charge of being a *witch*)

42   *privy to* cognizant of

47   *be drunk* be to go drunk

49–50   *E'en ... famine.* The overflowing of the Nile was of course the cause of Egypt's fertility, not of famine.

51   *wild* wanton

53   *oily palm.* A moist or oily palm was thought a sign of a sensual nature.

53–4   *fruitful prognostication* sign that she will have children

55   *workyday* commonplace, everyday

56   *Your fortunes are alike.* There is one difference in their fortunes: Iras dies before Cleopatra, Charmian after her. The Soothsayer may have forgotten that he has just told Charmian *You shall outlive the lady whom you serve.*

58   *I have said* I have no more to say

62   *husband's nose* (a phallic allusion)

63   *Our worser thoughts heavens mend!* Charmian pretends to be piously shocked.

65   *go.* This seems to mean 'enjoy sexual intercourse'.
        Isis (Egyptian goddess of the moon and of fertility)

71   *hear that prayer of the people!* Another mock-pietism. Charmian and Iras offer up prayers like priestesses. Iras now goes on to intone gravely, like a preacher.

the people (the Egyptians, the worshippers of Isis). Some editors emend to 'thy people'.

73   *loose-wived* with an unfaithful wife
     foul ugly

74   *keep decorum* do the appropriate thing

78–9   *they would make themselves whores but they'd do't* even if they had to make themselves whores they would do it

80   *Not he; the Queen.* The mistake suggests Antony's loss of his former public identity.

84   *A Roman thought* a thought of Rome (and so a sober reflection). Plutarch writes (immediately after the sentence quoted above in the note to I.1.52–4): 'Now, though most men misliked this manner, yet the Alexandrians were commonly glad of this jollity and liked it well, saying very gallantly and wisely that Antonius showed them a comical face, to wit, a merry countenance; and the Romans a tragical face, to say, a grim look' (page 206).

89   *field* battlefield

92   *the time's state* the needs of the moment

94   *better issue* greater success

96   *The nature of bad news infects the teller* bad news makes the teller seem vicious or even criminal, and so liable to harsh treatment

97–100   Compare II.5, where Cleopatra receives bad news in a way very different from Antony here.

100   *as* as if

100–   *Labienus . . . Parthian force.* Parthia occupied much the
101   same territory as modern Iraq and Iran. During the years of the triumvirate the Parthians were exceptionally troublesome to the Romans; Antony himself was to fail in his campaign against them. Labienus was a Roman general who had defected to the Parthians after the defeat of Brutus and Cassius at Philippi.

102   *Extended* (a legal metaphor) seized upon
     Euphrates (accented on the first syllable)

106   *home* plainly

106   *mince not the general tongue* don't soften what everyone is saying

108   *Rail thou in Fulvia's phrase* scold me in Fulvia's manner

110-12   *then we bring forth ... earing* when enlivening winds fail to aerate our soil, we produce nothing fruitful; a dose of home-truths is as good for us as ploughing (*earing*) is to the earth. Many editors unnecessarily emend F's 'windes' to 'minds'.

112   *Is.* In Elizabethan English it was not considered grammatically incorrect for a plural subject to govern a singular verb.

116   *stays upon your will* is waiting for your orders

122   *Forbear me* leave me

126   *By revolution lowering* moving around and down, as if on a wheel

128   *could* would like to

129   *enchanting* holding in her power as if under a spell

131   *idleness.* As well as its obvious sense, the word probably has the further connotation of 'lasciviousness'. Compare I.3.92.

138   *die.* Here, as often in amatory contexts, *die* refers to the sexual act, as well as having its obvious sense. Enobarbus mockingly insists on the idea five times in this single speech.

142-3   *upon far poorer moment* for a much slighter cause

143   *mettle* vigour, ardour. Enobarbus's phrase makes a satirical paradox: 'she finds something life-giving in "dying".'

145   *celerity* rapidity

152   *Jove* (Jupiter; one of his duties was arranging the weather)

154   *you had* you would have

155   *piece of work* masterpiece

156   *discredited your travel* lost you your reputation as a traveller (since a traveller was expected to see everything worthy of note on his route)

164–6   *it shows ... new* it shows man that the gods are the world's tailors (that is, makers of people, since 'the tailor makes the man'); and there is this comfort to be had – that when old clothes (or old wives) are worn out, there are always means (or men) to replace them. Enobarbus's notion of the tailor-shop is of course bawdy: *members* alludes to the male sexual role, *cut* and *case* to the female. The primary sense of *cut* is 'blow', 'misfortune'. For another bawdy use of 'tailor', with an implied reference to his needle, compare *The Tempest*, II.2.52: 'Yet a tailor might scratch her where'er she did itch.'

169   *smock* (a woman's undergarment; often used, as here, to mean 'woman')

170–71   *the tears ... sorrow* an onion would bring to your eyes the only tears this sorrow deserves

176   *abode* staying

177   *light* indecent

    our. This is the first of several uses in this speech of the royal plural – a means of quickly establishing an unanswerably authoritative tone.

178   *break* impart

179   *expedience* hasty departure

180   *part* depart

181   *touches* reasons, motives

183   *many our contriving friends* the many friends who work for my interests

184   *Sextus Pompeius* (the younger son of Pompey the Great; see the note to I.3.49)

186   *Our slippery people. Our* may be a royal plural, or it may have a larger, quasi-proverbial reference: 'We all know that the people always behave like this ...'.

188–9   *throw | Pompey the Great* bestow the title of 'Pompey the Great'

191   *blood and life* spirit and energy

191–2   *stands up | For the main soldier* presents himself as the world's leading soldier. But *main* may also mean 'sea';

he has just been said to command *The empire of the sea* (line 186).

192–3 *whose quality ... danger* who, if he continues as he has begun, may endanger the stability of the Roman world

192 *quality* capacity for effective action

193 *sides* frame

194 *the courser's hair*. A horse's hair was popularly supposed to turn into a snake when placed in water.

195–7 *Say ... hence*. This slightly indirect way of saying 'give the army orders to move' expresses Antony's position of absolute command (not he but his *pleasure* requires the move).

I.3.1 *I did not see him since* I have not seen him recently

3 *I did not send you* don't tell him I sent you
sad in a serious mood

10 *Thou teachest like a fool: the way to lose him*. This ten-line dialogue between mistress and maid is matched by that in IV.13, where, as a result of Charmian's advice, Cleopatra does in fact lose Antony.

11 *Tempt* try, test
I wish. Some editors plausibly emend to 'iwis', meaning 'certainly', 'trust me'.

14 *breathing* utterance, words. Antony begins in a tactfully courteous style.

16–17 *the sides of nature | Will not sustain it* the human frame cannot endure it

20–21 *What says ... come!* The two lines are probably based on a line in the verse epistle sent by Dido to Aeneas in Ovid's *Heroides* (vii.139), which Shakespeare is likely to have read at school: '*Sed iubet ire deus*'. *vellem, vetuisset adire* ... (' "But your god orders you to go." I wish he had forbidden you to come'). The entire situation, as developed by Shakespeare, recalls that of Dido and Aeneas, though of course with differences (see also the note to IV.14.53).

26   *planted* prepared, placed ready to grow

28   *Though you ... gods.* Cleopatra alludes hyperbolically
      to the notion that when Jupiter, king of the gods,
      swore an oath, the whole of Olympus shuddered to its
      foundations.

30   *mouth-made* formed on the tongue, not in the heart

31   *break themselves in swearing* are broken the moment
      they are spoken

32   *colour* pretext

33   *sued staying* begged to stay

35-7 *Eternity ... heaven.* These words are in indirect speech:
      they are what Antony in the past assured Cleopatra.
      He is now tartly reminded of his own lyric phrases.
      'According to you,' she tells him, 'eternity was in my
      lips and eyes ...'.

36   *our brows' bent* the curve of my eyebrows
      none our parts so poor none of my qualities, however
      poor

37   *a race of heaven* of heavenly origin or stock

41   *Egypt.* Here, as elsewhere in the play, this means Cleo-
      patra herself, as well as her country.

44   *in use with you* in your possession

45   *Shines o'er* is everywhere bright (with the flashing of
      the *swords*)
      civil swords swords of civil war

47-8 *Equality ... faction* when the management of a house
      is shared between two, squabbles will arise over in-
      significant points

48-9 *the hated ... to love* those who have been hated attract
      love when they acquire power

49   *The condemned Pompey.* Sextus Pompeius (see also
      I.2.184-93) was a serious threat to peace and had ac-
      cordingly been *condemned* (proscribed, declared an
      outlaw) by the Senate. His fleet commanded the western
      Mediterranean; he himself was in possession of Sicily.

53-4 *quietness ... change.* A long peace has produced dis-
      contents within the state; civic health must be restored

through purging – getting rid of impurities through the bloodletting of violence.

54   *My more particular* my own more personal reason

55   *should safe my going* should remove any trace of danger from my going

57–8 *Though age … childishness* I may be fool enough to love you, but at least I'm not such a child as to do so on the grounds that you may one day be free of your wife. (For the moment Cleopatra does not believe him.)

60   *at thy sovereign leisure* in your own royal good time (an instance of Antony's polite formality)

61   *garboils* trouble, disturbance
      best best item of news

63   *sacred vials*. The Romans were thought to place bottles of tears in the tombs of their loved ones.

64–5 The neat rhyme suggests something of the artificiality of Cleopatra's behaviour here.

68–9 *the fire | That quickens Nilus' slime* the sun that fertilizes the rich earth of the Nile valley

71   *affects* are inclined, are prompted to choose by your feelings
      Cut my lace. Cleopatra, tightly laced in a bodice, gasps for breath.

73   *So Antony loves* if Antony loves. Cleopatra may also mean that her health is as precarious as he is changeable.

74   *give true evidence* bear true witness
      stands will endure

81   *this is meetly* you are doing quite well

82   *target* (a small shield). 'Sword and target' was presumably a common collocation which Cleopatra ironically recalls.
      mends improves

84–5 *How this … chafe* how admirably this heroic descendant of Hercules assumes the part of an angry man.
      Carriage has the sense of 'demeanour', even 'bodily deportment'.

84   *Herculean.* Plutarch writes of Antony: 'He had a goodly
        thick beard, a broad forehead, crook-nosed; and there
        appeared such a manly look in his countenance as is
        commonly seen in Hercules' pictures, stamped or
        graven in metal. Now it had been a speech of old time
        that the family of the Antonii were descended from one
        Anton, the son of Hercules, whereof the family took
        name. This opinion did Antonius seek to confirm in all
        his doings, not only resembling him in the likeness of
        his body, as we have said before, but also in the wearing
        of his garments' (page 177).

90–91   *my oblivion . . . forgotten* (1) my memory, like Antony,
        has deserted me, so that I have forgotten what I
        wanted to say; (2) my mind – being entirely absorbed
        in the idea of Antony – is left a blank

91–2   *But that your royalty | Holds idleness your subject* if it
        were not clear that you are in perfect control of these
        follies, as a queen is of her subjects. For *idleness*,
        compare the note to I.2.131.

94   *bear* (as in childbirth, so linking with *labour* in line
        93)

96   *becomings* (1) graces; (2) changes, transformations

97   *Eye* look

100   *laurel.* A laurel wreath was an emblem of victory.

I.4   Caesar's first appearance establishes him as a man of
        cool temperance and efficiency. Yet if Antony is an
        instance of excess (one who *O'erflows the measure*),
        Caesar seems conversely to suffer from deficiency,
        something less than the true golden mean.

3   *competitor* partner, colleague. But inescapably the word
        also suggests rivalry and a potential hostility.

6   *the queen of Ptolemy.* Cleopatra had married her brother
        Ptolemy at the command of Julius Caesar; she was
        reported to have poisoned him.

8   *there* (in the letter)

9   *abstract* epitome, compendium

11 *enow* enough

12-13 *His faults ... blackness.* It is in keeping with the
       play's tendency to paradox that Lepidus should speak
       of Antony's faults as stars.

14 *purchased* acquired

18 *mirth* joke

19 *keep the turn of tippling* take turns in drinking toasts

20 *stand the buffet* endure the blows. See the note to
    I.1.52-4.

22 *As* although
    composure character

24 *foils* blemishes

24-5 *do bear | So great weight in his lightness* carry so heavy
      a burden as a result of his irresponsibility

26 *vacancy* free time (with a pejorative implication)

27-8 *Full surfeits ... for't* let stomach disorders and syphilis
      call him to an account

28 *confound* waste

29-30 *speaks as loud | As his own state and ours* counts as
       much as his and our public position (that is, as trium-
       virs)

30-33 *'tis to be chid ... judgement* should be reprimanded as
       we would rebuke boys who, old enough to know better,
       surrender what they have learned of life to secure
       immediate pleasure

39 *discontents* discontented people

40 *Give him* say he is

41 *from the primal state* since the first commonwealth
    that ever was

42 *he which is was wished until he were* the man who is now
    in power was supported only until he secured power

43-4 *the ebbed man ... lacked* the man whose tide is low
      (who has lost power), unappreciated till he has ceased
      to deserve it, wins favour by being absent

44 *Comes* becomes
    deared loved

common body common people

45   *vagabond flag* drifting reed

46   *lackeying*. F reads 'lacking'. Most editors accept the emendation *lackeying*, meaning 'following every aimless movement as a lackey does his master'. This emendation can be supported by line 967 of *The Rape of Lucrece*, where Time is addressed as 'Thou ceaseless lackey to Eternity'. On the other hand, 'lacking' is not impossible; the phrase would then mean 'without the firmly directed movements of the tide'.

48–54   *Menecrates . . . seen.* Plutarch writes: 'Sextus Pompeius at that time kept in Sicilia, and so made many an inroad into Italy with a great number of pinnaces and other pirates' ships, of the which were captains two notable pirates, Menas and Menecrates, who so scoured all the sea thereabouts that none durst peep out with a sail' (page 212).

48   *famous* notorious

49   *ear* plough

52   *Lack blood* turn pale (with fear)

       flush lusty

54–5   *Pompey's name . . . resisted* Pompey's mere name causes more trouble than would be caused if he actually made war on you

56   *wassails* carousals, drunken revelling. F's reading is 'Vassailes', that is, 'vassals', meaning 'low-born servants or followers'. This is possible, but the emendation *wassails* seems preferable.

56–71   The war referred to in these lines is the war of Mutina (Modena), 43 B.C., in which Antony was defeated by the army of the Roman Senate. Plutarch writes:

'Cicero . . . being at that time the chiefest man of authority and estimation in the city, he stirred up all men against Antonius; so that in the end he made the Senate pronounce him an enemy to his country . . .; and moreover sent Hircius and Pansa, then Consuls, to drive Antonius out of Italy. These two Consuls together with Caesar, who also had an army, went against Antonius that besieged the city of Modena, and there overthrew him in battle. But both the Consuls were slain there.

'Antonius, flying upon this overthrow, fell into great misery all at once; but the chiefest want of all other, and that pinched him most, was famine ... it was a wonderful example to the soldiers to see Antonius, that was brought up in all fineness and superfluity, so easily to drink puddle water and to eat wild fruits and roots. And moreover it is reported that, even as they passed the Alps, they did eat the barks of trees and such beasts as never man tasted of their flesh before' (pages 191–2).

57	*Modena* (accented on the second syllable)
59	*whom* (that is, famine)
60–61	*with patience ... suffer* with more fortitude than savages could show in suffering
62	*stale* urine
	gilded with glittering scum on the surface
63	*cough at* (and so refuse)
	deign not refuse
66	*browsèd'st* (used of animals) fed upon
71	*lanked* grew thinner
74	*i'th'field* in military array
78	*Both what by sea and land I can be able* what forces both by sea and by land I can muster
79	*front* confront
82	*stirs* events, happenings
84	*knew it for my bond* understood it to be my duty (or 'my commitment')

I.5   Antony's off-stage journey between Egypt and Rome continues, while Cleopatra, having nothing else to do in his absence, mentally accompanies him. As in the

previous and in the following scenes, the arrival of a
messenger with news provides a focusing point.

4   *mandragora* mandrake (a powerful narcotic)

11   *unseminared* emasculated

12   *affections* passions

16   *honest* chaste

18   *What Venus did with Mars.* The goddess of love and the
god of war once had an adulterous love-affair. In the
present play Venus is of course associated with Cleopatra and Mars with Antony.

22   *wot'st* knowest

23   *demi-Atlas.* In classical mythology the Titan Atlas
supported the heavens. Cleopatra seems to be speaking
without reference to the triumvirate, although at
I.1.12 Antony is said to be *The triple pillar of the world*
in virtue of being a triumvir.

23-4   *the arm | And burgonet of men* (he is pre-eminent both in
attack – *arm* – and in defence – *burgonet*). The *burgonet* was an exceptionally efficient helmet of Bur-
gundian origin; it was so fitted to the gorget or neck-
piece that the head could be turned without exposing
the neck.

27-9   *Think on me ... time.* Cleopatra sees herself as dark-
skinned (that is, sunburnt) from the pinches of her
lover *Phoebus* (the sun). The intonation of the sentence
is elusive: *wrinkled deep in time* may be humorously
meant.

29-34   Plutarch writes of Cleopatra, just before her first meeting with Antony, that, 'guessing by the former access
and credit she had with Julius Caesar and Cneius
[Gnaeus] Pompey, the son of Pompey the Great, only
for her beauty, she began to have good hope that she
might more easily win Antonius. For Caesar and
Pompey knew her when she was but a young thing,
and knew not then what the world meant. But now she
went to Antonius at the age when a woman's beauty is
at the prime, and she also of best judgement' (page 200).

29   *Broad-fronted Caesar. Front* can mean 'forehead' or
'face'. Julius Caesar had 'a rather broad face', according to Suetonius (in *The Lives of the Twelve Caesars*);
or the phrase may refer to his receding hair, also mentioned by Suetonius.

31   *morsel* tasty mouthful. Sexual experience is several
times in the play described in terms of eating; compare
II.1.12, 23–7, and 33; II.2.229–31 and 241–3; II.6.63–
5 and 124; III.13.116–20.

       great Pompey Gnaeus Pompey (elder son of Pompey
the Great). Shakespeare may be deliberately confusing
the two Pompeys so as to enhance the status of Cleopatra's former lovers. Plutarch clearly distinguishes
them (see the passage quoted in the note to lines
29–34).

33   *aspect* (accented on the second syllable) gaze

36–7   *that great medicine ... thee.* An alchemical metaphor:
in their experiments the alchemists sought the elixir
of life – the *great medicine* – by means of which they
hoped to transform base metals to gold and to prolong
life indefinitely. The metaphor is important and revealing, since the play is as a whole much concerned
with the transformation of 'base' human materials
into exalted ones; Cleopatra herself is the clearest
example of this.

37   *tinct.* 'Tincture' was another term for the elixir of life.

41   *orient* lustrous (originally applied to pearls from the
East, which were more brilliant than those found
nearer home)

42–50   *'Good friend' ... by him.* Alexas's report forms a
vignette of Antony in heroic posture. Though still a
lover, he has recovered his warrior's toughness. The
action of mounting his horse is perhaps emblematic:
the image of a rider in control of his horse is not un-
common in classical antiquity as well as in Shakespeare's period, and could signify a rational man in
control of his passions. See the Introduction, page 32,

for Plato's phrase 'the horse of the mind', as quoted by Plutarch.

43   *firm* resolute

45   *piece* augment

48   *arrogant.* F reads 'Arme-gaunt', and many attempts have been made to gloss this, such as 'battle-worn', 'lean from much warlike service'. The word occurs nowhere else and, if genuine, is probably a Shakespearian coinage. The emendation adopted here makes good sense and can be plausibly explained as being what the printer mistakenly read as 'Arme-gaunt' (for 'Arrogaunt', a common spelling of the word).

50   *beastly dumbed* (1) obliterated or negated in an animal-like way; (2) reduced to an animal-like inarticulateness

52   *nor . . . nor* neither . . . nor

53   *well-divided disposition* well-balanced temperament

54   *'tis the man* that's just what he's like

        but just, only

59–61   *Be'st thou . . . else.* Compare with this tribute Antony's to Cleopatra at I.1.49–51 and Enobarbus's at II.2. 240–45.

60   *violence.* The word suggests an exuberant commitment to whatever mood he happens to be in.

61   *posts* messengers

62   *several* separate

63   *Who's* anyone who is

65   *Shall die a beggar* (since bad luck will dog him throughout his life for being born on such a day)

67   *brave* excellent, fine

68   *emphasis* emphatic expression

71   *paragon* compare, match (so as to imply equality)

73–5   Compare the passage from Plutarch quoted in the note to lines 29–34.

74   *green* immature

77   *several* separate, different

78   *Or I'll unpeople Egypt* even if I have to send every one of my subjects out of Egypt as messengers to Antony

II.1   Sextus Pompeius, one of the seekers after power in the unstable world of Rome, affords a new viewpoint on Antony. Off stage, Antony concludes his journey to Rome (see the Introduction, page 13).

1   *shall* surely will

3   *what they do delay they not deny* a delay in answering prayers is not a refusal

4–5   *Whiles . . . sue for* even while we are begging something from the gods, it is ceasing to exist

10   *crescent* waxing like the moon
      auguring prophesying

12   *sits at dinner* (possibly a sexual allusion; see the note to I.5.31)

13   *without doors* out of doors (the only wars Antony will make are the wars of love)

17   *in the field* in military array

20   *Looking for* waiting for
      charms spells, enchantments

21   *Salt* lascivious
      waned faded (like the waning moon)

23   *Tie up . . . in a field of feasts.* This seems to mean 'tie (him) up like an animal in a rich pasture'.

25   *Sharpen* (subjunctive: 'May Epicurean cooks sharpen . . .')
      cloyless that will never satiate

26   *prorogue* suspend the operation of

27   *Lethe'd* oblivious, all-forgetting. Lethe was a river in the classical Hades; those who drank from it forgot their past. Pompey's words are interrupted by the arrival of the messenger – a way of bringing out the fact that he is out-of-date in his appraisal of Antony's situation.

30–31   *'tis | A space for farther travel* there has been time to travel even further than he has

35   *rear* raise

36   *our opinion* our opinion of ourselves

38   *hope* expect

39   *well greet together* meet each other like friends

40   *did trespasses to* committed offences against

42   *moved* prompted, encouraged

45   *'Twere pregnant they should square between themselves* they would probably quarrel among themselves

46   *entertainèd* received

48   *cement their divisions* firmly bring them together *cement* (accented on the first syllable)

50–51   *It only stands | Our lives upon* but it is a matter of life and death for us

II.2   This, the longest and weightiest scene so far, shows Antony back in Rome and the triumvirate in action. But the understanding reached by Antony and Caesar is precarious. As soon as the subordinates are left alone together, Enobarbus powerfully evokes Cleopatra's personal magnetism.

4   *like himself* in a way suitable to one so great *move* angers

5   *look over Caesar's head* treat Caesar as a man of small stature

8   *I would not shave't today* (that is, I would dare him to pluck it. To pluck another man's beard was to give him a grave insult.)

9   *stomaching* resentments, squabbles

15   *compose* reach agreement

19   *leaner* slighter

20–21   *debate . . . loud* violently argue over

23   *The rather for I earnestly beseech* the more readily for the fact that I am making a special request

25   *Nor curstness grow to th'matter* and keep ill-humour out of it

27   *thus.* Antony either refers to the moderation of Lepidus's speech or possibly embraces Caesar. The former seems more likely.

34   *being* being so

35   *or ... or* either ... or
36   *say myself* call myself
38   *derogately* disparagingly
43   *practise on my state* plot against my well-being
44   *question* business
45   *catch at* gather, infer
48   *Was theme for you* was a debate on your behalf
        You were the word of war you prompted the declara-
        tion of war
50   *Did urge me* used my name as a pretext
51   *true reports* reliable sources
54   *stomach* wish
55   *Having alike your cause* since I was involved for the
        same reason as yourself
56–7   *If you'll patch ... with* if you insist on making a quarrel
        for inadequate reasons, though in fact you have much
        better reasons
56   *patch* make up out of odd remnants
59   *patched up.* Caesar picks up Antony's word *patch*
        and throws it back.
60–68   The style of this and Antony's next speech seems
        deliberately tortuous, evasive, and graceless. Shake-
        speare no doubt meant it to express the double-
        talk of politicians.
61–2   *I know ... thought* I am sure you must have known
64   *graceful* favourable
        attend regard
65   *fronted* opposed
66   *I would you had her spirit in such another* I wish you had
        a wife like her
67   *snaffle* bridle-bit
68   *pace* (used of horses) train
71   *garboils* tumults
72   *not wanted* did not lack
75   *But* only
78   *missive out of audience* messenger out of your presence
79   *fell upon me, ere admitted, then* burst in on me there

and then, before he had been given permission to enter

80–81	*did want	Of* was not up to
82	*told him of myself* explained why I was not quite myself
84	*Be nothing of* have nothing to do with
86	*article* terms
87	*Soft* go gently (since the matter is so delicate)
94–5	*bound ... knowledge* kept me from all knowledge of myself
98	*Work without it.* This may mean 'operate without a due sense of my dignity (*greatness*)', or possibly *it* refers to *honesty*.
102	*noble* nobly
104	*griefs* grievances
104–6	*to forget ... atone you* to forget them completely would be a (wise) acknowledgement of the fact that the present emergency requires you to stand together
106	*atone* reconcile
114	*this presence* the present dignified company
115	*your considerate stone.* Enobarbus will be as mute as a stone, but nevertheless will have his thoughts (be *considerate*).
118	*conditions* dispositions
120	*staunch* firm
123	*by the mother's side.* Plutarch calls Octavia 'the eldest sister of Caesar – not by one mother' (page 210); in fact she was a full younger sister of Caesar.
126–7	*your reproof ... rashness* your reproof for rashness would be well deserved
132	*take Antony* let Antony take
133	*to* as
137	*jealousies* suspicions
138	*import* carry with them (with a further suggestion that the *dangers* are of importance)
139–40	*Truths would ... truths* inconvenient (or unwelcome) true things would be dismissed as fables, whereas now malicious half-truths are readily believed

143	*present* sudden
145–6	*touched	With* affected by
150	*so fairly shows* looks so promisingly
152	*of grace* gracious
157–8	*never ... again* may our love for each other never again desert us
160	*strange* exceptional
161	*thank him only* just thank him
162	*my remembrance suffer ill report* I am said to be ungrateful
	remembrance memory
163	*At heel of that* as soon as that is done
164	*presently* at once
166	*Mount Misena* (Mount Misenum, a port in southern Italy)
168	*fame* report
172	*do* I do
	view presence (where Antony can see her, and she him)
177	*Half the heart* the beloved friend
181	*digested* digested (that is, arranged)
	stayed well by't stood up to it well (a military expression, meaning 'stand firm', here used ironically of the soft living in Egypt)
182	*we did sleep day out of countenance* we put the day out of countenance by sleeping through it (so turning it into night)
184–5	*Eight wild boars ... there* (attested by Plutarch (page 204), though it was for supper, not breakfast)
186	*by* compared with
190	*square* true, fair
192	*pursed up* took possession of
194	*devised* invented
196– 231	The whole description follows Plutarch closely: 'Therefore when she was sent unto by divers letters, both from Antonius himself and also from his friends, she made so light of it and mocked Antonius so much that she disdained to set forward otherwise but to take

her barge in the river of Cydnus, the poop whereof
was of gold, the sails of purple, and the oars of silver,
which kept stroke in rowing after the sound of the
music of flutes, howboys, citherns, viols, and such
other instruments as they played upon in the barge.
And now for the person of herself: she was laid under
a pavilion of cloth-of-gold of tissue, apparelled and
attired like the goddess Venus commonly drawn in
picture; and hard by her, on either hand of her, pretty
fair boys apparelled as painters do set forth god Cupid,
with little fans in their hands, with the which they
fanned wind upon her. Her ladies and gentlewomen
also, the fairest of them were apparelled like the
nymphs Nereides (which are the mermaids of the
waters) and like the Graces, some steering the helm,
others tending the tackle and ropes of the barge, out
of the which there came a wonderful passing sweet
savour of perfumes, that perfumed the wharf's side,
pestered with innumerable multitudes of people.
Some of them followed the barge all alongst the river's
side; others also ran out of the city to see her coming
in; so that in the end there ran such multitudes of
people one after another to see her that Antonius
was left post-alone in the market-place in his imperial
seat to give audience. And there went a rumour in the
people's mouths that the goddess Venus was come to
play with the god Bacchus, for the general good of all
Asia.

'When Cleopatra landed, Antonius sent to invite
her to supper to him. But she sent him word again, he
should do better rather to come and sup with her.
Antonius therefore, to show himself courteous unto
her at her arrival, was contented to obey her, and went
to supper to her; where he found such passing sump-
tuous fare, that no tongue can express it' (pages
200–202).

202 *As* as if

204 *cloth-of-gold of tissue* (an especially rich fabric containing gold thread)

205–6 *O'erpicturing ... nature* surpassing those pictures of Venus in which we see the imagination transcending what is possible in nature

208 *divers-coloured* many-coloured (or perhaps iridescent)

209 *glow* make flush

210 *what they undid did* (although meant to cool, they seemed to warm)

211 *Nereides* (pronounced with four syllables) sea-nymphs

212 *So many mermaids* like so many mermaids

212–13 *tended her ... adornings* stood and moved about in front of her, seeing to it that their postures and movements were pleasing to look at

214 *tackle* rigging, cordage. But in view of the next line (*Swell*), presumably sails are also included.

216 *yarely frame the office* nimbly perform their tasks

218 *wharfs* banks

218–19 *cast ... out* expelled

219 *upon her* on her account, because of her

221 *but for vacancy* but for the fact that nature abhors a vacuum

230 *ordinary* (meal in a public eating-house or inn). The commonplace word is humorously chosen.

231 *Royal wench!* The phrase has the effect of an oxymoron: 'wench' would normally be applied only to a woman or girl of low birth.

233 *cropped* bore a child. Cleopatra's son by Julius Caesar was called Caesarion.

236 *That* so that

237 *breathless, power breathe forth.* F has 'breathlesse powre breath forth'. This might be read as 'breathless, pour breath forth', since F's spelling 'power' is normal for 'pour' in Shakespeare's period. The point would then simply turn on the contrast between having no breath and pouring it forth. But the more usual reading, adopted here, is preferable. F's 'breath' is a

well-attested spelling for 'breathe'; Cleopatra not
only pants for breath – which anyone might do – but
emanates *power* as she does so. See the Introduction,
page 14; and compare III.2.20-21, where Octavia is described as a *body rather than a life,/A statue than a
breather*.

244 *Become themselves* are made becoming, justify themselves

245 *riggish* wanton

248 *lottery* prize

II.3.6 *kept my square* kept to the straight line. A golden set-
square was an emblem of temperance.
   that that which is

10-31 Plutarch writes:

  'With Antonius there was a soothsayer or astronomer
of Egypt, that could cast a figure and judge of men's
nativities, to tell them what should happen to them.
He, either to please Cleopatra or else for that he found
it so by his art, told Antonius plainly that his fortune,
which of itself was excellent good and very great,
was altogether blemished and obscured by Caesar's
fortune; and therefore he counselled him utterly to
leave his company and to get him as far from him as he
could.

  '"For thy Demon," said he, "(that is to say, the
good angel and spirit that keepeth thee) is afraid of
his, and, being courageous and high when he is alone,
becometh fearful and timorous when he cometh near
unto the other"' (pages 215-16).

14 *motion* inward prompting

20 *daemon* guardian angel
  that thy spirit that spirit of thine

22 *Where* whereas

25 *no more but when* only when

27 *of* by, through

28   *lustre* light, glory
       thickens dims

33   *art or hap* skill or mere luck

34-9   Based on Plutarch: 'For it is said that as often as they
       two drew cuts for pastime who should have anything,
       or whether they played at dice, Antonius alway lost.
       Oftentimes when they were disposed to see cock-fight,
       or quails that were taught to fight one with another,
       Caesar's cocks or quails did ever overcome' (page 216).

35   *cunning* skill

36   *chance* luck
       speeds wins

37   *still* always

38   *it is all to nought* the odds are all to nothing (in my
       favour)

39   *inhooped* confined within a hoop or a circle (in order to
       make them fight)

II.4   This short scene reminds us of the main direction of
       the action – the coming meeting at Mount Misenum –
       and once more evokes the distances involved in the
       movements of its personages.

2   *Your generals after* after your generals

3   *e'en but* just, only

6   *conceive* understand, see

8   *My purposes do draw me much about* I have to go a
       long way round

9   *good success* (we wish you) favourable outcome

II.5   During this part of the play Cleopatra has nothing to do
       but wait for Antony's return. In this scene and its
       sequel (III.3) Shakespeare invents an episode which
       relates her to the main action. He adapts to Cleo-
       patra's dealings with the Messenger Plutarch's
       account of her ill-treatment of her treasurer Seleucus,

which occurred shortly before her death (see V.2.141–75). Plutarch writes: 'Cleopatra was in such a rage with him that she flew upon him, and took him by the hair of the head, and boxed him well-favouredly' (page 287).

1   *moody* melancholy

3   *billiards.* In George Chapman's comedy *The Blind Beggar of Alexandria* (published in 1598), the ladies also play billiards.

8–9   *when good will . . . pardon* (spoken as a good-humoured parody of a sententious maxim, with an indecent quibble on the words *come too short*)

10   *angle* fishing-tackle

11   *betray* deceive (into being caught)

15–18   Based on Plutarch: 'On a time he went to angle for fish; and when he could take none he was as angry as could be, because Cleopatra stood by. Wherefore he secretly commanded the fishermen that when he cast in his line they should straight dive under the water and put a fish on his hook which they had taken before; and so snatched up his angling rod and brought up fish twice or thrice. Cleopatra found it straight; yet she seemed not to see it, but wondered at his excellent fishing. But when she was alone by herself among her own people, she told them how it was and bade them the next morning to be on the water to see the fishing. A number of people came to the haven and got into the fisher-boats to see this fishing. Antonius then threw in his line; and Cleopatra straight commanded one of her men to dive under water before Antonius' men and to put some old salt fish upon his bait, like unto those that are brought out of the country of Pont. When he had hung the fish on his hook, Antonius, thinking he had taken a fish indeed, snatched up his line presently. Then they all fell a-laughing' (pages 206–7).

17   *salt* dried

18	*With fervency* excitedly
21	*the ninth hour* (9 a.m.)
22	*tires* apparel (or possibly 'head-dresses')
23	*sword Philippan* (named after the Battle of Philippi, where Antony defeated Brutus and Cassius)
28	*yield* grant, allow. Cleopatra treats the Messenger as if he himself were responsible for Antony's present condition.
33	*the dead are well* (a common euphemism, meaning that the dead are incapable of suffering further harm) *Bring it to that* if you take it to mean that
34–5	*The gold ... throat.* This was actually done to the Roman millionaire Crassus (see the note to III.1.2).
38	*so tart a favour* so sour an expression
40	*Fury.* In classical mythology the Furies were avenging goddesses, with snakes twined in their hair; they were associated with madness or frenzy.
41	*formal* sane, normal
50–51	*allay	The good precedence* spoil what had begun so promisingly
54	*Pour out the pack* empty your load (like a pedlar's pack)
58	*For what good turn?* Cleopatra assumes that Antony must be indebted to Octavia, since the Messenger says he is *bound unto* her.
59	*the best turn i'th'bed* (in the sexual sense)
63	*spurn* kick
64	(stage direction) *hales* drags
71	*boot* compensate
72	*Thy modesty.* This seems to mean 'someone as humble and deferential as yourself'.
75	*keep yourself within yourself* control yourself
78	*kindly* friendly, well-disposed
82–4	*These hands ... cause* I act ignobly in striking a person lower in estate than myself, since the person who ought to be punished is myself, the true culprit
92	*confound* destroy

94   *So* even if

96   *Narcissus* (in Greek mythology, a beautiful youth who fell in love with his own reflection)

99   *Take no offence that I would not offend you* don't take offence that I am unwilling to offend you (by giving an answer that is unwelcome)

101   *unequal* unjust

103   *That art not what th' art sure of* who are not as bad as the message of whose truth you are so certain

105-6   *Lie they upon thy hand,* | *And be undone by 'em* may you be unable to sell them and may you be ruined by them

112   *feature* physical appearance

113   *inclination* character

115   *him* (Antony)

116-17   *Though he be ... Mars.* The implied comparison is with a 'perspective' picture, a form of trick painting fashionable in Shakespeare's time. It showed two quite different images according to the viewpoint of the spectator.

116   *Gorgon* (one of three mythical female personages, with snakes for hair, whose look had the power to turn others to stone; hence, a hideous monster)

II.6   This and the next scene bring the business concerning Pompey to a conclusion. The triumvirate is seen in action for the last time: when Pompey is disposed of, there is nothing to prevent it from breaking up. Even now, the temporary concord is uneasy and strained. (stage direction) *one door ... another* (the entry doors at each side of the Elizabethan playhouse stage)

2   *meet* fit

7   *tall* brave, gallant

10   *factors* agents

10-23   Sextus Pompeius appeals to the events of recent Roman history, some of which had formed the subject of Shakespeare's previous Roman tragedy, *Julius Caesar*. Julius Caesar had defeated Pompey the Great at Pharsalus (48 B.C.); Antony and Octavius, avenging Caesar's assassination, defeated Brutus and Cassius at Philippi (42 B.C.). Sextus Pompeius now argues that, since Julius Caesar found avengers in them, Pompey should also find an avenger in his son.

11   *want* lack

13   *ghosted* haunted

17   *courtiers* wooers, questers

18   *drench* (in blood)

19   *but a man* only a man (not a king)

20   *rig* equip

22   *despiteful* cruel, malicious

23   *Take your time* (that is, don't get carried away by your anger)

24   *fear* frighten

25   *speak with* encounter

26   *o'ercount* outnumber

27   *o'ercount me of my father's house.* Pompey bitterly puns on Antony's word. The allusion is explained by Plutarch: 'when Pompey's house was put to open sale, Antonius bought it. But when they asked him money for it, he made it very strange and was offended with them . . .' (page 184).

28–9   *since the cuckoo . . . mayst* since cuckoos always use the nests of other birds, keep it while you can

30   *from the present* beside the point

32–3   *weigh | What it is worth embraced* think carefully how much you will gain if you accept it

33–4   *what may . . . fortune* (that is, how disastrous it may be for you if you pursue your ambitions (into war against us))

38   *unhacked edges* unused swords

39   *targes* (pronounced with a hard 'g') shields

43   *praise of* credit for

47   *well studied* well prepared by having given thought

51   *timelier* earlier (but also perhaps 'more opportunely')

54   *What counts harsh Fortune casts upon my face.* Fortune
has used Pompey as a tavern-board, working out
exactly what everything has cost and what he must
pay.

          counts sums

          casts calculates

58   *composition* agreement

62   *take the lot* accept the result of the lottery

66   *I have ... to them.* Pompey's tactless remark has just
earned a warning reproof from Antony (*You have heard
much*) and he hastily tries to placate him: *I have fair
meanings* ('My intentions are above-board'). Antony
accepts the implied apology by making him a trivial
compliment, which turns on a different meaning of
'fair': *And fair words to them* ('Your words are as
finely chosen as your intentions are proper'). For
the rest of the dialogue (lines 68–79), Antony
apparently moves out of earshot, leaving Pompey free
to pursue his offensive topic.

70   *A certain queen ... mattress.* The incident (familiar to
modern audiences from Shaw's *Caesar and Cleopatra*)
is described in Plutarch's *Life of Julius Caesar*. When
Caesar was in Alexandria, he 'secretly sent for Cleopatra, which was in the country, to come unto him.'
Plutarch goes on: 'She, only taking Apollodorus
Sicilian of all her friends, took a little boat, and went
away with him in it in the night, and came and landed
hard by the foot of the castle. Then, having no other
mean to come into the court without being known, she
laid herself down upon a mattress or flock-bed which
Apollodorus her friend tied and bound up together
like a bundle with a great leather thong, and so took
her up on his back, and brought her thus hampered in
this fardel unto Caesar, in at the castle gate' (page 69).

73   *toward* (accented on the first syllable) in the immediate
future

78   *Enjoy* continue to practise
      plainness blunt frankness

79   *It nothing ill becomes thee* it is in no way unbecoming to
      you

83   *known* met

94   *land service* military (as opposed to naval) service.
      There may have been an association between 'land
      service' and the idea of thieving: see *2 Henry IV*,
      I.2.127.

95   *authority* legal powers (to arrest)

96   *take* (into custody)
      two thieves kissing (their hands clasping)

97   *true* (1) honest; (2) without cosmetics

111   *Pray ye* I beg your pardon?

114   *bound to divine of* required to predict the outcome of

116   *policy* politics, statecraft
      made mattered

121   *still* quiet, silent
      conversation way of life

128   *use his affection* satisfy his appetite

129   *occasion* political opportunity, convenience

132   *used* exercised, made good use of (for drinking)

II.7   (stage direction) *banquet*. See the note to I.2.12.

2   *plants* (wordplay: the second meaning is 'feet' or
       'soles of the feet')

5   *alms drink*. This may mean 'drink taken as a work of
       charity', that is, to increase conviviality and to heal
       differences between friends. Another suggestion is
       'leavings', since 'alms drink' was ordinarily drink
       left over for alms people.

6-7   *pinch one another by the disposition* get on one another's
       nerves

7   *No more* no more bickering!

7-8   *reconciles...drink* gets them to yield to his plea (for amity)
       and at the same time consents to take a drink with them

12   *had as lief* would just as soon

13   *partisan I could not heave* long-handled spear too heavy for me to lift

14   *sphere.* See the note to IV.15.10.

15   *move* (1) revolve; (2) exert influence

16   *disaster* ruin (an astrological term, used of a star's malignant influence)

      (stage direction) *sennet* (trumpet notes signalling the entry of an important person)

17   *take* measure

18   *scales i'* measuring marks on

19   *dearth* famine

20   *foison* plenty

23   *shortly comes* it shortly comes

26-7 *Your serpent . . . sun.* This alludes to the belief, still common in the sixteenth century, that certain forms of organic life (for example, snakes and insects) could be created from inorganic matter. The colloquial use of *your* for 'the' suggests a complacent knowingness: Lepidus, now drunk, is showing off.

30   *I am not so well.* He takes the reference to *health* literally.

30-31 *I'll ne'er out* I won't be stand-offish, I'm with you

33   *in* (1) in drink; (2) indoors

35   *pyramises* (probably a drunken plural form)

39   *Forbear me till anon* leave me alone till a little later

44   *it* (the older form of 'its'; it probably has a slightly childish effect here, as elsewhere in Shakespeare)

45   *the elements once out of it* when it decomposes (in death)

      transmigrates decomposes and so passes into other forms of life

52   *epicure.* The Epicureans did not believe in an after-life.

55   *merit* my good service

57-80 Plutarch writes:

         'Now in the midst of the feast, when they fell to be

merry with Antonius' love unto Cleopatra, Menas the pirate came to Pompey and, whispering in his ear, said unto him:

'"Shall I cut the gables of the anchors, and make thee lord not only of Sicilia and Sardinia, but of the whole Empire of Rome besides?"

'Pompey, having paused awhile upon it, at length answered him:

'"Thou shouldst have done it and never have told it me; but now we must content us with that we have. As for myself, I was never taught to break my faith nor to be counted a traitor"' (pages 214–15).

57	*held my cap off* been respectful to
63	*But entertain it* just grant the possibility
65	*Will* who will
	Hast thou drunk well? have you been drinking a lot?
68	*pales* encloses
	inclips embraces
70	*competitors* partners (but see the note to I.4.3)
78	*Being done unknown* if you had done it without my knowledge
81	*palled* decayed, weakened
89	*'A* (a colloquialism) he
91	*go on wheels* (1) go smoothly; (2) whirl dizzily
92	*reels* (1) fun; (2) reeling movements
95	*Strike the vessels.* This may mean 'Broach the casks'. Other suggestions are 'Fill the cups full' and even 'Beat the kettledrums'. An injunction to drink seems the most likely.
97–8	*It's monstrous . . . fouler* (the more he rinses his brain with wine, the more hopelessly clogged it becomes)
99	*Possess it, I'll make answer* be master of the time, I say
102	*bacchanals* (a dance in honour of Bacchus, god of wine and revelry)
106	*Lethe* forgetfulness. See the note to II.1.27.
107	*Make battery to* assault, smite
108	*place you* put you in the right positions

the boy. A boy is provided at this point simply to sing the song.

109   *The holding every man shall beat* every man shall stamp in time to the refrain (*holding*). Editors usually emend F's 'beate' to 'bear' on the analogy of the common phrase 'bear the burden' (meaning 'sing the refrain'). But Shakespeare probably envisages a very lively drunken ring-dance with a great deal of rhythmic stamping. Horace's Cleopatra ode (I.37) opens with a reference to wine-heated dancers beating the earth with their feet:

Nunc est bibendum, nunc pede libero
pulsanda tellus ...

('Now is the time to drink and to beat the earth with unrestrained foot'). Shakespeare may well have recalled this poem; see the Introduction, pages 45–6, and the headnote to V.2.

111–16   *Come, thou monarch....* According to Richmond Noble (*Shakespeare's Use of Song*, Oxford, 1923) and F. W Sternfeld (*Music in Shakespearean Tragedy*, 1963), this bacchanalian song is modelled on the famous ninth-century Whit Sunday hymn, of which the following is the first stanza:

Veni Creator Spiritus
Mentes tuorum visita:
Imple superna gratia
Quae tu creasti pectora ...

('Come, thou Creative Spirit, visit the souls of thy people; fill with thy heavenly grace the hearts which thou hast created'). The opening word 'Veni' may have suggested the trochaic metre of *Come, thou monarch*. The song in Thomas Heywood's Roman tragedy *The Rape of Lucrece* (1603–8), 'O thou Delphian God, inspire', has a comparable rhythm. On the other hand, the resemblance to 'Veni Creator Spiritus' may be fortuitous. A more likely influence is Anacreon, the Greek lyric poet, whose drinking-songs were much imitated in the Renaissance, often in trochaic metre. No contemporary music for *Come, thou monarch* survives.

112   *pink* half-shut
        eyne (the old plural of 'eyes')
113   *fats* vats
115   *Cup us* ply us with drink, intoxicate us
118   *request you off* ask you to come ashore with me
122   *Spleets* splits. The *Oxford English Dictionary* recognizes this as a distinct word. It seems, in the context, more ludicrously expressive than 'splits', to which it is usually emended.
        The wild disguise the transformation effected by drunkenness
123   *Anticked us* reduced us to fools ('antics')
124   *try you* test your capacity (to hold liquor)
126   *my father's house.* See the note to II.6.27.

III.1   This scene, set in Syria, on the frontiers of the Roman Empire, follows on the previous scene without pause and implies an ironical comment on it. For a few moments we see the task of government through the eyes of subordinates.

        (stage direction) *as it were in triumph.* The phrase does not refer literally to the Roman 'triumph', which was a victory procession into Rome. It means 'in an exultant manner'. Historically, Ventidius was granted a 'triumph' by the Roman Senate, as Plutarch remarks (see the following note).

1–4   Antony had sent Ventidius into Asia to keep the Parthians at bay (see II.3.42). Plutarch writes:

        'Ventidius once again overcame Pacorus (Orodes' son, King of Parthia) in a battle fought in the country of Cyrrestica, he being come again with a great army to

invade Syria; at which battle was slain a great number of the Parthians, and among them Pacorus the
King's own son slain. This noble exploit, as famous as
ever any was, was a full revenge to the Romans of the
shame and loss they had received before by the death
of Marcus Crassus. ... Howbeit Ventidius durst not
undertake to follow them any farther, fearing lest he
should have gotten Antonius' displeasure by it. ...
Ventidius was the only man that ever triumphed of
the Parthians until this present day; a mean man born,
and of no noble house nor family, who only came to that
he attained unto through Antonius' friendship, the
which delivered him happy occasion to achieve to
great matters. And yet, to say truly, he did so well
quit himself in all his enterprises, that he confirmed that
which was spoken of Antonius and Caesar: to wit, that
they were alway more fortunate when they made war
by their lieutenants than by themselves' (pages
217–19).

1   *darting.* The Parthian horsemen used to advance
        flinging their darts, and then rapidly retreat shooting
        flights of arrows behind them.

2   *Marcus Crassus.* A man of enormous wealth, he was
        one of the first triumvirate along with Pompey the
        Great and Julius Caesar. He was defeated by the
        Parthians in 53 B.C. Orodes, father of Pacorus, put
        Crassus to death by pouring molten gold down his
        throat – as a punishment fitted to one who had thirsted
        for gold all his life.

7   *The ... Parthians follow* (that is, follow the ...
        Parthians)

9   *grand captain* great commander

10   *triumphant* triumphal

12   *lower place* man of subordinate rank

18   *place* rank
        his (Antony's)

20   *by th'minute* continually

229

24   *darkens him* eclipses him (that is, checks his advancement, so bringing loss rather than gain)

27   *perish* be worthless

27–9   *that ... distinction* that quality (discretion) without which a soldier and his sword can scarcely allow any distinction to be made between them

33   *The ne'er-yet-beaten horse of Parthia.* The Parthians were brilliant mounted soldiers.

34   *jaded* driven like worn-out nags ('jades')

III.2   The triumvirate appears for the last time.

1   *brothers* brothers-in-law (Antony and Caesar). The word is probably used with irony.
        parted departed

3   *sealing* finishing their arrangements

6   *green-sickness* (a form of anaemia supposed to affect lovelorn girls; Lepidus presumably has a hangover, which is mockingly attributed to his love for Antony and Caesar)

7   *A very fine one.* The Latin word *lepidus* means 'fine', 'elegant'. The following satire on Lepidus's 'love' for the other two triumvirs brings out obliquely the lack of sympathy with one another shown by all three.

11   *nonpareil* incomparable

12   *Arabian bird* phoenix (the mythical immortal bird, of which only one was supposed to exist at a time)

16   *figures* figures of speech

17   *cast* count, calculate
        number versify (put into 'numbers', that is, verse)

20   *They are his shards, and he their beetle* they are the dung patches (*shards*) between which the beetle Lepidus crawls to and fro. Enobarbus contemptuously rounds off the satirical flight.

21   *to horse* (the signal for departure)

23   *No further* you (or 'we') must go no further (that is, we must separate here)

26-7   *As my thoughts ... approof* as I think you will be, and as I would stake anything you will prove to be

26   *band* (a commercial term meaning 'bond', 'promissory note')

28   *piece* paragon

29   *cement* (accented on the first syllable) principle of union

32   *mean* means, intermediary

34   *In* by

35   *curious* exceptionally touchy and particular

48-9   *the swan's-down feather ... tide* she is like the swan's-down feather that floats in still water just before the tide turns. This delicately caught moment of silent immobility and indecisiveness on Octavia's part suggests that we are at or near the mid-point of the play.

52   *were he a horse.* A *cloud* on a horse's face – that is, the absence of a white star – impaired its value.

57   *rheum* running at the eyes

58   *confound* destroy

60   *still* constantly

60-61   *the time ... you* the passage of time will not out-distance my thoughts of you (that is, I shall think of you constantly)

63-4   *Look ... gods.* Antony embraces Caesar as an act of formal leave-taking.

II.3.2   (stage direction) *as before.* This means either that it is the same Messenger as in II.5 or that he is in the same ruffled condition as Cleopatra had left him in at the end of II.5.

3   *Herod of Jewry* (a proverbially fierce tyrant; see also the note to I.2.29-30)

14   *That's not so good.* This seems to treat Octavia's being *low-voiced* as a fault in her; Shakespeare may have intended to show Cleopatra's bad taste. But some editors take the phrase to mean 'That is less favourable

231

news'; the following *He cannot like her long* would then be an abrupt change of mood to optimism.

18   *creeps* shuffles

19   *Her motion and her station are as one.* She has so little vitality that it makes no difference whether she moves or stands still.

20   *shows* looks like

22   *observance* powers of observation

22-3   *Three ... note* few in Egypt have better powers of observation. *Three* is used vaguely here to mean a small or trifling number.

28-9   *thirty ... her face.* Cleopatra changes the subject; she was herself thirty-eight.

33   *As low as she would wish it* (a colloquialism, used to express petty malice: 'low, and serve her right too!')

35   *employ thee back again* send you back (to Rome) again as my messenger

37   *proper* good

39   *harried* maltreated
    by him according to him

40   *no such thing* nothing remarkable

42   *Isis else defend* Isis forbid anything else! (that is, I should jolly well think so!)

43   *serving.* The implied subject is *he* (line 42).

47   *I'll warrant you* I'll be bound

III.4   This and the following two scenes show the hostility between Antony and Caesar coming into the open. With the disposal of Lepidus, the Roman world is left with two 'competitors' for mastery. War suddenly seems imminent.

3   *semblable* similar

4-5   *made his will, and read it | To public ear.* In Plutarch (page 247) it is Antony's will which Caesar, having obtained possession of it from the custody of the vestal virgins, reads to the Senate and so arouses feeling against Antony. Possibly the text is corrupt at this point.

6   *scantly* grudgingly

8   most *narrow measure lent me* did me small justice

9   *hint* opportunity

10   *from his teeth* with obvious lack of conviction

12   *Stomach* resent

12-20 Plutarch writes that Octavia, meeting with Caesar, Maecenas, and Agrippa, appealed to them not to 'suffer her, that was the happiest woman of the world, to become now the most wretched and unfortunatest creature of all other.

    ' "For now," said she, "every man's eyes do gaze on me, that am the sister of one of the Emperors and wife of the other. And if the worst counsel take place (which the gods forbid!) and that they grow to wars, for yourselves it is uncertain to which of them two the gods have assigned the victory or overthrow. But for me, on which side soever victory fall, my state can be but most miserable still" ' (page 221).

13   *between* between the two

15   *presently* at once

24   *branchless* maimed

27   *stain* eclipse

34   *our faults* (the faults of Antony and Caesar)

III.5.5   *success* outcome

6-11   In his *Life of Octavius* Plutarch says that Lepidus betrayed Octavius in the war against Sextus Pompeius. Lepidus's soldiers deserted him for Octavius, who then deposed Lepidus from his position as triumvir but spared his life and allowed him to reside as a state prisoner in Italy. Shakespeare's account, which omits Lepidus's treachery and places Octavius in an unfavourable light, may have been intended to balance

the disclosure made shortly afterwards (line 18) that
Antony was responsible for Pompey's death.

7   *presently* after a short time
     rivality equal partnership

10   *his own appeal* his own (Caesar's) accusation

11   *up* shut up, imprisoned

12   *chaps* jaws

13–14 *throw ... the other* feed them with everything in the
       world, the jaws will still grind each other down

15   *spurns* kicks. Eros imitates Antony (*thus*).

17   *threats the throat* threatens the life
     that his officer the officer of his

17–18 In the *Life of Octavius* Plutarch writes that Antony's
       lieutenant Titius put Pompey to death in the isle of
       Samos 'by Antony's commandment'. For this deed,
       says Plutarch, Antony incurred the hatred of the people
       of Rome. He regrets the murder presumably because
       Pompey might have made a useful ally against Octavius.

21   *naught* something bad

III.6.1–19 Plutarch writes of the growing hostility against
            Antony felt by the Roman people:
            'But yet the greatest cause of their malice unto him
            was for the division of lands he made amongst his
            children in the city of Alexandria. And, to confess a
            troth, it was too arrogant and insolent a part, and done
            (as a man would say) in derision and contempt of the
            Romans. For he assembled all the people in the show-
            place where young men do exercise themselves; and
            there upon a high tribunal silvered he set two chairs
            of gold, the one for himself and the other for Cleo-
            patra, and lower chairs for his children. Then he
            openly published before the assembly that, first of all,
            he did establish Cleopatra Queen of Egypt, of Cyprus,
            of Lydia, and of the lower Syria, and, at that time also,
            Caesarion King of the same realms. (This Caesarion

was supposed to be the son of Julius Caesar, who had
left Cleopatra great with child.) Secondly he called the
sons he had by her "the Kings of Kings": and gave
Alexander for his portion, Armenia, Media, and
Parthia (when he had conquered the country); and
unto Ptolemy for his portion, Phoenicia, Syria, and
Cilicia. And therewithal he brought out Alexander in a
long gown after the fashion of the Medes, with a
high copped-tank hat on his head, narrow in the top,
as the Kings of the Medes and Armenians do use to
wear them; and Ptolemy apparelled in a cloak after the
Macedonian manner, with slippers on his feet, and a
broad hat with a royal band or diadem – such was the
apparel and old attire of the ancient kings and successors
of Alexander the Great. So, after his sons had done
their humble duties and kissed their father and mother,
presently a company of Armenian soldiers set there
of purpose, compassed the one about, and a like company of the Macedonians the other. Now, for Cleopatra, she did not only wear at that time, but at all
other times else when she came abroad, the apparel
of the goddess Isis, and so gave audience unto all her
subjects as a new Isis' (pages 242–3).

1	*Contemning* despising
3	*tribunal* raised platform, dais
6	*my father.* Julius Caesar had adopted Octavius.
9	*stablishment* confirmed possession
12	*showplace* place for public shows or spectacles, theatre
19	*so* (in those *habiliments*)
20	*queasy* disgusted
24–30	Closely based on Plutarch:

'Octavius Caesar reporting all these things unto the
Senate and oftentimes accusing him to the whole
people and assembly in Rome, he thereby stirred up all
the Romans against him. Antonius on the other side
sent to Rome likewise to accuse him; and the chiefest
points of his accusations he charged him with were

these: first, that having spoiled Sextus Pompeius in
Sicilia he did not give him his part of the isle; secondly,
that he did detain in his hands the ships he lent him
to make that war; thirdly, that, having put Lepidus
their companion and triumvirate out of his part of the
Empire and having deprived him of all honours, he
retained for himself the lands and revenues thereof
which had been assigned unto him for his part ...'
(page 243).

25   *spoiled* despoiled
      rated allotted

30   *revenue* (accented on the second syllable)

31   *'Tis done already, and the messenger gone.* Caesar's
extraordinary promptness and efficiency may recall a
famous line from Lucan's epic poem *Pharsalia*
(II.657), where Julius Caesar is described as *Nil
actum credens, cum quid superesset agendum* ('believing
nothing done while anything remained to do').

32   *Lepidus was grown too cruel.* Although based on Plutarch (page 244), this sounds unconvincing when said
of Shakespeare's Lepidus. This is one of many moments
in the play when we do not necessarily believe what
one character says of another.

40   *castaway* rejected

52   *ostentation* public display

52-3   *which, left unshown, | Is often left unloved* (love which is
not shown to exist may not exist in fact – or may be
thought not to do so)

61   *Being an obstruct* since you are an impediment

66   *nodded* beckoned with a nod

67   *who now* and they now

69-75   This list of kings is taken from Plutarch (page 250)

76   *more larger* even longer. The double comparative was
a common Elizabethan usage.

79   *withhold our breaking forth* restrain me from erupting
(into violent or decisive action)

80   *wrong led.* The sense is not very satisfactory, and some

editors have emended so that the line reads 'Till we perceivèd both how you were wronged'.

81   *negligent danger* danger from negligence
82   *the time* the present state of affairs
83   *content* happiness
86   *Nothing more dear to me* nothing is more dear to me than you
      abused deceived
87   *mark* reach
88–9 *makes his ministers | Of us* make us their servants
93   *large* licentious, free
94   *turns . . . off* dismisses, repudiates
95   *potent regiment* powerful rule
      trull harlot
96   *noises it* clamours
98   *known to patience* patient

III.7   The second movement of the play begins here with the Battle of Actium sequence. The battle (September 31 B.C.) was fought off the west coast of Macedonia. For his historical details Shakespeare closely follows Plutarch, whose account begins:

'Now after that Caesar had made sufficient preparation, he proclaimed open war against Cleopatra, and made the people to abolish the power and empire of Antonius because he had before given it up unto a woman. And Caesar said furthermore that Antonius was not master of himself, but that Cleopatra had brought him beside himself by her charms and amorous poisons, and that they that should make war with them should be Mardian the eunuch, Photinus, and Iras, a woman of Cleopatra's bed-chamber that frizzled her hair and dressed her head, and Charmion, the which were those that ruled all the affairs of Antonius' empire' (pages 248–9).

3–19   Plutarch says that 'Antonius, through the persuasions of Domitius [Enobarbus], commanded Cleopatra to return again into Egypt', and goes on to say that Cleopatra bribed Canidius to speak on her behalf to Antony: 'These fair persuasions won him; for it was predestined that the government of all the world should fall into Octavius Caesar's hands' (pages 244–5).

3   *forspoke* opposed

5   *Is't not denounced against us?* hasn't war been declared against me? She uses the royal plural; the Romans declared war not against Antony and Cleopatra but against Cleopatra only. Some editors keep the F reading, 'If not, denounc'd against vs', repunctuating it as 'If not denounced against us'. The speech would then mean 'Even if the war had not been declared against me, why shouldn't I be here in person?'

8   *merely* utterly

8–9   *the mares ... horse* the mares would carry the soldiers and copulate with the stallions

10   *puzzle* perplex, embarrass with difficulties

11   *heart* mind

13   *Traduced* calumniated, censured

14   *an eunuch.* The eunuch is Mardian, as Plutarch makes clear.

16   *charge* cost, expense

18   *for* in the capacity of

20   *Emperor.* Antony is called *emperor* three times in this short scene. In this way his stature is insisted on immediately before his fall. (According to Plutarch, Antony had been deprived of his title when war was declared on Cleopatra.)

21–3   *Tarentum and Brundisium ... Toryne.* Tarentum and Brundisium (modern Taranto and Brindisi) were the two chief ports of south-eastern Italy; Toryne was a few miles north of Actium.

23   *take in* occupy

24–5   *Celerity ... negligent.* In Plutarch, Cleopatra makes light of Caesar's brilliant efficiency: Shakespeare makes her administer a rebuke. See the Introduction, pages 34–5.

29   *For that* because

30–32   Plutarch mentions both these challenges (page 251). Pharsalia, the region where the decisive battle between Julius Caesar and Pompey the Great was fought, was not far from Actium.

35   *muleters* mule-drivers

36   *Engrossed by swift impress* hastily brought together by press-gangs

38   *yare* swift, easily manipulated

39   *fall* befall

43   *Distract* confuse

    most for the greater part

44   *footmen* foot-soldiers

    unexecuted unused

47   *merely* entirely

51   *head* promontory

57   *power* army

60   *Thetis* (a sea-nymph)

61–6   The speech is transcribed, with a few modifications, from Plutarch. A 'captain' cries out to Antony as he passes:

      'O noble Emperor, how cometh it to pass that you trust to these vile brittle ships? What, do you mistrust these wounds of mine and this sword? Let the Egyptians and Phoenicians fight by sea, and set us on the mainland, where we use to conquer, or to be slain on our feet' (page 255).

62   *misdoubt* doubt the existence of, disbelieve

64   *go a-ducking* get drenched in the sea

68–9   *his whole action grows | Not in the power on't* his entire strategy has been planned without regard to his real strength

75   *Carries* takes him forward

76   *distractions* divisions, small numbers

80–81   *With news ... some* (things are happening fast and every minute a new development is born). Some editors emend F's 'with Labour' to 'in labour', with a consequent idiomatic gain.

III.8 The battle scenes are managed with economy and even austerity. Since Actium was a sea-battle involving thousands of men, it had to be left to the imagination of the audience. There is no hand-to-hand fighting in Shakespeare's dramatization; the use of 'noises off' was therefore particularly important.

3 *whole* undivided (not weakened by division)
5 *prescript* written orders
6 *jump* hazard

III.9.2 *battle* line of battle

III.10 (stage direction) Exactly what *the noise of a sea fight* was on Shakespeare's stage is not certain. It probably involved gunfire from the cannon just outside the theatre – at least when the play was performed at the Globe. (See C. Walter Hodges, *The Globe Restored* (1968), page 82.)

1-23 Plutarch writes:

'Howbeit the battle was yet of even hand, and the victory doubtful, being indifferent to both; when suddenly they saw the three-score ships of Cleopatra busy about their yard-masts, and hoising sail to fly. So they fled through the midst of them that were in fight, for they had been placed behind the great ships, and did marvellously disorder the other ships. For the enemies themselves wondered much to see them sail in that sort with full sail towards Peloponnesus. There Antonius showed plainly that he had not only lost the

courage and heart of an Emperor but also of a valiant
man, and that he was not his own man, proving that
true which an old man spake in mirth: that the soul
of a lover lived in another body, and not in his own.
He was so carried away with the vain love of this
woman, as if he had been glued unto her and that she
could not have removed without moving of him also
....

'Many plainly saw Antonius fly, and yet could very
hardly believe it, that he, that had nineteen legions
whole by land and twelve thousand horsemen upon the
sea side, would so have forsaken them, and have fled so
cowardly; as if he had not oftentimes proved both the
one and the other fortune and that he had not been
throughly acquainted with the diverse changes and
fortunes of battles' (pages 258, 261–2).

1   *Naught* ruin, disaster

2   *Th' Antoniad, the Egyptian admiral.* Plutarch notes that
      'The admiral galley of Cleopatra was called *Antoniad*'
      (page 249).
      admiral flagship

5   *synod* assembly (usually used of the gods). Scarus is
      swearing by all the gods and goddesses at once.
      What's thy passion? what's the reason for your distress?

6   *cantle* segment of a sphere

7   *With very ignorance* through utter stupidity

9   *tokened pestilence* plague-spots (announcing imminent
      death)

10   *ribaudred* (much discussed and emended; presumably
      it means something like 'lewd' or 'filthy', perhaps
      'rotten with disease')

12–13   *When vantage . . . same.* Compare Plutarch: 'the battle
      was yet of even hand, and the victory doubtful, being
      indifferent to both' (page 258).

12   *vantage* chance of advantage

13   *elder* greater

14   *breese* gadfly. Scarus's fury, dismay, and horror result

in the heaped-up phrases and mixed metaphors of this
bellowed announcement. This is a very original vari-
ant on the traditional messenger-speech.

17   *loofed* luffed (with the head of the vessel turned into the
      wind, so as to prepare for departure)

18   *ruin of her magic* man ruined by her powers of en-
      chantment

19   *Claps on* puts on promptly
      sea-wing means of flight by sea (sails)
      mallard wild drake. Like *cow in June*, the word ex-
      presses contempt.

26   *what he knew himself* his true self

29   *are you thereabouts?* is that what you're thinking?
      good night indeed it's all up

31   *'Tis easy to't* it's easy enough to get there

35   *wounded chance* maimed fortunes

III.11   Plutarch describes Antony's desolation after his flight.
           First, when Cleopatra, who was in her own ship,
           'knew his galley afar off, she lift up a sign in the poop of
           her ship, and so Antonius coming to it was plucked up
           where Cleopatra was; howbeit he saw her not at his
           first coming, nor she him, but went and sat down alone
           in the prow of his ship, and said never a word, clapping
           his head between both his hands' (pages 258–9).
           It is a later passage that Shakespeare dramatizes in this
           scene: '. . . he returned again to his place and sat down,
           speaking never a word as he did before; and so lived
           three days alone, without speaking to any man.
           But, when he arrived at the head of Taenarus, there
           Cleopatra's women first brought Antonius and Cleo-
           patra to speak together and afterwards to sup and lie
           together' (page 260).
               Shakespeare leaves the location unspecified; it is felt
           to be vaguely Egyptian, so that editors usually give it as
           Alexandria.

3   *lated* belated (like a traveller who has lost his way after nightfall)

5–6   Based on Plutarch's account of Antony's solicitude for his followers: 'Then Antonius very courteously and lovingly did comfort them, and prayed them to depart; and wrote unto Theophilus, governor of Corinth, that he would see them safe and help to hide them in some secret place until they had made their way and peace with Caesar' (pages 260–61).

8   *show their shoulders* turn their backs (in flight)

12   *that* what

14   *rashness* folly

17   *Sweep your way* clear your path, make things easier

18   *loathness* unwillingness
           hint opportunity (or perhaps 'suggestion')

19–20   *Let that be left | Which leaves itself* leave the man (Antony) who is no longer himself

23   *command* the power to command others

35   *He* (Octavius. Antony is self-absorbed in an internal dialogue and does not at first hear the approach of the others.)

36   *a dancer* (who would wear a sword for ornament)

38   *mad Brutus.* A strange remark, since Marcus Brutus showed no signs of madness, although his ancestor Junius Lucius Brutus pretended in his youth to be simple-minded. (*Brutus* could mean 'stupid'.) Shakespeare may have meant to startle us with the sense that everyone has his own – often surprisingly partial – view of other people. Pompey's earlier references to *the good Brutus* and *the all-honoured, honest, Roman Brutus* (II.6.13 and 16) make an obvious contrast.

39   *Dealt on lieutenantry* depended on his subordinates to do his fighting for him

40   *squares* squadrons

41   *stand by* stand back

44   *unqualitied* beside himself

47   *but* unless

243

49   *reputation* honour

50   *A most unnoble swerving.* Antony takes up Eros's *Most
        noble sir, arise* (line 46) and retorts bitterly 'A most
        unnoble swerving'.

        swerving transgression, lapse

51–4   *See ... dishonour.* 'Convey' often meant 'remove by
        underhand means', and so 'steal'. In his acutely
        distressed state Antony sees himself as doing something
        comparably disreputable. 'See how I try to steal away
        (*convey*) my shame so that you can no longer see it, by
        brooding on the past and wishing vainly it had never
        happened.'

53   *looking back* looking back at

54   *'Stroyed* destroyed, lost

60   *beck* nod; mute signal

62   *the young man.* In the year of Actium, Antony was
        fifty-one, Caesar thirty-two.

        treaties terms (for negotiation)

62–3   *dodge | And palter* shuffle and prevaricate

63   *the shifts of lowness* the abject behaviour of those who
        have been brought low

67   *affection* passion

68   *on all cause* whatever the reason

69   *Fall not a tear* let not a tear fall

        rates is worth

71   *Even this* this alone

        schoolmaster (tutor to the children of Antony and Cleo-
        patra). See the headnote to III.12.

73   *viands* solid food

III.12   Plutarch's account of the exchange of ambassadors
                between the two sides is worked up by Shakespeare
                into a weighty episode which occupies this and the
                next scene. As so often in this play, key roles within
                individual scenes are given to messengers, ambassadors,
                go-betweens of various kinds, acting on behalf of

masters who seldom have the chance of meeting.
Plutarch writes:

'... they sent ambassadors unto Octavius Caesar in
Asia, Cleopatra requesting the realm of Egypt for
their children, and Antonius praying that he might be
suffered to live at Athens like a private man, if Caesar
would not let him remain in Egypt. And, because they
had no other men of estimation about them (for that
some were fled, and, those that remained, they did
not greatly trust them), they were enforced to send
Euphronius the schoolmaster of their children ...

'Caesar would not grant unto Antonius' requests.
But, for Cleopatra, he made her answer that he would
deny her nothing reasonable, so that she would either
put Antonius to death or drive him out of her country.
Therewithal he sent Thyreus one of his men unto her,
a very wise and discreet man, who, bringing letters
of credit from a young lord unto a noble lady, and that
besides greatly liked her beauty, might easily by his
eloquence have persuaded her. He was longer in
talk with her than any man else was, and the Queen
herself also did him great honour; insomuch as he
made Antonius jealous of him. Whereupon Antonius
caused him to be taken and well-favouredly whipped,
and so sent him unto Caesar; and bade him tell him
that he made him angry with him, because he showed
himself proud and disdainful towards him, and now
specially when he was easy to be angered, by reason of
his present misery' (pages 268, 269–71).

4 *pinion* pinion-feather
5 *Which* who
8 *petty to his ends* insignificant to his purposes
10 *To his grand sea* to the ocean that is its source
12 *Requires* requests
13 *lessons* disciplines. This gives a richer sense than 'lessens', to which it is often emended. But an audience
will probably hear it as 'lessens', despite the appro-

priateness of *lessons* to the schoolmaster who speaks it.

18   *circle* crown. The schoolmaster's speeches have a notable eloquence.

19   *hazarded to thy grace* dependent on your favour

21   *Of audience nor desire shall fail* shall not fail either to gain a hearing from me or to secure her wishes
     so if

25   *Bring* conduct
     bands (military) lines

26   *try* put to the test

27–9   *Promise . . . offers* use my authority to promise what she asks; offer in addition anything which you may at the time think effective. This edition keeps F's words; editors sometimes emend, so that the last clause reads 'and more, | From thine invention, offer' or 'add more, | As thine invention offers'.

30–31   *want will perjure | The ne'er-touched vestal* need will make the immaculate vestal virgin break her vows

31   *Thidias* (Shakespeare's name for North's Plutarch's 'Thyreus'; see the Account of the Text, page 288)

32   *Make thine own edict for thy pains* make your own judgement as to how your services should be paid

32–3   *which we | Will answer as* which (the *edict*) I will obey as if it were

34   *becomes his flaw* carries off his lapse

35–6   *what thou think'st . . . moves* what in your opinion he reveals (of his inner state) through every outward act

36   *power that moves* faculty of mind or body that is put in action

III.13.1   *Think, and die* brood and die (of depression). This is to be Enobarbus's own fate.

3   *will* desire, passion

5   *face* appearance, show
    ranges battle lines

7   *affection* sexual passion

246

8   *nicked* maimed, emasculated

9   *opposed* were in conflict

10   *The mered question* the sole ground of dispute (or since the verb 'mere' means 'to limit', 'the matter to which the dispute is limited')

11   *course* pursue

15   *so* if

16   *us* (royal plural)

17   *boy . . . grizzled head.* See the note to III.11.62.

20-22 *Tell him . . particular.* The oddly slack rhythm may indicate that the text is defective; perhaps some words have dropped out. As it stands, it seems to mean the following (with the sense of the second sentence here understood): 'Tell him he is now in the bloom of youth. But youth is common to all men at some time in their lives. From him the world has a right to expect some proof of personal distinction.' Antony goes on to say that the efficiency of Caesar's government and army prove nothing about his personal qualities, for they exist independently of him.

26   *gay comparisons* showy, specious advantages when we are compared. Perhaps there is also a suggestion of 'caparisons', meaning 'external trappings'.

27   *declined* past my prime (perhaps also 'having suffered ill fortune')

29   *high-battled* with great armies under him

30   *Unstate his happiness* lose his happiness by giving up his position

30-31 *be staged to th'show | Against a sworder* put himself on public display in a gladiatorial combat

32   *parcel* part

34   *suffer all alike* decay together

35   *Knowing all measures* having experienced every degree (of fortune)

36   *Answer his emptiness* meet in combat one as powerless as he

41   *square* quarrel

43   *faith* fidelity

46   *story* history, historical account

46-152 For Plutarch's account of Thidias's visit, see the head-note to III.12.

48   *haply* perhaps

50   *Or needs not us* or he needs no friends at all, being out of the running

55   *he is Caesar* (and therefore by definition magnanimous)
    right royal (that's very generous of him). Cleopatra's responses in this and her next two speeches are studiedly ambiguous.

61   *right* true

62   *merely* utterly

66   *require* request

71   *shroud* protection. The line is two syllables short; perhaps a word has dropped out before *shroud*.

74   *in deputation* by proxy

77   *Till from.* F reads 'Tell him, from'. The emendation adopted here was suggested by Kenneth Muir in *Notes and Queries*, 1961, page 142.
    all-obeying which all obey

78   *doom of Egypt* judgement on the Queen of Egypt

80   *If that the former dare but what it can* if a wise man has the resolution to persist in being wise

82   *My duty* (a kiss)
    Your Caesar's father (Julius Caesar; see the note to III.6.6)

83   *taking . . . in* occupying, annexing

85   *As* as if

87   *fullest* best and most fortunate

89   *kite* (a slang word for 'whore')

91   *muss* (a children's game in which small objects are thrown on the ground to be scrambled for)

93, 103 *Jack* (1) fellow, knave; (2) substitute (according to the *Oxford English Dictionary* 'jack' was sometimes 'Applied to things which in some way take the place of a lad or man, or save human labour')

96   *tributaries* (minor potentates who paid tribute)

103   *again* back

105   *blasted* withered, blighted

107-8   *Forborne ... women.* Historically, Antony had several children by Octavia.

107   *getting* begetting

109   *feeders* servants, parasites

110   *boggler* waverer. The word was usually applied to a restive horse, one given to sudden starting and shying. According to T. R. Henn, however, it here alludes to falconry – to 'the hawk that does not select and keep to one quarry, but turns backwards and forwards from one to another' (*The Living Image*, 1972, page 120).

112   *seel our eyes* blind us. In falconry the bird's eyes were sewn up ('seeled') as part of the taming process. Antony, to quote T. R. Henn again, 'like the blinded hawk, stumbles in the filth of the falconers' mews, surrounded by the jeering yard-boys who will see that she is given no sleep till she surrenders' (pages 120-21).

115   *confusion* destruction

117   *trencher* wooden plate
        fragment left-over

119   *vulgar fame* popular rumour

120   *Luxuriously picked out* lustfully selected

123   *fellow* mean subordinate

124   *God quit you!* may God reward you! (a phrase used by beggars)

125   *seal* token (something which confirms a covenant)

126-8   *O that I ... herd.* Antony sees himself as a cuckold with horns, and so eligible to take his place among *The hornèd herd*. The *hill of Basan* is mentioned in Psalm 68.15: 'As the hill of Basan, so is God's hill: even an high hill, as the hill of Basan'; and Psalm 22.12 mentions 'fat bulls of Basan'.

128   *savage cause* cause enough to run wild

129-31   *to proclaim ... him* to express myself in polite language would be as inappropriate as if a man about to be hanged were to thank the hangman for doing the job neatly

131   *yare* deft, quick

132   *Cried he? And begged 'a pardon?* Antony jeeringly treats Thidias as a schoolboy who has been flogged for a misdemeanour.

138   *fever thee* let (the *white hand . . .*) give you the shivers

140   *entertainment* treatment, reception
      Look see that

142–3 *harping on what I am, | Not what he knew I was.* Antony cannot accept what he has made of himself.

146   *orbs* spheres. See the note to IV.15.10.

147   *abysm* abyss

147–51 Based on Plutarch: ' "To be short, if this mislike thee," said he, "thou hast Hipparchus one of my enfranchised bondmen with thee. Hang him if thou wilt, or whip him at thy pleasure, that we may cry quittance" ' (page 271). Plutarch earlier remarks that Hipparchus 'was had in great estimation about Antonius. He was the first of all his enfranchised bondmen that revolted from him and yielded unto Caesar . . .' (page 261).

149   *enfranchèd* freed

151   *quit* requite

152   *stripes* weals

153   *terrene moon* (Cleopatra, the earthly Isis)

155   *stay his time* give him time, wait (till he recovers)

157   *one that ties his points* one who laces up his (Octavius's) clothes, a mere valet. *Points* were tagged laces for fastening clothes.

158–67 For Cleopatra's self-defence Shakespeare may have recalled the account in Exodus of the plagues that God inflicted on the Egyptians. These included the plagues of hail and of flies as well as the plague on the first-born. 'I . . . will smite all the first-born of Egypt', says Jehovah (Exodus 12.12); compare Cleopatra's *The next Caesarion smite* – Caesarion was her first-born child. These biblical resonances may have been felt to lend conviction to Cleopatra's words: hence Antony's *I am satisfied*. (See J. H. Walter, *Notes and Queries*, 1969, page 138.)

161   *neck* throat

      determines comes to an end, melts

163   *the memory of my womb* my children

165   *discandying* melting

      pelleted storm (hail-storm)

168   *sits down.* Plutarch has 'Caesar came, and pitched his camp hard by the city' (page 272). 'Sit down before' is a military term meaning 'besiege'; this is probably the sense here.

169   *oppose his fate* resist his destiny

171   *fleet* are afloat

      threatening most sea-like in a manner as threatening as the (stormy) sea's. Some editors take *sea-like* to mean 'in good sea-going trim'. Perhaps both senses are present.

172   *my heart* my courage. Some editors read this as addressed to Cleopatra, but it seems unlikely in view of the next phrase.

173   *field* battlefield

174   *in blood* (1) covered with blood; (2) in full strength

175   *chronicle* place in history

177   *hearted, breathed* treble-hearted, treble-breathed

178–9   *when mine hours | Were nice and lucky* when I was pampered by fortune

179   *nice* pampered, made wanton

179–80   *men did ransom lives | Of me for jests* men bought their lives from me for no more than the price of a joke (as if fighting were a game)

182   *gaudy* festive, joyous

184–6   Plutarch writes: 'Cleopatra, to clear herself of the suspicion he had of her, she made more of him than ever she did. For first of all, where she did solemnize the day of her birth very meanly and sparingly, fit for her present misfortune, she now in contrary manner did keep it with such solemnity, that she exceeded all measure of sumptuousness and magnificence ...' (pages 271–2).

191   *There's sap in't yet* there's life in me yet

192–3   *contend | Even with his pestilent scythe* kill as many as death does in time of plague

194   *furious* enraged to the point of frenzy

196   *estridge* goshawk (a large short-winged hawk; *not* an ostrich)

         still always

198   *heart* courage

IV.1.1   *boy.* This was an insult. Shakespeare probably knew from Suetonius's *Life of Augustus* that Octavius was in fact contemptuously called 'the boy' by some of his enemies. Compare III.13.17 and IV.12.48.

         as as if

3–5   *dares me ... die.* North's version of Plutarch reads: 'Antonius sent again to challenge Caesar to fight with him hand to hand. Caesar answered him that he had many other ways to die than so' (page 273). But in Plutarch's Greek, Caesar says that Antony might find many other ways of dying.

6   *Laugh at* I mock

7–8   *When one so great ... falling.* The image is of a hunted animal at bay; compare IV 13.2–3.

9   *Make boot of his distraction* take advantage of his frenzy

10   *heads* chief officers

12   *files* ranks

14   *fetch him in* close in upon him

16   *waste* lavish expenditure

IV.2   The sequence of short scenes from IV.2 to IV.12 focuses on the last stages in Antony's disintegration. All the incidents are based on Plutarch, but Shakespeare has rearranged them with a view to securing the most effective sequence. The most important departure from Plutarch's order is Enobarbus's defection. In Plutarch it comes before the Battle of Actium (pages 252–3). Shakespeare delays it until after Thidias's attempted overtures to Cleopatra; indeed it coincides with the night in which music is heard under the earth. Secondly, Antony's successful skirmish, given very little stress by Plutarch, is built up by Shakespeare so that for a brief time it seems a substantial victory. Antony's resurgence of high spirits and final military success are in this way interwoven with the desertion and death of the man who was closest to him. The final impression made by this brilliant sequence is one of dizzying instability and ultimate dissolution: Fortune is at her most treacherously inconstant, but within the individual personality there are equally volatile shifts of mood.

After Caesar's rejection of Antony's challenge, Plutarch goes on:

'Then Antonius, seeing there was no way more honourable for him to die than fighting valiantly, he determined to set up his rest, both by sea and land. So, being at supper as it is reported, he commanded his officers and household servants, that waited on him at his board, that they should fill his cups full, and make as much of him as they could.

' "For," said he, "you know not whether you shall do so much for me tomorrow or not, or whether you shall serve another master; and it may be you shall see me no more, but a dead body."

'This notwithstanding, perceiving that his friends and men fell a-weeping to hear him say so, to salve that he had spoken he added this more unto it: that he would not lead them to battle where he thought not rather safely to return with victory than valiantly to die with honour' (pages 273-4).

5   *Or* either

6-7   *bathe my dying honour ... again* revive my dying honour by giving it a blood-bath. A bath in warm blood was believed to be 'a powerful tonic in great debility from long-continued diseases' (*Oxford English Dictionary*: 'blood-bath'). Of course Antony implies also the other meaning of 'blood-bath': wholesale slaughter, massacre.

7   *Woo't* wilt

8   *Take all!* all or nothing

13   *kings have been your fellows* I have had kings as my servants

21   *Scant not my cups* provide liberally

23   *And suffered my command* and, like you, also acknowledged me as master
    What does he mean? In this incident Shakespeare seems deliberately to insist on an element of mystery or opacity in Antony: Cleopatra's question and Enobarbus's glib reply compel us to make our own interpretation.

25   *period* end

27   *mangled shadow* hideously disfigured ghost (like the ghost of Hector when he appears to Aeneas in Book 2 of Virgil's *Aeneid*)

33   *yield* reward

36   *Ho, ho, ho!* Antony attempts to laugh it off.

37   *the witch take me* may I be bewitched

38   *Grace* herb of grace (but also 'God's grace')
    drops tears
    hearty loving

44   *death and honour* honourable death

45   *consideration* serious reflection

IV.3   Plutarch writes, immediately after the passage quoted for IV.2:

'Furthermore, the self same night within little of midnight, when all the city was quiet, full of fear and sorrow, thinking what would be the issue and end of this war, it is said that suddenly they heard a marvellous sweet harmony of sundry sorts of instruments of music, with the cry of a multitude of people, as they had been dancing and had sung as they use in Bacchus' feasts, with movings and turnings after the manner of the Satyrs. And it seemed that this dance went through the city unto the gate that opened to the enemies, and that all the troop that made this noise they heard went out of the city at that gate. Now such as in reason sought the depth of the interpretation of this wonder thought that it was the god unto whom Antonius bare singular devotion to counterfeit and resemble him, that did forsake them' (pages 274-5).

5   *Belike* probably

10   *Here we* this is our place

      An if if

13   (stage direction) *hautboys* shawms. They would produce an eerie sound under the stage. Compare *Macbeth*, IV.1.105, where 'hautboys' are heard as the cauldron of the Three Witches sinks.

15   *signs* bodes

17   *the god Hercules.* Shakespeare substitutes Hercules (identified with Heroic Virtue) for Plutarch's Bacchus, whose relation with Antony he has suppressed.

25   *so far as we have quarter* as long as the period (of our watch) lasts

26   *give off* cease

IV.4.2   *chuck* sweet

3   *put thine iron on* help me on with the armour (of mine) which you are holding

5   *brave* defy

5–8   *Nay . . . must be.* F assigns these speeches differently. See the Account of the Text, page 293.

7   *False* you have put it on wrong

10   *Briefly* in a moment

13   *daff't* take it off

14   *squire* (whose duty was to give personal attendance to the knight)

15   *tight* skilled

17   *occupation* trade

18   *workman* professional, true craftsman

19   *charge* command

20   *betime* early

22   *riveted trim* (armour)

23   *port* gate

25   *well blown* (the trumpets). Some editors take it as referring to the *morning* ('the day is "blossoming" beautifully').

28   *well said* well done (a common Elizabethan usage)

31   *check* reprimand

32   *mechanic compliment* fussily commonplace civilities

IV.5   In Plutarch, Enobarbus is mentioned substantially only once, shortly before Actium: Antony 'dealt very friendly and courteously with Domitius, and against Cleopatra's mind. For, he being sick of an ague when he went and took a little boat to go unto Caesar's camp, Antonius was very sorry for it, but yet he sent after him all his carriage, train, and men; and the same Domitius, as though he gave him to understand that he repented his open treason, he died immediately after' (pages 252–3). From this brief passage, and from an earlier, even briefer reference (quoted in the note to III.7.3–19), Shakespeare built up the entire character of Enobarbus ('Domitius').

1   *happy* fortunate

2   *once* earlier. Compare III.7.61–6.

4   *revolted* deserted

14   *subscribe* sign

17   *Dispatch* make haste (or perhaps 'get it done with')

IV.6.5   *The time of universal peace is near.* Peace was for a time established under Augustus (the 'pax Romana'). Plutarch says at one point: 'it was predestined that the government of all the world should fall into Octavius Caesar's hands' (page 245).

6   *Prove this* if this proves
      three-nooked three-cornered (perhaps referring to Europe, Asia, and Africa)

7   *bear* bring forth. The *olive* was the emblem of peace.

8   *charge Agrippa* command Agrippa to

9   *vant* van, front line

10–11   *That Antony ... Upon himself.* Caesar's remark is in keeping with the more general impression that, since Actium, Antony is essentially in a state of isolation, undergoing a private and subjective ordeal of dissolution.

12–16   *Alexas ... hanged him.* Plutarch writes of Alexas: 'him Antonius had sent unto Herodes King of Jewry, hoping still to keep him his friend, that he should not revolt from him. But he remained there, and betrayed Antonius. For, where he should have kept Herodes from revolting from him, he persuaded him to turn to Caesar; and, trusting King Herodes, he presumed to come in Caesar's presence. Howbeit Herodes did him no pleasure; for he was presently taken prisoner, and sent in chains to his own country; and there by Caesar's commandment put to death' (page 269).

13   *dissuade* persuade. Some editors emend to 'persuade'.

16–17   *Canidius ... fell away.* Plutarch writes that after Actium 'Canidius, Antonius' lieutenant, flying by night and forsaking his camp, when they saw them-

selves thus destitute of their heads and leaders they
yielded themselves unto the stronger' (page 262).

17   *entertainment* employment
22   *bounty overplus* gift in addition
23   *on my guard* while I was on guard
26–7   *Best you safed the bringer | Out of the host* you had
         better see that the man who brought it is given a safe-
         conduct through the lines
27   *attend mine office* see to my duties
30   *alone the* the only, the greatest
31   *feel ... most* feel (it) more than anyone else
32   *mine* abundant store
34   *blows* swells to bursting point
35   *thought* melancholy, grief

IV.7   Plutarch writes: 'Antonius made a sally upon him, and
         fought very valiantly, so that he drave Caesar's horse-
         men back, fighting with his men even into their camp.
         Then he came again to the palace greatly boasting of
         this victory, and sweetly kissed Cleopatra, armed as
         he was when he came from the fight, recommending
         one of his men of arms unto her, that had valiantly
         fought in this skirmish. Cleopatra to reward his
         manliness gave him an armour and head-piece of clean
         gold; howbeit the man at arms, when he had received
         this rich gift, stale away by night and went to Caesar'
         (pages 272–3).
         (stage direction) *Alarum* call to arms
2   *has work* is hard-pressed
         our oppression the pressure on us
5   *droven* (an older form of the past participle) driven
6   *clouts* cloths, bandages
8   *H* (wordplay on the letter H and 'ache', which was
         pronounced 'aitch')
9   *bench-holes* holes of a privy
10   *scotches* gashes

12	*score* mark
15	*sprightly* high-spirited, cheerful
16	*halt* limp
	after after you

IV.8.1	*beat him to* driven him by blows into
	Run one let someone run
2	*gests* feats, deeds. The word has a chivalric colouring.
5	*doughty-handed* valiant in fighting. Like *gests* the word *doughty* is slightly archaic and romantic.
6–7	*Not as you served … mine* not as if you were merely obeying orders but as if you were as concerned as I am
7	*shown all Hectors* all behaved like Hector (the great warrior-hero of Troy)
8	*clip* embrace
11	*whole* well (fully healed)
12	*fairy* (another word with archaic romance associations) enchantress
13	*day* light
15	*proof of harness* impenetrable armour
17	*virtue* valour
20	*something* somewhat
21	*nerves* muscles
22	*Get goal for goal of youth* keep up with youth point for point
28	*carbuncled* embossed with jewels
29	*Phoebus' car* the sun-god's chariot
31	*targets* shields
	like the men that owe them as becomes the men who own them
33	*camp this host* accommodate this army
34	*carouses* toasts
35–9	*Trumpeters … approach.* This military command, delivered in a stentorian parade-ground voice, gives the

        scene a brilliant climax. The command is of course instantly obeyed. It marks Antony's last heroic moment in the play.

37   *tabourines* small drums

IV.9   The ear-splitting fanfare that concluded IV.8 is followed at once by the hushed silence of night – a carefully judged theatrical effect.

2   *court of guard* guard room

3   *shiny* moonlit

4   *second hour* (2 a.m.)

5   *shrewd* bad

8-9   *men revolted . . . memory* deserters receive an infamous report in the record of history

8   *record* (accented on the second syllable)

12   *mistress* (the moon). He alludes to the moon's supposed influence in inducing mental disease.
        melancholy melancholia

13   *poisonous damp* dampness that induces sickness
        disponge drop as from a sponge

15-18   *Throw my heart . . . thoughts.* According to current physiology, grief desiccated the heart.

19   *revolt* desertion

20   *in thine own particular* yourself

21   *rank me in register* put me down in its records

22   *master-leaver* runaway servant
        fugitive deserter. As Enobarbus here foretells, he was 'ranked in register' precisely as a deserter by Plutarch (see the headnote to IV.5).

23   (stage direction) *He dies.* Plutarch describes Enobarbus as 'sick of an ague' (see the headnote to IV.5); Shakespeare makes the cause of his death more ambiguous, so that his grief at having deserted Antony seems to assist in hastening his end.

27   *for* a preparation for

29   *raught* reached, laid hold of

30 *Demurely* with a low sound, gently

31-2 *Our hour | Is fully out* the period of our watch is over

V.10.3 *i'th'fire or i'th'air.* Antony is already fighting in two of the elements, earth and water (land and sea); *fire* and *air* would complete the four elements.

4-9 *our foot ... endeavour.* Some editors believe line 7 incomplete; the missing words may have been to the effect 'Let us go up' (to the hills, from which *we may best discover* ...). Other editors think line 7 essentially complete, taking *Where* (line 8) to refer back to *the hills* (line 5); in this case the words *Order ... haven* would be a parenthesis. For the Plutarchan source of these lines, see the first sentence quoted in the head-note to IV.12.

4 *foot* infantry

6 *for sea* to put to sea

7 *put forth* set out from

8 *appointment* equipment

V.11.1 *But being charged* unless we are attacked

   still on land inactive on land

2 *Which, as I take't, we shall* and I assume we shall be left unattacked

4 *hold our best advantage* take up the best possible position

V.12 Plutarch writes: 'The next morning by break of day he went to set those few footmen he had in order upon the hills adjoining unto the city; and there he stood to behold his galleys which departed from the haven and rowed against the galleys of his enemies; and so stood still, looking what exploit his soldiers in them would do. But when by force of rowing they were come near unto them, they first saluted Caesar's men, and then Caesar's men re-saluted them also, and of two armies made but one, and then did altogether row toward the city. When Antonius saw that his men did forsake him and yielded unto Caesar, and that his footmen were broken and overthrown he then fled into the city, crying out that Cleopatra had betrayed him unto them with whom he had made war for her sake. Then she, being afraid of his fury, fled into the tomb which she had caused to be made; and there locked the doors unto her, and shut all the springs of the locks with great bolts; and in the meantime sent unto Antonius to tell him that she was dead' (pages 275–7).

(stage direction) *Alarum afar off, as at a sea fight.* This edition follows F's arrangement. Many editors move this direction to line 3 or, less often, to line 9. In F's arrangement, the battle is joined before Antony and Scarus appear; Antony's first words show that he does not yet know that the fighting has begun. Editors unnecessarily move the direction to a later point on the assumption that Antony's words must correspond to the truth, but the situation gains in irony if they do not. For the noise of a *sea fight*, see the note to the opening stage direction of III.10.

1   *joined* (in battle)

     pine. Compare line 23 below.

3–4   *Swallows ... nests.* Plutarch mentions this as an ill omen before Actium: 'Swallows had bred under the poop of her ship' (page 249).

8   *fretted* chequered

13   *Triple-turned* (from Julius Caesar, from Pompey, from Antony himself)

15   *Makes only wars on thee* makes wars on you alone

16, 25 *charm* enchantress, witch

20   *hearts* men (his soldiers)

21   *spanieled.* F reads 'pannelled'; editors regularly emend to *spanieled*, meaning 'fawned on me like spaniels'.

In *Explorations in Shakespeare's Language* (1962) Hilda M. Hulme makes an original and attractive case for 'pannelled' as a verb formed from two Elizabethan nouns, 'panel' (earlier 'parnel'), meaning 'prostitute', and 'panele', meaning 'sugar'. But if Shakespeare did use this word, the subliminal echo in it of 'spaniel' (which could be spelt 'spannel' or 'spannell') was at least strong enough to produce the phrase *at heels* and dictate the image cluster (*discandy, melt, sweets*) that follows: Shakespeare several times associates dogs with soft or melting sweetmeats as a result of the common practice of feeding them under the table during meals. This and the absence of any firm evidence for the noun 'panel' meaning 'prostitute' in Shakespeare's time make *spanieled* the safer reading.

22   *discandy* become liquid

23   *this pine* (Antony himself)
    barked stripped bare

25   *grave* deadly

27   *my crownet, my chief end* the crown and end of all my activities

28   *right gypsy* true gypsy. Compare the note to I.1.10.
    fast and loose (a cheating game played by gypsies, who got their dupes to bet whether a coiled rope or trap was fast (fixed) or loose)

29   *Beguiled* cheated

30   *Avaunt* begone

33   *Caesar's triumph.* This is the first reference to the coming triumphal procession through Rome to which Caesar as victor in the war would be entitled. See V.1.65–6 and V.2.109–10 for his intention to lead Cleopatra in his triumph.

34   *plebeians* (accented on the first syllable)

35   *spot* stain, blemish

36–7   *most monster-like be shown | For poor'st diminutives, for doits* like a monster be exhibited to undersized weaklings on payment of their small coins. For *doits* some editors retain F's reading, 'Dolts', so that the phrase means 'exhibited to undersized weaklings and fools'; other editors adopt *doits* but interpret *diminutives* as 'small coins'. In favour of *doits* is *The Tempest*, II.2.27–32: 'Were I in England now, as once I was, and had but this fish painted, not a holiday fool there but would give a piece of silver. There would this monster make a man. . . . When they will not give a doit to relieve a lame beggar, they will lay out ten to see a dead Indian.'

37   *doits* coins of very small value

39   *preparèd* (grown long for the purpose)

43–5 *The shirt of Nessus . . . moon.* Antony recalls the death of his supposed ancestor Hercules (sometimes called *Alcides*). The centaur Nessus gave Deiani a, the wife of Hercules, his shirt soaked in poison, assuring her that if she sent it to Hercules it would act as a love-potion. She accordingly sent it, using Lichas as a messenger. When Hercules put on the shirt, it burnt him to death; in his agony he hurled Lichas into the sea. The death of Hercules is the subject of Seneca's tragedy·*Hercules Oetaeus*, which was probably known to Shakespeare.

47   *Subdue my worthiest self* overcome the most heroic part of my nature (that which was most like Hercules)

48   *To the young Roman boy.* The line would be metrically and stylistically improved by the deletion of *young*. Perhaps Shakespeare forgot to remove it after writing *boy*, which makes *young* tautologous.

IV.13.2 *Telamon* (Ajax, who went mad when the shield of Achilles was awarded not to him but to Odysseus)
         the boar of Thessaly (sent by Diana to ravage Calydon, and killed by Meleager)

3   *embossed* (a hunting term) driven to extremity
     monument. See the quotation from Plutarch in the headnote to IV.12.

5   *rive* rend, cleave
6   *going off* departing
10   *bring me* bring me word

IV.14   For Antony's death, Shakespeare follows Plutarch very closely, keeping even the impression of lifelike anti-climax which attends Antony's failure to kill himself at once. He has just received the report of Cleopatra's death:

'Antonius, believing it, said unto himself:

' "What dost thou look for further, Antonius, sith spiteful fortune hath taken from thee the only joy thou hadst, for whom thou yet reservedst thy life?"

'When he had said these words, he went into a chamber and unarmed himself; and being naked said thus:

' "O Cleopatra, it grieveth me not that I have lost thy company, for I will not be long from thee. But I am sorry that, having been so great a captain and Emperor, I am indeed condemned to be judged of less courage and noble mind than a woman."

'Now he had a man of his called Eros, whom he loved and trusted much and whom he had long before caused to swear unto him that he should kill him when he did command him; and then he willed him to keep his promise. His man drawing his sword lift it up as though he had meant to have stricken his master. But turning his head at one side, he thrust his sword into himself and fell down dead at his master's foot. Then said Antonius:

' "O noble Eros, I thank thee for this; and it is valiantly done of thee, to show me what I should do to myself, which thou couldst not do for me."

'Therewithal he took his sword and thrust it into his belly; and so fell down upon a little bed. The wound he had killed him not presently, for the blood stinted a little when he was laid; and when he came somewhat to himself again, he prayed them that were about him to dispatch him. But they all fled out of the chamber, and left him crying out and tormenting himself; until at last there came a secretary unto him called Diomedes, who was commanded to bring him into the tomb or monument where Cleopatra was' (pages 277–9).

2   *that's dragonish* that looks like a dragon

4   *pendent* overhanging

8   *black vesper's pageants* the spectacular moveable shows of evening. *Pageants* were originally floats or wheeled stages of the medieval Mystery plays. Antony's description may owe something to the new moveable scenery of the Jacobean court masque.

9–10   *even with a thought | The rack dislimns* as quick as thought, the drifting cloud (*rack*) wipes out. But there is also a wordplay involving the idea of a *body* (compare line 13) being 'dislimbed' – torn limb from limb – on a rack.

12   *knave* boy

19–20   *Packed cards . . . triumph* shuffled the cards in Caesar's favour and treacherously allowed him to trump my glory. Antony plays on *triumph*, which in Shakespeare's day could also mean a trump card.

23   *robbed me of my sword* (unmanned me)

25   *saucy* insolent

26   *die the death* undergo the punishment of death

29   *unto thy hand* already for you

33   *rendered* surrendered

38   *sevenfold shield of Ajax* (made of brass, lined with seven folds of oxhide)

39   *battery* bombardment

40   *thy continent* what contains you, what holds you in

41   *Apace* quick

42   *pieces* (of armour)

46   *length* (of life)

48–9   *very force entangles | Itself with strength* (the fiercer the struggle, the more tangled and exhausted he becomes – like a trapped animal). J. Dover Wilson compares Sonnet 23, lines 3–4:

> [Like] ... some fierce thing replete with too much rage,
> Whose strength's abundance weakens his own heart.

49 *Seal* finish (as in sealing a will)

50 *Eros! ... Eros!* The repetition of Eros's name in this scene is very insistent. In classical mythology Eros was the god of love.

51 *couch* lie

52 *sprightly* high-spirited, lively. (But a secondary meaning – 'ghostly' – may also be present.)
  port bearing, demeanour

53 *Dido and her Aeneas.* In Book 6 of Virgil's *Aeneid*, when Aeneas visits the underworld, Dido refuses to meet her former lover. Antony chooses to recall them simply as famous lovers. But there are further similarities and significant differences between Dido and Aeneas and Cleopatra and himself. Dido, like Cleopatra, was queen over an African realm; but, unlike Cleopatra, she did not succeed in deflecting her lover from his Roman 'duty'.
  want troops lack followers, retinue

54 *all the haunt be ours* everyone will follow us. (But since everyone there will be ghosts, they will be 'ghost-haunted' too.)

58 *Quartered* cut into quarters
  o'er green Neptune's back on the sea

59 *to lack* for lacking

60 *less noble mind* (in apposition with *I* in line 57)

61 *our Caesar* (that is, our Roman Caesar)

63 *exigent* final emergency, moment of extreme need

65 *inevitable prosecution* pursuit from which there is no escape

72 *windowed* placed as in a window

73   *with pleached arms* with hands bound behind him.
      Another possible explanation, 'with folded arms'
      (the conventional melancholy posture), seems less
      likely.

74   *corrigible* submissive

74-5 *subdued | To penetrative shame* humbled with the sense
      of piercing shame

76   *branded* exposed with brutal clarity (as with a brand)

77   *His baseness that ensued* the abject humiliation of the
      man who followed

80   *pardon me* excuse me from doing it

83   *precedent* (accented on the second syllable) former

86   *worship* worth, honour

87   *Lo thee!* there you are

98   *by their brave instruction* by teaching me a lesson in
      bravery

98-9 *got upon me | A nobleness in record* have beaten me in
      winning a noble place in history

104   (stage direction) *Decretas.* In North's Plutarch this
      character's name is given as 'Dercetaeus'; in F the
      name occurs twice in full in the form adopted in this
      edition, and once in full as 'Dercetus'. The abbreviated
      speech prefixes '*Decre.*' (once) and '*Dec.*' (three times)
      also point to 'Decretas' as Shakespeare's preferred
      form.

107   *his period* its end

113   *enter me with* recommend me to

117   *Sufficing strokes for* strokes sufficient for

122   *Which never shall be found* a thing that will never hap-
      pen (that Cleopatra should *dispose with Caesar*)

123   *disposed* come to terms

124   *purged* allayed, cured

133-4 *live to wear ... out* outlive

136   *To grace it* by favouring it

136-7 *Bid ... and we* if we bid ..., we

268

V.15   Plutarch writes:

> '... and so he was carried in his men's arms into the
> entry of the monument. Notwithstanding, Cleopatra
> would not open the gates, but came to the high
> windows, and cast out certain chains and ropes, in the
> which Antonius was trussed; and Cleopatra her own
> self, with two women only which she had suffered to
> come with her into these monuments, triced Antonius
> up.
>
> 'They that were present to behold it said they never
> saw so pitiful a sight. For they plucked up poor
> Antonius, all bloody as he was and drawing on with
> pangs of death, who holding up his hands to Cleo-
> patra raised up himself as well as he could. It was a hard
> thing for these women to do, to lift him up. But Cleo-
> patra stooping down with her head, putting to all her
> strength to her uttermost power, did lift him up with
> much ado and never let go her hold ...' (pages 279–
> 80).

(stage direction) *aloft*. The staging of the scenes in the
monument has provoked much discussion; and whatever is said must be conjectural. It may be, as J. Dover
Wilson suggests, that a flat-roofed wooden structure
was brought on to the stage; it would be placed over
the trapdoor, through which Cleopatra and her maids
would enter it. They would then take their places on
the roof.

4–5   *we ... Our ... our* (royal plural)

10   *sphere*. In the Ptolemaic astronomy the sun was fixed
in a crystalline sphere and, along with the other
planets, revolved round the earth. If it burned its
sphere, it would fly off into space, leaving the earth in
darkness (*darkling*).

11   *varying shore o'th'world*. This is usually taken as a
sublime pictorial image – the world seen as an island
with an irregular coastline, or possibly a coastline
variegated in light and darkness. The word *shore* may,

however, be a term of contempt, meaning 'sewer'. 'Common shore' was regularly used for 'common sewer' in Shakespeare's day. Cleopatra would then mean that the world without Antony is nothing but a ceaselessly flowing sewer – just as later, when Antony dies, she finds *this dull world . . . No better than a sty* (lines 61–2). In these concluding scenes there are several other expressions of contempt for the world, which take up Antony's reference, at the beginning of the play, to *Our dungy earth* (I.1.35). (The terms 'common shores' and 'sty' occur in a single scene of *Pericles*, probably written not long after *Antony and Cleopatra*: see *Pericles*, IV.6.93 and 174.)

13–31   It has been argued, by J. Dover Wilson and others, that Shakespeare made a false start which he then failed to delete. The result, according to this argument, is that we have an unnecessary passage (from line 13, *Peace!*, to line 31, *Assist, good friends*) and consequently two sets of unnecessary repetitions: Cleopatra's instructions to pull Antony up, and Antony's line *I am dying, Egypt, dying*. Against this, the integrity of the F text has been defended by David Galloway (*Notes and Queries*, 1958, pages 330–35). It seems, on balance, preferable to hold to the F text, since this is a play uncommonly concerned to render – in some of its scenes, at least – the feel of life as it is lived and especially its tendency to untidiness and anti-climax. That tendency is nowhere more apparent than in this sequence of Antony's death. If the passage objected to by Dover Wilson seems confused and repetitive, that may be exactly what Shakespeare intended.

19   *importune death* keep death waiting

21   *dare not* (she dare not open the gate or descend)

23   *imperious* imperial

25   *Be brooched with me* have me as its chief ornament (*brooch*)

26   *operation* power (referring to *drugs*, line 25)

28   *still conclusion* quietly impassive judgement

29   *Demuring upon me* looking at me demurely (with an irritatingly complacent sobriety)

33   *heaviness* (1) weight; (2) sorrow

34   *Juno* (the wife of Jupiter; the queen-goddess of heaven)

35   *Mercury* (the winged messenger of the gods)

38   *Die when thou hast lived* (that is, don't die until you have lived once again)

39   *Quicken* come to life

42–58   This is closely based on Plutarch: 'Antonius made her cease her lamenting, and called for wine, either because he was athirst, or else for that he thought thereby to hasten his death. When he had drunk, he earnestly prayed her and persuaded her that she would seek to save her life, if she could possible without reproach and dishonour; and that chiefly she should trust Proculeius above any man else about Caesar; and, as for himself, that she should not lament nor sorrow for the miserable change of his fortune at the end of his days; but rather that she should think him the more fortunate for the former triumphs and honours he had received, considering that while he lived he was the noblest and greatest prince of the world, and that now he was overcome not cowardly, but valiantly, a Roman by another Roman' (pages 280–81).

44   *false* treacherous

       housewife (pronounced 'huzzif') hussy

45   *offence* insults

59   *woo't* wouldst thou

64   *garland* crown, glory

65   *The soldier's pole.* The meaning is disputed. Suggestions include 'polestar', 'standard', 'maypole', and, as a possible secondary meaning to one of these, 'phallus'. The first of these seems the best.

66   *The odds is gone* there is now no difference of value between things

67   *remarkable* wonderful

72   *No more but e'en a woman* no more than just a woman (perhaps in reply to Iras's *Empress!*)

73   *such poor passion.* The reference is probably not simply to passionate grief but to *hysterica passio*, a condition common to women, according to medical views current in Shakespeare's time. It was caused by strong passion; its symptoms included swooning. As a woman, Cleopatra is as subject to it as any other woman, irrespective of rank. (See J. H. Walter, *Notes and Queries*, 1969, pages 138–9.)

74   *chares* chores, tasks

77   *naught* worthless, useless

78   *sottish* stupid, foolish

84   *Good sirs* (addressed to the women; an Elizabethan usage)

90   *briefest* swiftest

V.1   Plutarch narrates how one of Antony's guardsmen called Dercetaeus took Antony's sword 'and brought Octavius Caesar the first news of his death, and showed him his sword that was bloodied. Caesar hearing these news straight withdrew himself into a secret place of his tent, and there burst out with tears, lamenting his hard and miserable fortune that had been his friend and brother-in-law, his equal in the Empire, and companion with him in sundry great exploits and battles. Then he called for all his friends, and showed them the letters Antonius had written to him, and his answers also sent him again, during their quarrel and strife; and how fiercely and proudly the other answered him to all just and reasonable matters he wrote unto him' (pages 281–2).

2–3   *Being so frustrate . . . makes* tell him that, since he is so helplessly defeated, his delays are a mere mockery

5   *thus* (with a naked sword)

14   *breaking* (1) destruction, end; (2) disclosure, telling

15   *crack* (1) explosive sound; (2) breach, rift (perhaps 'convulsion')

16   *civil* city

19   *moiety* half

21   *self* same

30   *Our most persisted deeds* what we most persist in doing

31   *Waged equal with him* were equally matched in him

36   *followed* pursued
        launch lance

38   *such a declining day* a declining day (or sun) such as you have shown

39   *stall* dwell

41   *sovereign* potent

42   *competitor* partner (but see the note to I.4.3)

43   *In top of all design* in worthiest enterprise

46   *his* its

46   *Unreconciliable* in perpetual conflict with each other

47-8   *should divide | Our equalness to this* should sunder us, who were so equally partnered, in this way

49   *meeter season* more suitable moment

50   *looks out of him* shows from his appearance

57   *by some of ours* from some of my representatives

63   *passion* grief

64   *greatness* loftiness of spirit

65-6   *her life in Rome . . . triumph* her presence alive in Rome in my triumph would make it famous for ever

74   *hardly* reluctantly

75   *still* constantly

V.2   For his last scene, by far the longest in the play, Shakespeare runs together several occasions which in Plutarch are distinct. The immediate result is a condensation of time: Shakespeare's Cleopatra dies very shortly after Antony; in Plutarch events are more protracted. A perhaps more important difference concerns Cleopatra's emotional state during this final

273

phase in her story. In Plutarch, overwhelmed with grief, she physically maltreats herself: 'she had knocked her breast so pitifully, that she had martyred it and in divers places had raised ulcers and inflammations, so that she fell into a fever withal'; and when, shortly after, Caesar visits her he finds her 'marvellously disfigured; both for that she had plucked her hair from her head, as also for that she had martyred all her face with her nails; and, besides, her voice was small and trembling, her eyes sunk into her head with continual blubbering, and moreover they might see the most part of her stomach torn in sunder' (pages 286-7). Shakespeare could make no use of this, or of the account of her visit to Antony's grave; his Cleopatra, who has twice mentioned her *resolution* in IV.15 (at lines 49 and 90), is an altogether less broken figure, though at the same time her *desolation* is convincingly established. For his conception of her inner transformation, Shakespeare may have owed something to Horace's Cleopatra ode (I.37), especially its last three stanzas:

Yet she preferred a finer style of dying:
She did not, like a woman, shirk the dagger
   Or seek by speed at sea
To change her Egypt for obscurer shores,

But, gazing on her desolated palace
With a calm smile, unflinchingly laid hands on
   The angry asps until
Her veins had drunk the deadly poison deep,

And, death-determined, fiercer then than ever,
Perished. Was she to grace a haughty triumph,
   Dethroned, paraded by
The rude Liburnians? Not Cleopatra!

       (*The Odes of Horace*, translated by James Michie,
                  Penguin Books, pages 86-7)

For the rest, Shakespeare closely followed Plutarch, except for Cleopatra's 'dream' of Antony, which was his own invention.

2   *A better life.* The philosophical values of the Stoics are adopted here. The good man (or woman) despised the gifts of fortune and triumphed over adversity by showing resolution or inner constancy. Compare Antony's words to Eros at IV.14.60–62 and to his other followers at IV.14.136–8.

3   *knave* servant

5   *that thing* (suicide)

7–8   *never palates more the dung, | The beggar's nurse and Caesar's* never more tastes the produce of the mere earth (*dung*), which gives life to all men, whatever their place in society. Compare I.1.35, *Our dungy earth.*

10   *study on* think carefully about

14   *to be deceived* whether I am deceived or not

15   *That have* since I have

17   *keep decorum* do the appropriate thing

20   *as* that

23   *Make your full reference* refer yourself wholly (that is, put yourself wholly into his hands)

26   *sweet dependency* willingness to be submissive

27   *pray in aid for kindness* ask you to help him in being kind to you

29–30   *I am ... got* I do homage to his good fortune and I formally acknowledge his authority

29   *send him* send him acknowledgement of

34   (stage direction) *The soldiers approach Cleopatra from behind.* This direction is editorial. The stage business here is unclear and can only be conjectured. Shakespeare may have left it deliberately vague so as to make it adaptable to different stage conditions. What seems to happen is that the soldiers reach Cleopatra from behind, possibly using ladders from the pit up on to the main stage.

41   *Relieved* rescued

42 *languish* (lingering disease)

45 *well acted* duly exercised. But *acted* is ambiguous; it also suggests 'assumed as a role', 'imitated'.

46 *let come forth* allow to be displayed

48 *babes and beggars* (those to whom 'relief' is usually given)

50 *If idle talk ... necessary* if useless words have to be used for once

51 *This mortal house* (her body). According to Plutarch, Cleopatra did in fact maltreat herself; see the headnote to this scene.

53 *pinioned* (1) with arms tied behind, shackled; (2) like a bird with its wings clipped

54 *once* ever

   chastised (accented on the first syllable)

56 *varletry* mob

60 *Blow* deposit their eggs on

   into abhorring so that I become an object of disgust

61 *pyramides* (four syllables, accented on the second)

62 *extend* magnify

71 *empress.* The title, used by a Roman, implies considerable respect. Dolabella is flattering Cleopatra.

75 *trick* way, habit

79–92 With Cleopatra's 'dream', compare Lady Percy's elegiac description of the dead Hotspur (*2 Henry IV*, II.3.17–38).

79 *stuck* were set

81 *The little O o'th'earth.* F has 'The little o'th'earth'. Most modern editors read 'The little O, the earth'. But it seems essential to keep the very Shakespearian phrase *o'th'earth*; and the likeliest explanation is that a monosyllabic noun has dropped out, so that Shakespeare wrote something like 'orb o'th'earth' (*Coriolanus*, V.6.126), though he is perhaps unlikely to have used 'orb' here, since it occurs four lines later (line 85). *O*, meaning 'tiny circle', is paralleled in *Henry V*, Prologue 13, 'this wooden O', and, meaning 'zero',

'nothing', in *King Lear*, I.4.188–9, 'an 0 without a figure'.

82–3   *his reared arm | Crested the world* (a metaphor from heraldry: a coat of arms could have a raised arm as a crest)

83–4   *propertied ... spheres* as musical in quality as all the spheres (alluding to the Pythagorean doctrine of the harmonious sound created by the movement of the planetary spheres, which was normally inaudible to human beings)

84   *and that to friends.* The meaning required seems to be 'when speaking to friends' and is contrasted with what follows. The text may be corrupt here.

85   *quail* make quail

87   *an Antony it was.* This is F's reading. Most editors adopt the emendation 'an autumn 'twas'. This is plausible, but emendation does not seem absolutely necessary. If it is objected that the F reading does not make sense, it should be remembered that Cleopatra is speaking rhapsodically and with startlingly abrupt metaphors (as the following lines show, for example, *In his livery | Walked crowns and crownets*). The idea of Antony as a perpetually plenteous harvest is amply prepared for in *bounty* and *winter*; an audience would understand with no difficulty. For the phrase *an Antony*, compare II.5.14, IV.2.18, and line 99 of this scene.

88–90   *His delights ... lived in* just as dolphins show their backs above the water, so Antony rose above the pleasures that were his element. Dolphins were themselves thought to be highly sensual creatures.

90   *The element* (the sea)
       livery service

91   *crowns and crownets* kings and princes

92   *plates* silver coins

96   *if ... one such* if there neither is nor ever was such a man. This reading keeps F's 'nor', and takes the con-

	struction to be 'neither [understood] ... nor'. Some editors emend *nor* to 'or'.
97	*It's past the size of dreaming* no mere dream could approach it
97–100	*Nature wants stuff ... quite* nature lacks the material to compete with fancy in the creation of fantastic (*strange*) forms, yet to imagine an Antony would be a masterpiece of conception, natural rather than fantastic, and entirely discrediting the figments of fancy
99	*piece* masterpiece
103	*but I do* if I do not
104	*rebound* reflection
105	*My very heart at root* to the bottom of my heart
111–90	Shakespeare precedes and follows Caesar's visit to Cleopatra with Dolabella's clear assurances that Caesar intends to make her walk in his triumph. In her interview with Caesar, and particularly in her dealings with Seleucus, Cleopatra is probably deceiving Caesar into believing that she wants to live. Shakespeare leaves room for doubt, but Plutarch's account is unambiguous:

'... Cleopatra began to clear and excuse herself for that she had done, laying all to the fear she had of Antonius. Caesar, in contrary manner, reproved her in every point. Then she suddenly altered her speech, and prayed him to pardon her, as though she were afraid to die and desirous to live. At length, she gave him a brief and memorial of all the ready money and treasure she had. But by chance there stood Seleucus by, one of her treasurers, who to seem a good servant, came straight to Caesar to disprove Cleopatra, that she had not set in all but kept many things back of purpose. Cleopatra was in such a rage with him that she flew upon him, and took him by the hair of the head, and boxed him well-favouredly. Caesar fell a-laughing and parted the fray.

' "Alas," said she, "O Caesar, is not this a great

278

shame and reproach, that thou having vouchsafed to
take the pains to come unto me, and hast done me this
honour, poor wretch and caitiff creature brought into
this pitiful and miserable estate, and that mine own
servants should come now to accuse me; though it may
be I have reserved some jewels and trifles meet for
women, but not for me, poor soul, to set out myself
withal. but meaning to give some pretty presents and
gifts unto Octavia and Livia, that, they making means
and intercession for me to thee, thou mightest yet
extend thy favour and mercy upon me?"

'Caesar was glad to hear her say so, persuading himself thereby that she had yet a desire to save her life.
So he made her answer that he did not only give her
that to dispose of at her pleasure which she had kept
back, but further promised to use her more honour-
ably and bountifully than she would think for. And so
he took his leave of her, supposing he had deceived
her. But indeed he was deceived himself' (pages
287–9).

120   *sir* lord, master
121   *project* (accented on the first syllable) set forth
122   *To make it clear* as to make it seem innocent
125   *enforce* emphasize
126   *apply yourself* conform
129   *lay on me a cruelty* make me look cruel (that is, inflict
      on me an appearance of being cruel)
134   *may* (that is, may leave, or set out on a journey (for
      anywhere in the world))
135   *scutcheons* (captured) shields
138   *brief* summary
140   *Not petty things admitted* except for trivial items
146   *seel* sew up (see the note to III.13.112)
151   *pomp is followed* people in high estate are served
      Mine my followers
152   *shift estates* change places
153–4 *does | Even make me wild* simply makes me mad

279

155   *hired* paid for, bought

158   *rarely* exceptionally

163   *Parcel* number off one by one, read out a list of. But this merges with another sense: 'extend', 'augment'.

164   *envy* malice

165   *lady* suitable for a lady

166   *Immoment toys* unimportant little things
        dignity worth

167   *modern* ordinary

169   *Livia* (Caesar's wife)

170-71   *unfolded | With* exposed by

171   *one that I have bred* one of my household

173   *cinders* burning coals

174   *chance* fortune
        a man (not a eunuch)

175   *Forbear* leave, go

176   *misthought* misjudged

178   *We answer others' merits in our name* we are responsible for the faults committed by others in our name
        merits deserts (good or bad; here bad)

183   *make prize* haggle, bargain

185   *Make not your thoughts your prisons* don't think yourself a prisoner, since you are free

191   *words me* puts me off with mere words

194   *Hie thee again* hurry back

198-203   Based on Plutarch: Dolabella '. . . did bear no evil will unto Cleopatra. He sent her word secretly, as she had requested him, that Caesar determined to take his journey through Syria, and that within three days he would send her away before with her children' (pages 289-90).

199   *makes religion* binds me absolutely

208   *puppet* (actor in a pantomime). Cleopatra imagines herself and Iras drawn along on a wheeled stage, taking part in an 'Egyptian' tableau.

209   *Mechanic slaves* common labourers

212   *Rank of gross diet* smelling of bad food

213 *drink* inhale

214 *Saucy* insolent
     lictors (magistrates' officers). They will be treated by
     the lictors, so Cleopatra imagines, as ungently as
     beadles treated prostitutes in Elizabethan England.

215 *scald* scurvy, contemptible

216 *Ballad us* sing our story in ballads
     quick quick-witted

217 *Extemporally* in improvised performances

220 *boy my greatness* reduce my greatness to what an in-
     competent boy-actor can manage. Shakespeare's
     Cleopatra was, on the contrary, written for a boy-actor
     to whose skill and virtuosity these lines implicitly
     pay tribute.

228 *Cydnus.* See II.2.191–231.

229 *Sirrah* (an address used to inferiors, male or female)

230 *dispatch* (1) hasten; (2) finish. Cleopatra plays on both
     senses.

231 *chare* chore, task

232 (stage direction) *Exit Iras.* This is not in F. Some
     editors give Charmian an exit too, bringing her back
     with Iras at the Clown's departure.

233–79 Plutarch writes: 'Now whilst she was at dinner there
     came a countryman, and brought her a basket. The
     soldiers that warded at the gates asked him straight
     what he had in his basket. He opened the basket and
     took out the leaves that covered the figs, and showed
     them that they were figs he brought. They all of them
     marvelled to see so goodly figs. The countryman
     laughed to hear them, and bade them take some if they
     would. They believed he told them truly, and so bade
     him carry them in' (page 291).

236 *What* how

238 *placed* fixed

240 *fleeting* changeful. Since the moon 'changed' monthly,
     it presided over the realm of mutable nature. In choos-
     ing to die, Cleopatra is leaving the moon's domain.

There is also a possible allusion to Isis, the Egyptian moon-goddess, in whose *habiliments* Cleopatra had earlier appeared (see III.6.16–19).

241 (stage direction) *Clown* countryman, rustic

242 *Avoid* go

243– In the period after Actium Cleopatra had investigated
312 the most painless ways of dying. Plutarch writes: 'So, when she had daily made divers and sundry proofs, she found none of them all she had proved so fit as the biting of an aspic, the which causeth only a heaviness of the head, without swounding or complaining, and bringeth a great desire also to sleep, with a little sweat in the face, and so by little and little taketh away the senses and vital powers, no living creature perceiving that the patients feel any pain' (page 267).

243–78 *the pretty worm . . . joy o'th'worm.* In the scene with the Clown, *worm* has three applications: (1) snake, asp (as at line 243); (2) the male sexual organ (as at line 255); (3) earth-worm (as at line 270).

247 *immortal* (the Clown's mistake for 'mortal'. But compare Cleopatra's words at lines 279–80.)

250 *of* from

251 *honest* (1) truthful; (2) chaste

252 *lie* (1) tell lies; (2) have sexual relations with a man

253 *died* (another sexual allusion; see the note to I.2.138)

257 *falliable* (another mistake by the Clown, presumably for 'infallible')

262 *do his kind* act according to his nature

264–76 *the worm is . . . mar five.* Shakespeare seems to be making, through the Clown, a detached comment on the powers of sex, which, according as they are used, may be good or evil. The Clown's drily unromantic admonitions sound an astringent note immediately before the play's exalted conclusion.

267 *Take thou no care* don't worry

273 *dress* prepare for cooking. There may also be a secondary sense of 'put on clothes'.

274   *whoreson* (Elizabethan slang) accursed

280   *Immortal longings* longings for immortality

282   *Yare* quickly

285   *The luck of Caesar.* Octavius was noted for his good
       fortune or 'felicity'. Compare Antony's phrase at
       IV.14.76, *fortunate Caesar.*

285-6 *which ... wrath* (the gods give men good fortune in
       order that they may punish them for having enjoyed
       it)

286   *after* subsequent

288-9 *I am fire ... life.* Man was thought to be composed of
       four elements, two higher (*fire* and *air*) and two lower
       (earth and water).

289   *baser* lower (but also with a contemptuous connota-
       tion)

291   (stage direction) *Iras falls and dies.* F has no direction
       here. Some editors take it that Iras dies simply of grief,
       but it seems best to assume that she has already applied
       an asp to herself by the time Cleopatra kisses her.

292   *aspic* asp

299   *This* (Iras's death)

300   *curlèd* with curled hair. Perhaps Cleopatra thinks of
       Antony as she first met him, *barbered ten times o'er*
       (II.2.229).

301   *spend that kiss* slake his passion on her

302   *mortal wretch* deadly little thing. *Wretch*, like *fool*
       (line 304), was often, as here, an affectionate term.

303   *intrinsicate* mysteriously intricate

307   *Unpolicied* outwitted in 'policy' or statecraft
       eastern star (the morning star, Venus)

308   *my baby at my breast.* Plutarch reports that Cleopatra
       was bitten in the arm (pages 292–3). With Shake-
       speare's version compare Thomas Nashe's *Christ's
       Tears over Jerusalem* (1593): 'at thy breasts (as at
       Cleopatra's) aspises shall be put out to nurse' (*Works*,
       ed. McKerrow, II.140).

312   *What* why

313   *vile* worthless, contemptible. F reads 'wilde', which is possible. But 'vile' was often spelt 'vilde', and 'v' and 'w' were not uncommonly confused, so that the emendation adopted here is not difficult. *Vile* seems preferable to 'wild' on grounds of meaning; for other dismissals of the world, compare I.1.35 (*dungy earth*) and IV.15.61–2 (*dull world . . . sty*).

315   *windows* eyelids

316   *Phoebus* (the sun-god)

317   *Of* by
        awry crooked

318   *and then play* (alluding to lines 231–2)
        (stage direction) *rustling* clattering

320   *Too slow a messenger.* For once Caesar's administrative efficiency is defective; compare the note to III.6.31.

322   *beguiled* deceived

324–6   Based on Plutarch:

'. . . But when they had opened the doors they found Cleopatra stark dead laid upon a bed of gold, attired and arrayed in her royal robes, and one of her two women, which was called Iras, dead at her feet; and her other woman called Charmion half dead and trembling, trimming the diadem which Cleopatra ware upon her head. One of the soldiers, seeing her, angrily said unto her:

'"Is that well done, Charmion?"

'"Very well," said she again, "and meet for a princess descended from the race of so many noble kings."

'She said no more, but fell down dead hard by the bed' (pages 291–2).

329   *Touch their effects* meet with realization, are realized

334   *levelled at* guessed at

337   *simple* of humble condition

329–42   See the note to lines 324–6.

344   *like sleep* as if she were asleep

345   *As* as if

346   *toil* net, snare

grace beauty, seductiveness

347   *vent* discharge

       blown deposited (compare the note to line 60). The usual explanation, 'swollen', seems less likely. In the next speech the First Guard explains what the *something* is.

353   *conclusions infinite* innumerable experiments

357   *clip* (an amatory metaphor) embrace

359   *Strike* touch, afflict

360   *than his glory which* than is the glory of him who

364   *solemnity* ceremonious occasion

AN ACCOUNT OF THE TEXT

THE date of the composition of *Antony and Cleopatra* has to be conjectured. A terminal point is provided by the Stationers' Register for 20 May 1608, when the publisher Edward Blount entered two 'books', *Pericles, Prince of Tyre* and *Antony and Cleopatra*. Secondly, in 1607 Samuel Daniel's tragedy *Cleopatra*, which was first published in 1594, appeared in a new edition, 'newly altered', and this edition contains revisions which can be argued to have been influenced by Shakespeare's play as it was performed on the stage. An earlier limit is less easy to fix. Most scholars nowadays assign the play to the years 1606–7, its immediate predecessor probably being *Macbeth* (1606).

The only authoritative text of *Antony and Cleopatra* is the one included in the collected edition of Shakespeare's plays, the first Folio (1623). It was probably printed direct from Shakespeare's own manuscript and not from some intermediate source such as a regularized prompt-copy. It shows many signs of the author's hand which would probably have been eliminated had a copyist working for the theatre been the writer of the manuscript. These authorial signs may be grouped under three heads: evidence from spelling; evidence from which conjectures may be made about Shakespeare's handwriting; and evidence from stage directions.

Textual critics have assembled a good deal of information about Shakespeare's probable spelling habits. They seem to have been rather old-fashioned, even archaic, by the standards of the 1620s. The Folio text shows a number of such individual spellings which suggest the presence of a Shakespearian manuscript, for instance, 'reciding' (for 'residing'), I.3.103; 'triumpherate' (for 'triumvirate'), III.6.28; and 'arrant' (for 'errand'), III.13.104. Some of the proper names are also of interest, since they can be compared with the originals which Shakespeare found in North's Plutarch, for example, 'Scicion' for North's 'Sicyon', and 'Camidius', 'Camidias', and 'Camindius' for North's 'Canidius'. The spelling 'Scicion', with its unusual initial 'Sc', may be Shakespearian, since in the scene in the anonymous play *Sir Thomas More* which is thought by good judges to be very probably in Shakespeare's handwriting the form 'scilens' (for 'silence') occurs; in the first Quarto of *2 Henry IV*, 'Scilens' occurs eighteen times for the name of the character 'Silence'; and in *Coriolanus* the form 'Scicinius' several times occurs for North's 'Sicinius'. In the case of 'Camidius' etc., the question arises whether Shakespeare did not deliberately intend a form beginning with 'Cam', since the form 'Canidius' nowhere occurs in the Folio text. Another odd form is 'Thidias' for North's 'Thyreus'. This may be a deliberate change, as J. Dover Wilson suggested, to make for ease of speaking.

Secondly, it can be argued that some of the misprints in the Folio text arose from the peculiarities of Shakespeare's handwriting. An instance is 'foretell' for 'fertile' (I.2.40), where Shakespeare probably wrote 'fertill' in such a way as to make the confusion easily possible.

Thirdly, the stage directions are such as to suggest an authorial imagination rather than a mind more narrowly intent on directives for a stage performance. Some of them leave the particulars vague, for example, '*Enter two or three Seruants, with a Banket*' (II.7.0). In others the wording suggests a mind in the process of conceiving an effect, as in '*Enter the Guard rustling in, and Dolabella*' (V.2.318). Some are of special interest in showing how Shakespeare imagined a stage grouping, for example, '*Enter Anthony, Cæsar, Octauia betweene them*' (II.3.0), or elsewhere possibly the order in which characters entered the stage, for example, '*Enter Agrippa, Mecenas, and Cæsar*' (III.6.0), where the chief character appears last, or '*Enter Proculeius, Cæsar, Gallus, Mecenas, and others of his Traine*' (V.2.110), where Proculeius is placed first because he has supervised the capture of Cleopatra and is now leading his master to her.

The Folio text is least reliable in its punctuation and lineation: in many cases both clearly need correction. It is, finally, noteworthy that (leaving aside '*Actus Primus. Scœna Prima*' at the beginning) the Folio text is entirely without act and scene division.

COLLATIONS

These lists are selective. Quotations from the first Folio (F) are given in the original spelling, except that 'long s' (ʃ) has been replaced by 's'.

I

The following is a list of departures in the present text from that of F, whose reading is given on the right of the square bracket. Only those readings are included which affect meaning; obvious misprints are not listed. Many of the emendations accepted here were first made by eighteenth-century editors of the play. Those first found in seventeenth-century reprints of the Folio (F2 and F3) are indicated.

THE CHARACTERS IN THE PLAY] *not in* F

I.1.	39	On] One
	50	whose] F2; who
I.2.	4	charge] change
	40	fertile] foretell
	63–4	CHARMIAN Our . . . mend! Alexas – come] *Char.* Our . . . mend. *Alexas.* Come
	81	Saw you my lord?] F2; Saue you, my Lord.
	114	ho, the news] how the newes
	115	FIRST ATTENDANT] 1. *Mes.*
	116	SECOND ATTENDANT] 2. *Mes.*

I.2.	119	MESSENGER] 3. *Mes.*
	138	occasion] an occasion
	180	leave] loue
	185	Hath] F2; Haue
	194	hair] heire
	196	place is under us, requires] F2; places vnder vs, require
I.3.	43	services] Seruicles
	80	blood; no more.] blood no more?
	82	my] F2; *not in* F
I.4.	3	Our] One
	8	Vouchsafed] vouchsafe
	9	abstract] F2; abstracts
	30	chid] chid:
	44	deared] fear'd
	46	lackeying] lacking
	56	wassails] Vassailes
	66	browsèd'st] F2; brows'd
	75	we] F2; me
I.5.	5	time] time:
	24	burgonet] F2; Burganet
	48	arrogant] Arme-gaunt
	50	dumbed] dumbe
		he, sad] he sad,
	61	man] F2; mans
II.1.	16,18, 38	MENAS] *Mene.*
	21	waned] wand
	41	warred] F2; wan'd
	43-4	greater. .... all,] greater, ... all:
II.2.	111	soldier only.] Souldier, onely
	120-21	staunch, from ... world I] staunch from ... world: I
	125	not so,] not, say
	126	reproof] proofe
	151	hand.] hand
	166-7	ANTONY What ... strength? CAESAR By land, great] *Anth.* What ... land? *Cæsar.* Great,

199 lovesick with them. The] Loue-sicke. | With them the

209 glow] gloue

II.3.   23 afeard] a feare

25 thee; no more but when to thee.] thee no more but: when to thee,

31 away, 'tis] alway 'tis

II.5. 10–11 river; there, | My ... off,] Riuer there | My ... off.

12 Tawny-finned] Tawny fine

28 him, there] him. | There

43 is] 'tis

II.6.   16 the] F2; *not in* F

39 ALL THE TRIUMVIRS] *Omnes.*

53 There is] ther's

66 meanings] meaning

69 of] F3; *not in* F

II.7.   4 high-coloured] F2; high Conlord

90 part then is] part, then he is

98 grows] F2; grow

111 BOY (*sings*)] The Song.

118 you off. Our] you of our

126 father's] Father

127–8 ENOBARBUS Take heed you fall not. | Menas, I'll not on shore. MENAS No,] *Eno.* Take heed you fall not *Menas:* Ile not on shore, | No

130 a loud] aloud

III.1.   5 SILIUS] *Romaine.*

27,34 SILIUS] *Rom.*

III.2.   10 AGRIPPA] *Ant.*

16 figures] Figure

59 wept] weepe

III.4. 6–7 of me; when ... honour,] of me, | When ... Honour:

8 them, most] then most

9 took't] look't

24 yours] F2; your

III.4.	30	Your] F2; You
	38	has] F2; he's
III.5.	12	Then, world, thou hast] Then would thou hadst
		chaps,] chaps
	14	the one the other] the other
III.6.	13	he there] hither
		kings of kings] King of Kings
	29	and, being, that] And being that,
	61	obstruct] abstract
III.7.	5	Is't not denounced] If not, denounc'd
	14	Photinus, an eunuch,] *Photinus* an Eunuch,
	35	muleters] F2; Militers
	69	leader's led] Leaders leade
	72	CANIDIUS] *Ven.*
	78	Well I] Well, I
III.10.	14	June] F2; Inne
	27	he] his
III.11.	19	that] them
	47	seize] F2; cease
	58	tow] stowe
	59	Thy] The
III.13.	55	Caesar] *Cæsars*
	56	embraced] embrace
	74	this: in deputation] this in disputation,
	77	Till from] Tell him, from
	90	me. Of late, when] me of late. When
	112–13	eyes, | In our own filth drop] eyes | In our owne filth, drop
	137	whipped for] whipt. For
	162	Caesarion smite] Cæsarian smile
	165	discandying] discandering
	168	sits] sets
	198	preys on] prayes in
IV.1.	3	combat] Combat.
IV.2.	19	ALL THE SERVANTS] *Omnes.*
	38	fall! My hearty friends,] fall (my hearty Friends)
IV.3.	9	THIRD SOLDIER] I

IV.4.   5 too.] too, *Anthony.*
        6–8 ANTONY Ah ... this. CLEOPATRA Sooth, la,]
             for? Ah ... this, | Sooth-law
         13 daff't] daft
         24 CAPTAIN] *Alex.*
         25 ALL THE SOLDIERS] *All.*

IV.5. 1, 3, 6 SOLDIER] *Eros*
         17 Dispatch. Enobarbus!] Dispatch *Enobarbus.*

IV.6.   36 do't, I feel.] doo't. I feele

IV.8.   2 gests] guests
         18 My] F2; Mine
         23 favouring] sauouring

IV.12.   4 augurers] Auguries
         21 spanieled] pannelled
         37 doits] Dolts

IV.14.   4 towered] toward
         10 dislimns] dislimes
         19 Caesar] *Cæsars*
        104 ho!] how?

  107, 134 ALL THE GUARDS] *All.*
        111 DECRETAS] *Dercetus.*

IV.15. 25–6 me. If ... operation,] me, if ... operation.
         40 ALL THE GUARDS] *All.*
         72 e'en] in
         82 What, what,] What, what

V.1. 28, 31 AGRIPPA] *Dol., Dola.*
         59 live] leaue
         70 ALL CAESAR'S ATTENDANTS] *All.*

V.2.   34–5 it. GALLUS You] it. *Pro.* You
         81 little O o'th'earth] little o'th'earth
        104 smites] suites
        216 Ballad] F2; Ballads
             o'tune] a Tune
        223 my] F2; mine
        313 vile] wilde
        317 awry] away

293

2

Rejected emendations

Below are listed instances where the present text either preserves readings of F (modernized according to the principles of this edition) that have often, with some plausibility, been emended, or introduces an emendation different from the one usually accepted. Emendations found in some modern editions of the play are given after the square brackets, separated by semi-colons where there are more than one.

I.1.	47	now] new
I.2.	71	the] thy
	111	winds] minds
	124	doth] do
	131	How] Ho
I.3.	11	I wish] iwis
	20	What says ... woman – you may go?] (F: What sayes ... woman you may goe?); What, says ... woman you may go?; What says ... woman? You may go.
	100	laurel] laurelled
I.4.	21	smells] smell
	47	motion.] motion. *Enter a second Messenger*
	49	Makes] Make
	84	knew] know
I.5.	48	arrogant] (F: Arme-gaunt); arm-girt; termagaunt; war-gaunt; rampaunt
II.1.	39	greet] gree
II.2.	7	Antonio's] Antonius'
	48	theme] then
	57	you have] you have not
	64	graceful] grateful
	75–6	you	When, rioting ... Alexandria, you] (F: you, when rioting ... Alexandria you); you	When rioting ... Alexandria; you

II.3.	8	lady. Good] lady. OCTAVIA Good
II.5.	24	Ram] Rain
	26	Antonio's] Antonius
	103	That art not] That sayst but; That art but
II.6.	16	honest, Roman] honest Roman,
II.7.	109	beat] bear
	122	Spleets] Splits
III.2.	49	at the full] at full
III.3.	18	look'st] looked'st
III.6.	22	knows] know
	39	lord] lords
	78	does] do
	80	wrong led] wronged
	88	makes] make
		his] them
III.7.	80	with labour] in labour
III.11.	44	He's] He is
III.12.	13	lessons] lessens
	28–9	add more,	From thine invention, offers] and more	From thine invention offer
	31	Thidias] Thyreus (*also at* III.13.73 *and in prefixes and directions*)
III.13.	26	comparisons] caparisons
	103	The] This
IV.2.	12	Thou] And thou
IV.5.	17	Dispatch. Enobarbus!] (F: Dispatch *Enobarbus*.); Dispatch my Eros; Eros, dispatch
IV.6.	9	vant] van
	13	dissuade] persuade
IV.12.	0	*See the Commentary*
IV.13.	10	death to the monument.] death. To the monument!
IV.14.	35	Unarm] Unarm me
IV.15.	22	dare not] dare not descend; dare not open
	38	when] where
	54	lived; the] (F: liued. The); lived the
	86	do't] do it

V.1.   5 Decretas] Dercetas; Dercetus (*also in prefixes and directions here and in* IV.14)

        26 Look you, sad friends.] (F: Looke you sad Friends,); Look you sad, friends?

        27 tidings] a tidings

        31 Waged] Weighed

        36 launch] lance

        52 Egyptian yet. The] Egyptian, yet the

V.2.   7 dung] dug

        66 sent for] sent me for

        81 little O o'th'earth] (F: little o'th'earth); little O the earth

        87 Antony it was] autumn 'twas

        96 nor] or

       146 seel] seal

       197 Where's] Where is

       226 absurd] obscene

       257 falliable] fallible

       324 here, Charmian? Is] here? Charmian, is

       351 caves] canes

3

Stage directions

The stage directions in this edition are based on those in F, although they have sometimes been modified and others have been added where necessary to clarify the action. The more interesting F stage directions that have been altered are given below in their original form on the right of the square bracket. Also listed are the more significant additional stage directions; asides and indications of the person addressed are not included.

I.1.   10 *Charmian and Iras*] *not in* F

I.2.   0 *Enter Charmian, Iras, and Alexas*] *Enter Enobarbus, Lamprius, a Southsayer, Rannius, Lucillius, Charmian, Iras, Mardian the Eunuch, and Alexas.*

         6 *Enter a Soothsayer*] *not in* F

	11	*Enter Enobarbus]* not in F
	87	*and Attendants]* not in F
	88	*Exeunt all but Antony, Messenger, and Attendants]* Exeunt.
	113	F has 'Enter another Messenger.'
	122	*He gives him the letter]* not in F
		Exit Messenger] not in F
I.3.	60	*He gives her the letter]* not in F
I.5.	34	*Enter Alexas]* Enter Alexas from Cæsar.
II.2.	32	*They sit]* not in F
II.5.	81	*Exit Charmian]* not in F
	84	*Enter Charmian and the Messenger]* Enter the Messenger againe.
II.6.	0	*Pompey and Menas at . . . Agrippa, with]* Pompey, at . . . Agrippa, Menas with
II.7.	16	*and a Boy]* not in F
	39	F has 'Whispers in's Eare.' after 'anon'
	52	*Menas whispers to Pompey]* not in F
	56	*He rises and they walk aside]* not in F
	87	*pointing to the servant who is carrying off Lepidus]* not in F
	127	*Exeunt all but Enobarbus and Menas]* not in F
	132	*He throws his cap in the air]* not in F
III.1.	0	*Enter Ventidius, as it were in triumph, with Silius and other officers and soldiers. Before Ventidius is borne the dead body of Pacorus]* Enter Ventidius as it were in triumph, the dead body of Pacorus borne before him.
III.2.	20	*Trumpet within]* not in F
	42	*weeping]* not in F
III.8.	0	*and Taurus, with their army]* with his Army
III.10.	0	*with his army]* not in F
		Enobarbus] Enobarbus and Scarus.
III.11.	24	*Exeunt attendants. Antony sits down]* Sits downe
		Iras] not in F
III.12.	0	*and Thidias]* not in F
III.13.	82	*She gives him her hand]* not in F

III.13. 93 *servants*] *a Seruant.*
IV.1.   0 *their army*] *his Army*
IV.3.   13 *hautboys*] *the Hoboyes is*
IV.4.   0 *Charmian and*] *not in* F
          2 *with armour*] *not in* F
IV.5.   0 *a Soldier meeting them*] *not in* F
IV.7.   0 *and others*] *not in* F
          8 *Retreat sounded far off*] *Far off. (after* 'heads'.
            in line 6)
IV.8.   0 *Enter Antony, with Scarus and others, marching*]
            *Enter Anthony againe in a March. Scarrus, with
            others.*
         39 *Trumpets sound*] *not in* F
IV.9.   0 *the watch*] *not in* F
         23 *He dies*] *not in* F
         33 *with the body*] *not in* F
IV.14.   87 *He turns from him*] *not in* F
        103 *He falls on his sword*] *not in* F
        104 *Enter Decretas and a company of the Guard*]
            Enter a Guard.
        115 *Exit Decretas*] *not in* F
IV.15.   6 *below*] *not in* F
          9 *Enter, below, the Guard, bearing Antony*] *Enter
            Anthony, and the Guard.*
         62 *Antony dies*] *not in* F
         68 *She faints*] *not in* F
V.1.   0 *Maecenas, Gallus, Proculeius*] *Menas*
V.2.   8 *Enter, to the gates of the monument, Proculeius,
            Gallus, and soldiers*] *Enter Proculeius.*
         34 *The soldiers approach Cleopatra from behind*] *not
            in* F
         35 *They seize Cleopatra*] *not in* F
         36 *Exit Gallus*] *not in* F
         39 *She draws a dagger*] *not in* F
            He disarms her] *not in* F
         70 *Exeunt Proculeius and soldiers*] *Exit Proculeius*
        136 *She gives him a paper*] *not in* F

140 *Enter Seleucus*] not in F
190 *Dolabella ... attendants*] *and his Traine.*
192 *She whispers to Charmian*] not in F
232 *Exit Iras*] not in F
241 *with a basket*] not in F
259 *He sets down the basket*] not in F
278 *Enter Iras with a robe, crown, sceptre, and other regalia*] not in F
291 *She kisses them. Iras falls and dies*] not in F
311 *She applies another asp to her arm*] not in F
318 *rustling in*] *rustling in, and Dolabella.*
320 *She applies an asp to herself*] not in F

READ MORE IN PENGUIN

In every corner of the world, on every subject under the sun, Penguin represents quality and variety – the very best in publishing today.

For complete information about books available from Penguin – including Puffins, Penguin Classics and Arkana – and how to order them, write to us at the appropriate address below. Please note that for copyright reasons the selection of books varies from country to country.

In the United Kingdom: Please write to *Dept. JC, Penguin Books Ltd, FREEPOST, West Drayton, Middlesex UB7 0BR*

If you have any difficulty in obtaining a title, please send your order with the correct money, plus ten per cent for postage and packaging, to *PO Box No. 11, West Drayton, Middlesex UB7 0BR*

In the United States: Please write to *Penguin USA Inc., 375 Hudson Street, New York, NY 10014*

In Canada: Please write to *Penguin Books Canada Ltd, 10 Alcorn Avenue, Suite 300, Toronto, Ontario M4V 3B2*

In Australia: Please write to *Penguin Books Australia Ltd, 487 Maroondah Highway, Ringwood, Victoria 3134*

In New Zealand: Please write to *Penguin Books (NZ) Ltd, 182–190 Wairau Road, Private Bag, Takapuna, Auckland 9*

In India: Please write to *Penguin Books India Pvt Ltd, 706 Eros Apartments, 56 Nehru Place, New Delhi 110 019*

In the Netherlands: Please write to *Penguin Books Netherlands B.V., Keizersgracht 231 NL–1016 DV Amsterdam*

In Germany: Please write to *Penguin Books Deutschland GmbH, Friedrichstrasse 10–12, W–6000 Frankfurt/Main 1*

In Spain: Please write to *Penguin Books S. A., C. San Bernardo 117–6° E–28015 Madrid*

In Italy: Please write to *Penguin Italia s.r.l., Via Felice Casati 20, I–20124 Milano*

In France: Please write to *Penguin France S. A., 17 rue Lejeune, F–31000 Toulouse*

In Japan: Please write to *Penguin Books Japan, Ishikiribashi Building, 2–5–4, Suido, Tokyo 112*

In Greece: Please write to *Penguin Hellas Ltd, Dimocritou 3, GR–106 71 Athens*

In South Africa: Please write to *Longman Penguin Southern Africa (Pty) Ltd, Private Bag X08, Bertsham 2013*